Club

Club

Bill James

A Foul Play Press Book

The Countryman Press, Inc.
Woodstock, Vermont

ISBN 0-88150-331-2

10 9 8 7 6 5 4 3 2 1

Printed in the United States of America
by Quebecor Printing Book Press, Inc.

Club

Chapter 1

From where he stood at the door near the back of the courtroom, Detective Chief Superintendent Harpur watched Sarah Iles push her way across the second row in the public gallery to the one spare space. She was very pregnant. People closed up to give her more room but she signalled no gratitude. Probably they thought she belonged to one of the five men coming back now from the cells into the dock for the verdicts and had made a special effort to get here. In a sense she did, and she had, even though she was an Assistant Chief Constable's wife. Appearing here today was not one of Sarah's wisest moves, but Harpur knew from way back that whenever a clash came between what she wanted and what was wise she did what she wanted. Harpur liked that.

The jury forewoman rattled out the Guilty judgements on Ron Preston, Tyrone Gullen, Hoppy Short and Barry Leckwith: Preston, Tyrone and Hoppy for armed robbery, Leckwith as an accessory. Then it was the last man, Aston, also charged as an accessory. But, coming to him, the forewoman lifted her head from the sheet in her hand and said, 'Not guilty.' Harpur immediately looked back at Sarah and saw a fat, happy grin spread fast over her lovely face and stay there. Desmond Iles was not going to be anything like as pleased, when he heard. Sarah leaned forward, as if trying to get Aston to glance her way, so they could share the joy. His eyes stayed on the judge, though, as he waited to be freed.

When that order came, he left the dock at once, before the sentencing of the others began, and made swiftly for the door of the court. He walked past Harpur, ignoring him, and went out, that youthful, snub-nosed face utterly blank. Still he had not looked up at the public gallery. Sarah stood suddenly and started pushing her way urgently back across the row. She was too big to move fast, and he saw the grin had gone now: she seemed terrified she might fail to get downstairs in time to intercept Aston. Again people were nice to her in her state and made way. Harpur could not leave to see if she was quick enough: there might be commendations from the judge for the police ambush which caught Preston and the rest, and someone had to be present to look grateful.

Chapter 2

They spoke in whispers.

'Is he here, Harpur?' Desmond Iles asked.

'Who, sir?'

'Aston,' Iles said.

'In the church?' Harpur asked.

'Of course in the fucking church,' the Assistant Chief replied.

'Almighty and everlasting God,' the vicar said, 'who of thy great mercy didst save Noah and his family in the ark from perishing by water; and also didst safely lead the children of Israel, thy people, through the Red Sea, figuring thereby the holy baptism; and by the baptism . . .' The baby stirred a little in Sarah's arms but made no noise and the vicar, who had paused for a moment, resumed the service.

'No, I don't think Aston's here, sir,' Harpur murmured.

Iles glanced back over his shoulder towards the decently crowded seats. 'Sarah thinks he'll show.'

'She said so?'

'For Christ's sake, I can feel it. She's as tense as buggery.'

In a while, the vicar began to address Harpur and the other god-parents. 'Dost thou in the name of this child renounce the devil and all his works, the vain pomp and glory of the world, with all covetous desires of the same, and the carnal desires of the flesh, so that thou wilt not follow nor be led by them?'

Harpur and the others replied: 'I renounce them all,' and Iles nodded with approval and seemed to mouth several times to himself the words 'vain pomp and glory of the world'.

There were more questions for the god-parents and when they were over the vicar took the child from Sarah and moved to the font. Harpur himself had the chance now to glance behind and scan the congregation in case Aston really had turned up. It

9

was possible: an acquittal made some people cocky and convinced they were fireproof for ever, let alone for three months. It would be a fine bit of insolence to sit in on this. Harpur could not see him there, though.

Sarah must have sensed he had shifted attention from the baby and herself as she turned urgently and stared towards the rear of the church, perhaps imagining he had spotted Aston. Not finding him, she switched her gaze questioningly for a second from the congregation to Harpur. The vicar was completing the service and wished to return the child to her. Harpur signalled to Sarah with his eyes and she remembered why they were there and put out her arms for the baby.

'Ye must remember that it is your part and duties to see this infant be taught, so soon as she shall be able to learn, what a solemn vow, promise and profession she hath made here by you,' the vicar told Harpur and the two women. Again the ACC nodded gravely in agreement.

He had laid on a white wine party for guests afterwards at their house in Rougement Place.

'You did quite beautifully, Col,' he told Harpur. 'Exceptionally plausible. Of course Aston wasn't going to be there. Touchy of me.'

'That bastard will lie very low for a long time, sir.'

'Think so?'

'Sarah looked so happy,' Harpur said.

'Indeed she did, and very lovely,' Mark Lane, Chief Constable, remarked. He had joined them with his wife, Sally. 'Motherhood brings so much.'

'The vicar spoke well,' Sally Lane said.

'I like christenings best of all, even more than weddings,' the Chief commented.

'Who do you think she's like, the baby?' Mrs Lane asked them all, pleasantly.

For a moment nobody answered. Then Harpur said: 'She has the Assistant Chief's colouring.'

'Oh, yes, very definitely,' Lane added.

'Most say that,' Iles declared.

'There's Sarah now, with the little mite,' Mrs Lane cried. 'I must have a real look.' Iles went with her.

The Chief said: 'I'll be glad when this lot's over, Colin.'

10

'Some edginess, yes.'

Lane spoke sadly. 'Normally, what I like about christenings is the lovely sense of family, and then of the wider family, through the god-parents. Today, I feel something troublesome gnawing.'

'You're right that motherhood suits Sarah.'

'Oh, you really think so? I know I said that, but there's a restlessness, as if she's wondering what the hell she's let herself in for.'

'Yes, well, she's pretty bright.'

Lane glanced about and gave a couple of official smiles to guests. 'Tell me, Colin, after the acquittal, I hear that in the street . . .'

'I was still in the court, sir.'

'This story that she pursued Aston outside, yelling for him to stop. This is a woman eight and a half months gone, the wife of an Assistant Chief, in the middle of the town.'

'I didn't see anything like that, sir.'

'And are they still in contact?'

'No idea, sir.'

Lane was gazing across the room. 'My wife sees this simply as a joyful, celebratory occasion.'

'Well, I feel the same, sir. The Assistant Chief looks transformed.'

Chapter 3

Standing near the Monty's fine old mahogany bar, Sarah could tell it embarrassed the proprietor to see her in his club. Too bad.

'I'm sorry to say he comes here much, much less these days, Mrs Iles,' Ralph Ember told her. 'Well, not at all, as a matter of fact. Since the court business, you know? But you? You've been seeing him since then? Well, you're special, of course. And now he's disappeared for you, too? For us, he just dropped right out of sight straight after.'

'Why?'

'That I can't answer,' Ember said. 'Ian's very much his own man. Well, I don't have to tell you. Business elsewhere? And then there's the matter of some potential unpleasantness. A man gets off and four or five mates are convicted. People do wonder. Most of my members are as good as gold, but there are some difficult ones, too, I'll admit that. They can turn.'

'Do wonder what?'

'Wheels within wheels, Mrs Iles.'

'What the fuck does that mean?'

Ember winced at the language and Sarah saw him glance apologetically around the club. There were not many customers in yet. Sarah had noticed before how close he came to being handsome, in a sallow, jagged, sombre style: like Charlton Heston, they said, without the cash. The knife scar along the line of his jaw would always be there, but it was fading very nicely. He leaned across the bar and spoke quietly. 'It means, did Ian get special treatment on some account? I don't say that, personally. But it's what's perceived by others. In business you learn that what others think is true is almost as important as what really is true.'

'They think he sold them, you mean?'

'People in some trades are very sensitive.'

'They weren't his mates, anyway.'

'They were in the dock together, Mrs Iles. Some would say that ought to bring kinship.'

'You're telling me there are people really looking for him?'

Behind the bar, Ember began polishing some of the brasswork. In the old days, the Monty had been a very decent club for businessmen. All that had ended long before Panicking Ralph took it over, but he liked to pretend the links remained and keep up appearances. 'Have you tried the flat?' He smiled. 'I'm always more than happy to see you in my little club, Mrs Iles, with or without Ian, but I do ask myself whether it's wise for you to come here searching now. One wonders about, well, the baby. Me, I'm always inclined to think in terms of family.'

'This was the part of the evening Ian liked to come here, wasn't it? Before the full cascade of dregs arrive.' She glanced around. A couple of men were playing pool and another three sat at a table drinking wine and pretending to ignore her.

Ember winced again. 'Yes, this was his special hour or two. Should I mention that you've looked in, Mrs Iles? If I were to see him, that is.'

'When?'

'I did say if. Mrs Iles, may I mention this further point: your husband's not really going to like your coming here, is he?' His voice hardened. 'I do not want the club involved. Reputation? It doesn't do me a lot of good to cross Desmond Iles. He's a man who can bear a grudge. And he's not without power. The living sod.'

'He doesn't know I'm here.'

Ember shrugged. 'Who can be sure what the ACC knows? That's always the, as it were, crux.'

Chapter 4

'God, this takes me back to the Iles child's christening, all those weeks ago, Colin,' Lane said, his nice-natured, heavy face grave again. 'Didn't I tell you then something was desperately wrong? Well, you felt it yourself.'

'Sir, I can't see that this incident . . .'

'You'll tell me no proven connection, obviously. I wish I could accept that.'

'As I see it so far, sir, this is an appalling but essentially simple bit of typical gangland business.'

The Chief stared past him. 'Sometimes, I wonder what I'm presiding over here.'

'This is a man who might have run into terminal aggro at any time, sir – flirting with rival outfits, selling bits of information and bits of loyalty, and working entirely alone, no protection.'

Lane pointlessly opened and closed a drawer in his desk. 'Do you know, almost the whole time I've headed this Force I've wanted to be somewhere else,' he said. To Harpur, it sounded less like a whine than a startling discovery, suddenly just come upon the Chief. 'Colin, is that the way to run an outfit? Call it leadership?'

'Everyone believes you've settled very well, sir.'

'I don't run the thing, it runs me. So, yes, I've settled, as you say. I'm acceptable.'

Now, the tone did seem to be sinking into self-pity, as well as a helping of truth, and Harpur offered no more consolation.

Seeming to read the silence right, Lane tried to shake off his mood. 'So, this simple bit of gangland business, Colin – how did he die?'

'Seven or eight blows to the head. A heavy instrument.'

In shirt sleeves at the desk, Lane swallowed and passed a hand across his features. 'Identification? What poor sod's had to do that?'

'There was plenty on him. We didn't have finger-print records any longer, and we failed to contact the parents, but we brought down Panicking Ralph, owner of the Monty club, plus one of the members. They couldn't manage it from the face, of course, and said they hadn't seen him for a while, anyway. But they thought the build was right and the clothes style.'

'And no definite leads?'

'Not for the moment, sir.'

Lane's mouth tightened. 'Look, there are going to be very considerable pressures, Colin. All the inter-connections are well known, not least to the media.'

'Yes.'

'We've had something damn similar here before. As you know. Two villains last time, yes? All right, every Force has messy killings, obviously, but not every Force—'

Iles knocked and came in. Wearing his Prince of Wales check grey suit and what might be a rugby club tie from one of his refereeing trips, the Assistant Chief looked routinely masterful and dynamic, his walk cheery. He carried a green folder.

'Ah, Desmond,' Mark Lane said. 'We were talking about this terrible killing.'

'Yes, quite unlovely. That lad had certainly crossed someone,' Iles replied. He sat down near Harpur, in front of Lane's desk, and, opening the folder, pushed it across to the Chief. There were three colour photographs of the naked body taken from above and lying on its back. 'These blows were very thorough.'

Lane seemed to force himself to gaze at the pictures for a few seconds and even separated them, so none obscured another. 'Colin says this character had it coming to him.'

Iles put his handsome, lean head back and considered this for a moment. 'Had it coming to him? Yes, I'll buy that.'

Lane said: 'I mean, sailing very dangerous waters between various competing villains.'

'I like that, "sailing very dangerous waters". Exactly it.' Iles brought a pencil from his jacket pocket and, with a flourish, made a note on the bottom of the folder. 'I'm shameless when it comes to lifting other people's phrases for future use, sir.'

15

'This is going to be a real dossier trawl, through all his criminal contacts,' Lane said.

'Something will show very soon. Don't worry,' Iles told him. 'But you'll naturally be wondering what Sarah makes of it all, sir.'

'Sarah?' Lane exclaimed. 'No, not at—'

Iles pulled the pictures back towards him. 'As you might imagine, I find it quite affecting to be looking down on this one's body, and to know that my wife has been in prolonged, deep contact with it.' Iles turned one of the pictures around and concentrated on the midriff. 'Yes.'

Lane stood and walked away from the pictures. As often happened, he had no shoes on in the office and a pair of heavy khaki socks hung loosely on his feet, like a clown's shoes. The Chief habitually went for the relaxed touch. He hoped to disarm.

'Sarah's not taking it at all well, as a matter of fact,' Iles said. 'Very shrill grief. The doc has given her a bit of sedation, but she's strong, you know, fights it off.'

'I'm really very sorry, Desmond,' Lane remarked over his shoulder, looking out from the window.

'Thank you, sir. She will get through it. That's another aspect of her strength. Obviously, she had to be told at once about the death, but I haven't disclosed the skull pulp details.'

'Obviously,' Lane said.

'Though there are parts of me that long to do exactly that.' Iles somehow kept his voice just clear of snarling. 'Even show the pictures.'

Lane gasped and turned. 'Those are not to leave this building, Desmond.'

Iles brought along one of his saddest smiles: 'Of course not, sir. Just my malevolent dreams.'

'Not to be intrusive in any way, but I thought it was a thing of the past, anyway, that relationship,' Lane said.

'It's helpful, sir, the way you always wish the best for people. Perhaps it is "a thing of the past". Naturally, since the child was born, Sarah is much less free. But . . .' He pondered. 'I can't say that I've ever known what Sarah is thinking. Tell me, do you find it easy to tune in to Megan, Col?' he asked Harpur, then at once held up a hand. 'No, don't answer. I mustn't pry, nor into your marriage, either, Chief, clearly. Frankly, though, I simply do not know whether it was "a thing of the past". And even if it was, it is not the very distant past, so Sarah is still liable to be devastated. I worry about her mind. Post-natal women are vulnerable. Sarah's touch and go just now, I fear. Still, what one can rely on is that, after this, the affair certainly will be a thing of the past.' He gathered the corpse portraits of Ian Aston together, looked at each dotingly in turn, then put them back in the folder.

'And the girl child?' Lane asked, returning to his desk from the window. 'How is she? My wife will press me. Must be nearly six months old now.'

'Fanny? People do shy off speaking the name. But both Sarah and I thought it should be rescued from lewd public bar talk. Yes, she's lovely and passably amiable. Safe, to date.'

'Still with your colouring, sir?' Harpur asked.

Iles opened the folder and looked long at the photographs again. 'Oh, yes. Even more so.'

Chapter 5

From Harpur's right in the darkness came a woman's sudden, hoarse shout, almost a scream: 'The law. Here. Now.' He swung the flashlight around and at the same time heard from upstairs a brief, frightened grunt, as if a man had just been woken up. This was followed by the sound of someone moving hurriedly, maybe the man getting to his feet and then stepping quickly across a room or a landing, possibly stumbling over debris in the rush.

The woman had made herself a bed on the floor out of sheet cardboard, a couple of pieces of tattered carpet, a duffel coat and newspapers. She was propped up on one elbow in the bed, like a temptress ad for a porn video, but in the torch beam her skin said she could be over sixty, or twenty-eight on a meths diet, and she seemed to be fully dressed in an army greatcoat, pullovers and a woollen hat that came down over her ears. She smiled into the glare and waved gently with her free hand. Someone else groaned and whimpered in another part of the room, outside the little area of light, but then resumed steady snoring.

'I can't see you behind that torch, but if I could I believe I'd hate the look of you,' the woman said.

'Many do, yet some get hooked,' Harpur replied.

'Myself, I still believe in exercise, night or day. It keeps the glow on the body.' She sat up properly in the rough bed and put her arms and hands out together in front of her, then languidly moved them wide and back a couple of times, maybe slowed by the army coat and other clothes.

Harpur took the beam off her and picked his way as fast as he could across the room through bricks and rubbish towards the stairs. Join the police and see the world. It was one of the last, big, old derelict houses left around Valencia Esplanade, ineffectively boarded up and awaiting demolition. Most had already gone, to make space for a dockland and marina redevelopment. Once, winos and down-and-outs and people on the run could take their pick from whole streets of these ruins. Now, they had to crowd into the remaining few, like rabbits pushed back to the shrinking central circle of wheat in a threshed field. This woman and the rest might be all right for a while, though, because here, like everywhere, prestige redevelopment suddenly had money troubles.

'It's a community,' she said. 'Arrant thieving non-stop, but never someone's cardboard. A filthy sin to take someone else's cardboard. Don't bloody laugh. Every society lays down limits.'

'I wish you hadn't shouted when I came in,' Harpur replied.

'This is a community. You want Les Reid?'

Harpur was at the bottom of the stairs when he heard a window shatter somewhere above in the back and he climbed at a rush. A man sat sleeping about halfway up, his head propped on his knees and a cider bottle between them. Harpur kept moving. In these places the banisters always went early for firewood and he stayed close to the wall. Reaching the first landing, he turned the flashlight beam towards the back of the house. He was standing near what had once been a lavatory and obviously still was, but with no water supply. Most doors had gone for fuel like the banisters and he could see that the glass in the window in a small rear room had been knocked out. He went in. On the floor was another cardboard and newspaper bed, unoccupied. Switching off the flashlight, he crossed to the window and looked down. The remains of a garage joined to the house stood below. Its roof had been stripped but the walls remained and Chickenfeed Reid had lowered himself from the window on to one of them and was seated for a moment with his legs hanging down towards the garden. He dropped. Perhaps he had heard Harpur. Chickenfeed glanced back up for a second at the window and then turned and ran awkwardly over the weeds and scattered junk in the garden to where the lane door had been. Just before he reached it, Francis Garland stepped through from outside, arms open, like a mother welcoming a child.

Harpur put on the flashlight again and went back downstairs. He found that Garland had brought Reid into the house through the piece of loosened boarding that everyone used.

'We like Les,' the woman said from her bed. 'Style and

tolerance. These are his qualities. It's a testing ground here, like the Civil Service selection board.'

'We like him, too,' Harpur said. 'We know him from way back.'

'We'd like him to help us with our inquiries,' Garland told her.

'Oh, God,' she replied, 'that means bone fragments all over the décor.'

'We've been round your place and guessed you were sleeping rough, Chickenfeed. But as rough as this?' Harpur said.

'Expecting us, were you?' Garland asked.

'I knew you'd have thoughts, Mr Harpur.'

'What thoughts?' Garland said.

'About Aston, of course.'

'I can vouch for this: he said to me you'd have thoughts,' the woman told them.

'As far as we can make out, Les, you were among the last to see him alive,' Garland said.

'Tell me this: is there a dossier anywhere that says Chickenfeed Reid does violence?' Reid replied. 'Some business connections with Aston, but always amicable.'

The woman said: 'Our view here, as a sort of cooperative, is this: you boys will be around everywhere, framing and scapegoating because you've got to keep the heat off someone else.'

'I don't say that,' Reid muttered, 'but—'

'Namely ACC Iles,' the woman said. 'This is a considered view, using certain background information relevant to motive.'

'In fact, I'd say Ian Aston was a real friend,' Reid went on. 'All right, it might be stupid to leave my place and hide here, but am I going to hang about waiting for you lads?'

The three of them were standing in the middle of the big, once noble room, Harpur with the torch pointed down at the ground. In the bit of reflected light Reid looked almost distinguished. He had a heavy, solemn face, with a thick, fair, officer-quality moustache, and a neat, middle-height body. His overcoat had not been doing well lately but was obviously a bit of genuine cloth.

'Here, in this haven, he can get counselling,' the woman said.

Behind Harpur a snoring sleeper woke up suddenly and a man's voice howled: 'What? What?'

'Counselling, Jerome,' the woman replied. 'A haven.'

'I hate the light,' he said.

'Police light. Only shines where they want it to,' she told him.

20

Jerome settled down to sleep again. As he rearranged himself in his papers the sound was like a vast church congregation simultaneously turning a missal page.

'What business?' Garland asked.

'Aston and I?' Reid replied. 'Oh, agency work. Bringing buyers and sellers together. Entrepreneurial.'

'We heard you'd had a nasty disagreement, Les,' Garland told him.

'What kind of business?' Harpur asked.

'Various. Very various.'

'Didn't *The Sunday Times Business News* do a feature on you?' Garland asked.

'No disagreements,' Reid said. 'Healthy competition. I can account for my movements.'

The woman said: 'Ask him if this dead boy ever said he felt threatened. Ask him if he ever said who by. Ask him that. But would you?'

'This is no place for a conversation,' Garland commented. 'The stench. Could all this here possibly tick over without you for an hour or two, do you think, Chickenfeed?'

Chapter 6

'Boys, these days, normally, as you know, I don't touch anything outside running the club. Not worth the risk. I've got to be damn careful,' Ember explained.

'Rightly famous for it, Ralphy.'

'The name of the Monty. In a word, reputation.' But Ember wondered whether two full-time, heavy-duty villains could have any idea what he was talking about.

'Ralph, this is not going to expose you or we wouldn't ask.' Caring Oliver could do a very gentle, respectful voice, which was one reason they called him Caring. Only one reason. He had something there that could be kind and considerate, but it got lost often.

'A liaison matter, nothing more,' Pete Chitty added.

'I'll tell you, things have been tough here,' Ember said, looking at Caring. He was youngish but had come on famously in his game these last few years. His face was about success now, calm and sharp, even if a bit sad looking, too. 'Since right after the fucking Aston acquittal: diabolical,' Ember told them. 'And then, worse still, he has to go and get himself found stove in like that. Police coming here and taking me to identify, like I'm his nearest and dearest, or something. I mean, he's got parents – West Country way – but they come for Ralph W. Ember to look at the body. All sorts have stopped visiting the Monty. Well, pardon me, but I've got to say it – you boys yourselves.'

'We've felt bad about it, Ralph. It got too hot,' Caring said, and he did sound ashamed.

Ember explained: 'The word's out that Aston must have spilled to the police. A deal: they soft-pedal evidence to get him off.

Immediately, people go to ground, scared over who else he talked about.'

'Right.'

'And suddenly the Monty's dangerous territory,' Ember went on. 'Can't you hear the whispering: "Ralph's involved: they took him to inspect the damage." See that bloody bottle of armagnac? No change in it since he walked free. I've still got a mortgage and poll tax and school fees for two.'

'That's a fine place your daughters go to, Ralph. Really ladylike uniform,' Caring said. 'Red and black – tasteful. Once I honestly believed in the comprehensive system. But can it deliver?'

'And then he gets his head smashed in and half of the few who were still coming to the club and spending a bit disappear,' Ember remarked. 'They just did an oratorio at my kids' school.'

'Well, it's a genuine establishment,' Oliver commented.

'But it costs,' Ember said. 'Not just uniform. Fees. Games gear. Travel right across the city every day.'

'You know why people lie low,' Peter Chitty said. 'This is full chaos we're living in. Romania before the mutiny. The law doing what the hell it likes. Call it the fucking law!'

Caring said: 'This boy, Aston, he was going to do a little assignment for us, you know. I felt sorry for him after the acquittal. I never believed he shopped Ron Preston and his crew. That's not Ian at all.'

'Of course, banging a police wife three times a week didn't help. People put two and two together and make five,' Chitty added.

'Anyway, he was given the freeze by every trade after the case, Ralph. Well, we put some little job his way. He was dealing with it very sweetly. And now, suddenly, he's mortuarised – eight cracks on the head, eight! – and we're a man short.' He leaned forward and touched Ember's arm for a moment, deferentially but heartfelt, like helping royalty into the lifeboat. 'We were wondering if you'd assist, Ralph. Being aware you're up against it, too. I've asked you along these lines before and you've always said no. I fully respected your point of view. What else could I do, you with your experience and brain?'

The thing about Caring was, although he had started harvesting the money, he stayed a nobody. Big but no stature. He had no history, knew none of the calibre impresarios from the past.

These were the things he seemed to see in Ember and wanted to get close to – like the jumped-up new rich, desperate to buy a bit of class as well as the possessions. Once or twice Caring had asked about the knife scar on Ember's jaw and encouraged him to talk about the old days.

Oliver stood suddenly as Margaret came in with the two girls. 'Mrs Ember, this *is* nice,' he said. Peter Chitty got up as well. They had some style, these two, although blood under their nails.

'Hello, darling,' Ember said. He had to stand, also. 'Kids. Have a good day? Any more news about that Latin?' He turned to Oliver. 'This school's thinking of dropping Latin. I ask you! I'm just talking a bit of business with Peter and Ollie, Maggie.' They were in the bar of the Monty, empty of customers at this part of the afternoon. Margaret Ember chatted for a moment, then took the children through towards the stairs up to the flat. He only let Venetia and Fay spend brief times in the club.

'Can you tell me the law's really looking for the one who broke Aston's shell?' Chitty asked.

They were all drinking straight tonic water but now Ember went and brought to the table the bottle he had spoken about and poured three armagnacs. 'Ah, that makes it look a bit more lived in,' he said.

Chitty took a drink. 'Top stuff, as ever, Ralphy. Look, what I'm saying is this – someone murdered by a cop for knocking off his wife on a regular basis, so are they going to try and get the cop for it? Do they want that known?'

Chitty was Caring's sidekick. Every big one had a sidekick. Probably Pete always would be a sidekick. He was clever, no getting away from it, but narrow as hell and crude. He had to go straight at a subject.

'It's not just any cop we're discussing,' Oliver remarked.

'Super-cop. They act how they like,' Chitty went on. 'That's what frightens people and hits your business, Ralphy. Who's safe if they can go around settling scores, no come-back? People are attached to their skulls.'

Oliver said: 'Chickenfeed Reid even left home, for God's sake. He knew the way things would go. Moved into Urbanmiraclestrasse. Naturally, they found him – bloody Harpur found him – and took him in. All rot, of course. Reid was out in an hour.'

'Harpur himself – is he above board?' Chitty said. 'I hear he was doing something with another cop's wife. And that cop shot him where it matters, if you know what I mean, during the Preston ambush, so it could be made to look an accident. That finally put a stop to Harpur's little affair, yes. Ruth Cotton? Wife of a sergeant? Marksman?'

Venetia came down from the flat, wearing her jeans and a T-shirt now, and went out to get something from the car. He noticed that Pete and Ollie took a lot of care not to stare at her legs and arse, or at her chest when she came back. He appreciated that. This was a girl not fourteen yet: pretty, yes, and with a body on the way, but still only a child.

Ember said: 'If this is a job I like the sound of, and there's a reasonable return, I'll think about it, Ollie, this time. Enough to tide me over.'

'It would make me feel really grand, Ralph.'

'I'm not so special,' Ember replied. Suddenly, he realised he was sliding too fast into agreement. 'But listen, boys, the kind of work Aston used to take on was always on the edges, nothing front line. Am I right?'

'Right,' Chitty said. 'You won't get dirty, Ralph.'

'We wouldn't have approached you otherwise,' Oliver added. 'As for my own daughter, Lynette, she goes away to school. This is in Cheltenham. Well known. Her mother wanted that.'

Chitty kept to the point: 'Intermediary only. When it comes to buying weaponry for a job we don't like having direct contact ourselves.'

'Never,' Oliver added. Ember felt that one of the great things about him was the grey hair brushed back behind his ears, which, on top of the sad face, made him look like one of those chairmen of soccer supporters' clubs, anguishing about yob violence, even though he was not old. 'This Cheltenham school is good, Ralph. Cost? An arm and a leg.'

Anyone could see he had to talk about that school to show he had picked up the right things about life-style, as well as picking up loot.

'This is a job that will be done miles from here, Ralph, and the gun dealer's miles from here, also,' Chitty explained. 'No way any shit that flies will stick to you or the Monty.'

'Not that any will fly,' Oliver said.

'I'm just taking things at the very worst possible,' Chitty went on. 'This dealer's in London. Absolutely clear.'

Chitty always looked pretty good, too. All right, a bit teenage with his clothes, like A Day In The Eternal Life of Cliff Richard, but not grab-all looking or savage. Sometimes newcomers at the Monty made a very bad mistake and took these two for soft.

'Guns we buy new, every time,' Oliver remarked. 'Pete's idea from some old Robert Mitchum movie.'

'No tracing. The price is agreed. All you do is hand over the cash and collect, Ralph.'

'Five or six hours. Use a stolen car, so no possible connection. Back in time for evening opening.'

'No rush for that,' Ember said. 'Hardly any bugger here.'

'The way we see it, getting work under way again like this will help bring things all round back to normal,' Chitty went on. 'People will hear about this and have a pretty good idea it's us. They'll see we haven't just collapsed because Iles's gone jungle over his wife.'

'Gone jungle yet again,' Oliver said.

'People will start stirring, recovering some of their guts. A drift back to the Monty, Ralph.'

'I bring them with me?' Ember asked.

'The guns? Yes,' Chitty replied. 'Six. Smith and Wesson K-frames. No problem. Put them and the shells with the spare wheel or something and drive back nice and carefully.'

'Bring them out to my place right away. Obviously not items you want on Monty premises. Lose the car somewhere. That's the last you'll have to do with any of it.'

'This dealer's able to forget you as soon as you drive away, Ralph. Called Leopold.'

'Lovely chap, I hear, although we have no direct contact,' Oliver said. 'Two sons. Both at Belmont Abbey. Mick, but good.'

Ember poured three more armagnacs. He spoke slowly: 'You know they call me Panicking Ralph. This is an unspoken factor in all this.'

'It's rubbish,' Chitty said at once. 'Would we risk it?'

'It's because you're the opposite that we want you, Ralph. This is one of those nick-names that say the reverse – like Shorty for a tall guy.'

'Thanks, lads. I never reckoned I deserved it.' He took another soothing pull at the armagnac. 'Aston getting roof trouble – you sure it was to do with Iles, not, well, not this deal for you, such as something gone sour? These people in London? Leopold. Might he have turned nasty? That can happen over guns. I mean, if I'm walking into something problematical.'

'Iles,' Chitty said. 'Any other Force he'd be inside by now.'

'This gun deal is on established lines, Ralph. The people are discreet. Leopold's socially very acceptable. This is an area called Kew. Well, the Botanical Gardens and fine trees. Nothing ever goes wrong. There could be no reason for violence.'

'Fucking Iles written all over Aston's death,' Chitty added. 'Except all the other cops pretend they can't read. And lately a story that Harpur's moving over towards his wife – that's Iles's wife, instead of the Cotton woman. Wonderful? Some crew, though, yes? A mother now, too. They must have patched him up down below – where it counts – after the Preston ambush shooting.'

'So, welcome aboard, Ralph. I feel very proud.'

Chapter 7

'I'm afraid you'll have to attend, Colin,' the Chief said. 'This is a very bloody murder and technically the lad has nothing against him on the books. We have to make the routine gesture of respect.'

'I'm getting used to Church occasions, sir.'

'In the normal course I might have gone to the funeral myself, or the ACC. Not as things are.'

'I see the point, sir.'

'But I hear the ACC's wife might wish to be there.' Lane opened and closed that drawer in his desk, to no purpose again. Harpur wondered how a cop brought up to recognise displacement activities in others could be so incapable of controlling his own.

Harpur said: 'For Sarah, attending could mark the end, sir. Funerals act as a therapy. The grief is given expression and disperses. I know that's how Mr Iles is thinking about it. Finale.'

'Grief? Grief for a baggage-man to villains from the wife of— From a beautiful woman I would otherwise admire greatly, and do admire, anyway. You can't talk her out of it?'

'You know Sarah, sir.'

Lane, looking passably smart and fit in uniform today, said: 'If she does go, it must not be in your company, Colin. Her attendance is private. Yours is as a representative of the Force.'

'She understands that, sir.'

'Why the hell does she have to be there?' He gave a small groan as a new idea came to him. 'Jesus, will she take the baby?'

'That I don't know. She says she feels duty-bound to see him off. And she wants to discover what his life was, so her memories of him are full. That's the term she used. I mean beyond the Monty and the court and the injuries and the smelly

28

little jobs he did. His family. We had trouble finding them, but there's a mother and father.'

'Well, yes, smelly. What in God's name explains this desperate loyalty to him from a woman of her calibre, Colin?'

'Such relationships are never simple, sir.'

Lane shrugged impatiently. 'I take your word for that.' Almost at once he was obviously sorry: 'Forgive me, Colin. I sound like a nun. But Sarah could be standing there, at some would-be crook's graveside, a kid in her arms? It's like a Victorian lithograph. Cameras.'

'Cremation, sir.'

'That's something. So, I take it Sarah was still seeing him, child or not?'

'Off and on, yes, she tells me.'

Agitation rushed him. 'Christ, this could have a bearing on the death, Col. You've talked to her formally – as part of the inquiries?'

'Informally, to date.'

'And the ACC?'

'Did he know she was still seeing him?'

'Yes.'

'He says not.'

'But?'

'He says not, sir.'

Lane leaned across the desk and spoke in a tone of apology again: 'I'm going to have to think about bringing in someone from another Force to look at all this you know. It's reaching too deep.' From in front of him, he picked up a photostat document and passed it across to Harpur. 'This is a copy of something that came to our Complaints people. Looks as if it was written on cardboard with a nail and boot polish. A woman saying we victimised a guy called Reid, took him from his legitimate domicile, as she calls it, and that it's all part of a police cover-up over Aston. Are these accusations general gossip then?'

'Reid tells us Aston was on some go-between job for Pete Chitty and Oliver Leach.'

Lane bucked up. 'Working for Caring Oliver? The Met and others fail to take him for armed robbery from time to time in different parts of the country, yes? What sort of job?'

'That Chickenfeed didn't know, or said he didn't. Garland's

digging. It could be quartermaster's messenger. Transporting armament.'

'It might be to the point then? That's dangerous traffic.'

'Could easily be, sir.'

'If we could turn this killing away from Desmond Iles, Colin.'

'We will, sir.'

'I don't want people digging here – an outside Force, the media. God, the media.'

'We'll handle it.'

The funeral was at Bristol, Aston's home town, and in Jericho Gospel Hall, not a church. Harpur found it moving and dignified, and felt glad Lane had sent him. Despite what the Chief had said, he drove there with Sarah Iles, though they stayed apart at Jericho and at the crematorium, except for a few moments. Harpur had decided it would be stupid to travel such a distance alone, particularly as Sarah might need support. She set out as if in her own car but left it in a multi-storey and Harpur picked her up in the street. Sarah did bring the baby and for most of the time Fanny slept serenely in her carry-cot on the back seat. Once on the way down and once on the way back they pulled off the road so she could be fed and changed. It might have been a family outing. Or not.

Almost as the Chief had feared, Sarah carried the child in her arms, both at Jericho and the crematorium. Fanny remained quiet until the curtain moved slowly across the coffin at the crematorium, just before powered rollers took it away. For a second, it seemed as if this baby had divined the pain of the moment, but then Harpur realised that the curtain made a sharp, grating sound on its rail, and must have frightened Fanny. She began to yell. He turned and saw that Sarah herself was already weeping helplessly and was too distressed to comfort the baby. Harpur moved out of his place and went to them. Fuck the cameras, if there were any. This was his godchild. He took Fanny and rocked her gently until she grew peaceful again. Sarah put her face against his shoulder and in a while brought the sobbing under control. Fanny looked up and grinned at him, just as the sound of the box rollers stopped. He grinned back.

It had been an almost cheerful service at Jericho, conducted by a man with no dog-collar in a lovely, booming West Country

30

accent. Harpur liked his bottom-of-the-heart style better than the church christening. He had been brought up in a similar sort of place, a Hall primitively bare except for text scrolls painted on the walls, like Jericho, and with plenty from the platform about the blood of the Lamb. The preacher said Aston as a youngster had accepted Christ as his saviour and that, as a result, 'The flames that will devour his poor, abused body are as nothing, because the flames of the devil's kingdom shall never touch our brother.' Harpur wondered, but found himself saying 'Amen', from a habit he had thought long gone.

Sarah and the baby went ahead of him from the crematorium and outside Harpur talked with Aston's mother and other relatives.

'We know you must seek to find whoever has done this thing to Ian,' Mrs Aston said, 'and yet I wonder if it is so very important. Did you know my boy?'

'No, I'm afraid not.'

'It is all just one of those duties of this world for you, then?'

'Well, yes. It's the law, Mrs Aston.'

'Ah, the law. I prefer to think of grace.' She was heavily built, with kindly eyes, kindly voiced, big featured and plain. He remembered so many women like her teaching at his Sunday School. 'What I can only describe as unhelpful stories about his life in that other place have come to us here. None of it seems to matter now, does it? Of course, you know a Mr Iles? I simply don't want to hear such stories.'

Another woman, built the same and possibly her sister, said: 'The young lady with the child and wearing no hat. You know her? I saw you minister to her, so kindly. She isn't local.'

'A friend of Ian, I believe,' Harpur replied.

'Perhaps she cannot see beyond the ashes, poor young thing.'

In the car on the way back, Sarah said: 'There might have been more there if so many of his friends weren't locked up.'

'He'd understand.'

'Colin, he didn't shop those people, did he – Planner Preston and the rest?'

'Of course not. Someone else did.'

'He should never have been in the dock, should he?'

'Maybe not.'

'Desmond wanted him locked up.'

'Not just the ACC. We all thought we had a case.'

'All right. And then, when he got off, Desmond decided he'd . . .'

'We have some strong leads on the killing, Sarah. Aston had gone back to his old sort of work. It was always dangerous.'

She became thoughtful for a while. 'But I don't believe Desmond would hurt the child, whatever he thinks. I won't contemplate that.'

'He adores her.'

'I do believe that, Colin. Adores her regardless.'

Chapter 8

Ember grew alert.

'This job to do with those two who were in the club the other day, Ralph?'

He knew Margaret wanted to sound nice and casual, but she could not speak of Monty customers without making them sound like child molesters who had popped in for a break. Ember replied: 'It's a little assignment and I'm in no position to be sniffy, love.'

'Well, I don't say turn it down. Anyway, that sort – Caring and Chitty – if they offer you something, can you turn it down? I see how rough things are with the club just now. But go carefully. It's been a long time and you might have forgotten some of the old survival tricks.'

'Turn it down? Of course I can turn it down if I want to.' Did she think he feared people like those two? Had his own wife swallowed that Panicking Ralph crap?

'So why are they suddenly asking you?' she said. 'Don't they know you jacked in all that ages ago?'

It was Saturday and they were having a late breakfast on their own in the bar of the club. Venetia and Fay had gone riding. Sometimes he enjoyed moments alone like these.

Ember said: 'They thought this was up my street, Maggie. I could take it or leave it.'

'Maybe you're the only one they could find. Everybody else hiding under stones since the crisis – crises.'

He laughed. He had nearly let his temper really take over then, but decided it was best to keep things looking like no big deal. 'That's it. They must be desperately hard up, Maggie.' He put on an Irish accent for this last bit. Apparently, there was a touch of Irish somewhere far back on his mother's side, and he would bring it out occasionally if he needed to sound playful.

But, of course, she would spot that: 'What sort of thing is up your street, then, Ralph?'

'Messenger boying. No sweat. But needing a bit of polish. Someone who can put a couple of words together.'

She looked past him, in that sodding considerate way she often did when meaning to say something sticky: 'Isn't this the kind of work Ian Aston handled?'

'Aston? How does he come into it, for God's sake?'

'Don't know. Does he?'

'I told you: Caring thought this was something I could handle. What happened to Aston was nothing to do with any job for Caring. Higher-echelon pussy. He couldn't leave it alone. Aston was light on brains.'

'He got lighter.' Margaret gathered up the dishes and left it at that.

Well, sod you. That was his first reaction. She did not want to understand his situation. Yes, this outing would involve a step back towards the shadows and towards hazard, no question. Work was work, though.

Just the same, he hated to see Margaret upset or anxious and was never able to stay evil towards her for long. Decent families could not operate like that. He followed her into the kitchen now and began to wipe the dishes as she washed. She glanced up and grinned at him. 'Sorry,' she grunted. 'I shouldn't have said that about the poor sod.'

'It won't hurt him now.' He touched her warm, soapy hand for a second. A gesture like that said so much. She and he had something good going, and he valued it. Maggie had looked after him well, given him lovely daughters and stayed rock loyal through some bloody difficult stretches, including those problematical days when he collected the knife wound, and almost collected a lot worse: his jaw, but nearly his throat. Despite time and all the stress, she had hung on to some of her looks, and he could never imagine being long-term with anyone else. He remained proud to be seen out with her and knew that many men around the Monty and elsewhere envied him, though she gave no encouragement, he was sure. For himself, as a tribute, he would never shag any other woman inside their flat or, indeed, on Monty premises at all, even when the family were away. Often he thought he could

34

take faithfulness further still, but when you were running a club the opportunities came too often, and not just with boiling pieces.

'All right, Maggie,' he said. 'You read Ralph Ember so damn well. Yes, as a matter of fact, it *is* a job that Aston was handling for them. But that doesn't mean it was why he got what he got. Anyway, look, no fretting. I can easily run a check. There's that friend of Ian, in the club sometimes, Chickenfeed Reid. I'll pop down and ask him if Aston had any fears about the job.'

'I'll come with you.' At once, she took off her apron to show she was ready.

'Well, I don't know, love. From what I hear, he moved out of his place as soon as Aston was found and took a débris suite in Urbanmiraclestrasse. It's no fun in some of those houses, darling.'

'So I'll still come.'

He prized that in her. She would have a go.

They drove down and found that Reid had quit days ago, after a visit from detectives. Ember might have given up then, but Margaret wanted to try Reid's flat and when they knocked they found him at home alone. 'What's this?' he yelled, 'my Monty subscription lapsed? Bailiffs in pairs?'

Ember studied his face, but Chickenfeed had been around the perimeters a long time and you did not see anything there except what he wanted you to see. He was wearing one of his great old-time suits and a great old-time shirt and a great old-time reddish military tie, the one Harold had on when the arrow got him, with some of the genuine battlefield horseshit on it. Chickenfeed could hold a smile longer than anyone Ember knew. 'Enter,' he cried, smiling.

'Harpur took you in, I hear, Chickenfeed,' Ember said.

'Well, he would, wouldn't he? They'll take in every bugger except the one they ought to take. It's known as *esprit de* cops. But no point in holing up in that tip any longer if they know I'm there. They realise I can't tell them anything.'

'We're not stopping, Les,' Margaret said. 'The girls are back soon. It's just that . . .'

Reid re-smiled. 'I know, it's just that people hear I've been down there with Mr Bloody Harpur and Co and want to know what I said, for their own purposes. What are you up to then, Ralphy?' He paused. 'No. All right. I've said nothing, because I had nothing to say. Ian told me bugger all about his other business activities. That's how we both liked it.'

'Wise.'

'What I did tell them was Ian had woman trouble and husband trouble, as everybody in the world knows, including the police, naturally. Especially the police. The trouble wasn't new, but it was getting much worse. Not to put too fine a point on it: the baby. Yes, he was scared about that. And Mrs Iles wouldn't let him go. This was something deep – I mean, noble in its way, but very, very fraught. I kept telling Harpur and sidekick this, but do they wish to listen? They've got orders to fix it somewhere else.'

'Rough you up?' Ember asked.

'Pushing and shoving. Humiliations. You've had it, too, Ralph? Harpur won't allow any welly. I'll say that for him. That Garland would be a different commodity if he had a chance.'

'So do we believe Chickenfeed?' Margaret said, when they reached home.

Ember was uncertain. Reid had talked very fast. 'I believe him, because I'm sure he's got it right about Aston's death.'

'But my God, Ralph, an Assistant Chief? That ought to be unthinkable.'

'Yes, it ought to be.'

The girls came in then, with talk of a gymkhana about fifty miles away in a couple of weeks, which would mean hiring a bloody double horse-box for the day again, and maybe two days. Venetia said that as a matter of fact they were very lucky to have been selected to take part.

'Yes, really well done, kids,' he said.

Chapter 9

Harpur watched the Chief summon strength and courage. 'As will be apparent to you, Desmond, our problem is that we have a murdered man for whom in my view you would have been very justified in feeling great jealousy, hatred indeed,' Lane said. 'This is bound to come out.'

'That's entirely fair,' Iles declared at once, as if they were discussing someone else. 'Oh, yes, there's motive. He'd been fucking my wife for God knows how long.' He nodded a couple of times at Lane, giving encouragement, reminding Harpur of a teacher with a nervous child. 'Aston is not the father of my daughter, however.'

Lane raised his hands, like a priest about to bless, and wrinkled his face to show shock. 'That's not my suggestion at all, Desmond.'

'Which, sir?'

'Which what?' Lane asked.

'Which is not your suggestion, sir: that he'd been fucking my wife, or was, or was not, the father of my daughter?'

Lane paused and sighed: 'Oh, the second, of course.' Harpur thought the Chief might begin to wish he had never started this.

Iles replied: 'I see. It's not your suggestion that he is the father of Fanny, but it is your suggestion that he had been having my wife?'

Lane said: 'I wonder if we could conduct things in a passably civilised way, Desmond.'

Iles thought about this. 'Yes, sir, jealousy and hatred would be valid terms for what I felt about Aston. Obviously, I'm glad he's dead and the method is acceptable – to me, personally, that is. Not from a professional point of view, obviously.'

They were in the Chief's room, Lane not at his desk today but trying to look relaxed in an easy chair. The Chief gave plentiful, genial thought to making people feel at ease, and was strong on sensitivity: Iles always said catastrophically strong. Lane had discarded his suit jacket and put on an old office cardigan in beige, and also removed his shoes again. His face was, as ever, kindly but also pale even by his standards, and his breathing had become noisy and shallow. You would think he was the one being questioned. Iles sat upright on a straight chair, also without a jacket, his shirt sleeves turned. back a little, legs crossed. He was very still, also a little whiter than usual and perhaps not as much in command of himself as seemed.

'You valued your wife deeply, regardless,' Lane said.

'Regardless, sir?'

'Well, regardless of her behaviour.'

'She was, is, my wife, sir. I come from a tribe where marriages continue. Sarah does, too. She might go out looking for it and consulting counsellors, but she comes home. We're tediously lower-middle-class in origins, the sort the to have and hold bit was specifically written for.'

'Anyone who endangered your marriage could be seen as a threat?' Lane asked.

'My marriage and my family.'

'As a threat?'

Iles had another period of thought. '*Anyone* who endangered the marriage? Not sure about the *one* in anyone. It took two you know, sir. She wanted him. Sarah has her own mind. One of the things I love in her, but which brings its hazards. Its pain.'

'Yes, but Desmond, Aston was . . .'

Iles spoke in a quiet, expository voice, from which he tried to keep any trace of sadness, though Harpur spotted the misery there well enough: 'I couldn't give her whatever it was she wanted, sir. It's not the first time in our marriage that this sort of thing has happened. Sarah isn't one to accept what she regards as a second-rate state of affairs and simply sit on her thumb. Thumbs are not what she likes best to sit on, and especially not her own. Possibly you've never run into that sort of situation, sir. Perhaps you can adequately fill Mrs Lane's wants. Very enviable. If I may add, I've noticed the way she looks at you.'

Lane glanced down at her framed picture on the desk and Iles said: 'And on your, part, too, sir. It would make the sort of

38

seething dissatisfaction present in Sarah quite difficult for you to understand.'

At the start of this interview, Harpur had stood near the door of Lane's room, ready to leave, if it came to that, and uncertain whether he wanted to stay or go. He had not looked forward to watching someone forced to talk about the most agonising parts of his life, even someone like Iles. But, Christ, what did that mean, 'even someone like Iles'? He could suffer as much as anybody. Suffering might have helped make him the way he was now. No one started out like that, police star or not.

Very tentatively, the Chief had opened up with: 'Desmond, as a professional you'll understand the situation. Colin and I think you have to be interviewed about Aston's death. A matter of—'

'Eliminating me from inquiries?' Iles had affably remarked.

'Disposing of certain matters. Obviously, Colin can't properly handle this: questioning his senior.'

'Oh, I'd never pull rank on dear old Col.'

'Would you be willing if I did it?' Lane had said.

'But of course, sir. I'm in the best of hands.'

Although Harpur felt sympathy, a part of him longed to hear the truth dredged from Iles now, if that was possible. The wish had nothing to do with being a policeman. Since the trip with Sarah to Aston's funeral, and especially since that moment when she wept against his shoulder, he had begun to feel something approaching jealousy of Iles, jealousy even of the weak, on-off hold the ACC seemed to have over his wife. Harpur's feelings had surprised him, and so far he had not examined them too closely. They were there, all right, though. That link with Ruth Cotton must really have been broken, then? He had not felt sure till now. Today, things could happen here that might weaken Iles's hold on Sarah even further, perhaps brush it right away, and Harpur found he wanted that. Iles had spoken of her mind going. She might need someone to look after her, someone other than the ACC. Certainly that.

'This is totally informal, naturally – no warning or tape recorder or any of that rubbish,' the Chief had declared, as they began, and then asked whether Iles would prefer Harpur to leave. 'It can be done just man to man.' Lane had put a lot of soul into that, trying to sound as if the two of them were nothing but friends and equals. Iles would regard it as unforgivably impertinent.

'Colin?' he replied. 'As I've said, Colin's great. He must stay.'

In that endearing, civilised way of his, the Chief had remained apologetic. 'In case I have to bring in someone from outside the Force, Desmond, I must be able to say I've covered certain ground with you. A key question is whether the affair between Sarah and Aston was over.'

' "Key" in the sense that it would remove motive?'

'Certainly diminish motive.'

'If he was no longer a "threat", there'd be no point in smashing his head?' Iles remarked.

'*Was* it over, Desmond? Had the coming of the child transformed the situation?'

Iles thought only briefly about this. 'No. For a time I hoped so. Men regard pregnancies as rather more magical matters than women do, sir. Their desires are not transformed by bearing a child. I don't think she could leave him alone.'

Harpur, sitting there watching and listening, not sure whether he should speak, thought what a bizarre trio they were. Iles, neat, emotionally scarred, ferociously contemptuous of almost everyone, and especially of the Chief, was the natural focus: someone Harpur had worked with and talked with as closely as with any man ever, and whom he knew as well as he had known any man ever. Probably the ACC was capable of pretty much anything, including what they were discussing here, the removal of Sarah's lover. Did Mark Lane understand that? In his nice, hopeful way, the Chief had said the interview was a formality. Did he really believe it? And, then, when Harpur thought about himself, and the divided interests he had just found, he was forced to ask whether he wanted those certain matters removed 'once and for all' and Iles left in the clear.

'You'll know, sir, that we've been able to fix the time of Aston's death quite accurately.' Harpur felt they had done enough on motive and that he could reasonably hit Iles with some basics.

'Yes, I've seen the findings, of course, Col. You'll want to know where I was then.'

'Look, Desmond, it does seem outrageous to be asking an ACC for an alibi,' Lane stated.

Iles generously waved a hand to show no objection. 'I have thought about this, naturally, and been able to pin-point my movements pretty exactly for that time.'

Smiling hugely with relief, the Chief said immediately: 'Wonderful! Wé can dispose of the thing and then get on properly with the inquiry. Colin has substantial leads. Aston was back into quite perilous work, apparently. Can you tell us, then, where you were?'

'With a tart. In my car. Yes, at just that time,' Iles said.

For a moment, Lane fell silent, the smile instantly dead.

'A warehouse yard behind Nott Street. Say an hour and a half, possibly a little longer.' Iles became like a teacher again, addressing Lane: 'This is what's known as a middling session, sir, as distinct from the famous short time, or, of course, all night. Colin will be familiar with the various terms. The fees vary.' He glanced about Lane's room. 'Are we bugged, sir?'

Lane looked profoundly hurt. 'Certainly not, Desmond.'

Iles shrugged.

'You were with this girl in your Orion, sir?' Harpur asked.

'Yes. You're right, Col. It might have been noticed. That would be a help, I suppose. The reg is probably known to a lot of the riff-raff. Quite a few girls and clients use that area.'

Lane said helplessly: 'Are we talking about circularising ponces, whores and punters to provide information about my Assistant Chief Constable's sex life?'

'I do wish it could be otherwise, sir. May I say by way of explanation that there's been very little physical activity between Sarah and me for a long time,' Iles replied, adding forcefully, 'though the child is certainly mine. And, then, Sarah was always so damn conventional – limited – in what she would do, at least with me, sir. One felt circumscribed. You'll have read that President J. F. Kennedy liked a woman to provide three particular sexual experiences. But as for Sarah . . .'

'Do the ninety minutes or so you were in the car with this girl exactly cover the time when Aston was killed?' Lane said.

'I believe they do,' Isles replied.

'Was this a regular girl of yours, sir?' Harpur asked. 'Someone we could find?'

'No, not regular. One does look for change. And if a girl got to know who I was it could lead to embarrassment. Not good for the Force. You'll understand the need for supreme discretion, sir,' he told the Chief. 'Of course, I know where I picked her up. It could be her routine beat. We might be lucky. But these girls travel.

41

Football matches, business exhibitions, Amsterdam. I imagine she could be anywhere by now. She gave a name – Veronica. But, I ask you.'

'Do you think you'd recognise her, sir?' Harpur asked. 'Or she you?'

'It is difficult. It was dark, of course. And they see a lot of men. I don't expect I'm especially memorable.'

'Well, there was the Kennedy New Frontiers aspect, sir, the three different acts,' Harpur suggested.

'You think that might stick in her mind, Col? Possibly. You believe most of their business is straight up the middle?'

'Fair or dark, sir?'

'Blonde, I think.'

'Age?'

'Eighteen? Perhaps a bit younger.'

Lane winced. 'How much younger?'

'Oh, of legal age, sir, no question. I wouldn't have you worrying yourself about that.'

'Accent?' Harpur asked.

'Well, there were only very few words.'

'What?'

'Forty-five quid. Followed by: All right, thirty-five, but it's a bleeding steal. Could be local intonation, I think, though the "bleeding" might suggest Cockney.'

Lane said: 'God, I wish I'd never—'

'In some ways I confess to feeling a touch of guilt, sir, bringing you into all this louche behaviour.'

42

Chapter 10

When Caring Oliver came out next time on a visit to the Monty he was alone, wearing what Ember would call a real Institute of Directors blue pin-stripe suit, and a grey tie with gleaming silver dots on, the sort that usually went with distinguished capital and integrity. Good Taste was written all over him, but in very nice, plain letters, not garish. This was afternoon again, nobody much about in the club. If you did not know who and what Caring Oliver was, it could be a real plus for the Monty having someone like that seen going in: gleaming, grey hair tidy around his ears, and the gold-card garments, including a waistcoat and cut-away collar shirt.

'When there's a job coming, Pete Chitty and I don't get seen together,' Oliver said. 'Well, I mentioned Welcome aboard last time we talked, but I need to be certain you're in, Ralphy.'

Probably Oliver coming on his own was a gambit. He always handled the diplomatic, gentle stuff. The caring. 'Ralph Ember will definitely do it,' Ember replied. It boomed out big, cocky, empty, all-friends-together, and Ember suddenly thought he sounded exactly the way Maggie had said: shit-scared to turn it down.

'Grand,' Oliver cried and took Ralph's hand and shook it hard. You could see he really believed he had achieved something, and given himself a leg up. It made Ember feel good. On the whole, he had decided to believe Les Reid, and shelve the worries about Aston.

Caring waved a thin, green leather document case he was carrying. 'Ralphy, I was so sure you wouldn't leave us in the lurch I've brought some of the papers with me, for a briefing.' They sat at one of the tables near the bar and Oliver put the case in front of them and unzipped it. He pulled out a transparent plastic bag as big as an LP, full of fifties. 'Here's the object of the exercise then. Cash outward journey, freight inward. Those buggers at the other end kick up about fifties sometimes, on account of they're conspicuous, supposedly, but stuff them. I'm not lugging great stacks of paper about and I'm not having my people do it, either.'

'It's certainly fulsome quantity,' Ember said, picking up the bag and feeling the weight. There was something hearty about the way a stack of fifties sat on your hand. It had been a long time.

'We pay far over the odds. They think we're out-of-town suckers and don't notice, but it's one of those things we accept. This is weapons brought in from the States somehow – I don't ask – brand new, first class, no jamming and no tracing. All that's pricey, Ralph. You'll remember, I expect. These are K-frames, Model Thirteen, .357. FBI use them, so you can see why they cost. Plus there's a fee in here for one of Leopold's lads for an assignment. Your commission comes out at a percentage of the whole amount, Ralph, which made it six hundred and fifty pounds, so we put it to a round seven hundred and fifty for luck and a golden hello.'

'Nice. Another lad? What assignment is that, Caring?'

Under the plastic bag were some photographs, as if Oliver had pulled them out by accident. 'Oh, look,' he said. The first three were of some big, beautiful stone buildings with very good lawns in front, lead on the windows and a couple of cars parked near.

'This is it,' Caring said.

'What? I thought this job was just to—'

'The school. In Cheltenham. This is where the daughter goes.'

'Looks great. A stack of tradition. Something you don't buy in Tescos.' He touched the bag of money. 'So, just hand it over and they give me a parcel?'

'That's the first part of your little mission, yes.'

Ember's breath went for a second. Then he said: 'First? Something else, Caring? This other lad you spoke of? What assignment? Now, look—'

'Hand it over and they count. Then they give you six Model Thirteens, one at a time, and *you* count. Look good at these guns, Ralphy. You still remember about armament?'

'Well, counting to six I can do.' He laughed.

Caring laughed, too, a bit late, a quick, executive-type laugh, unmerry. 'You'd know a new piece, yes? No fucking stuff that went through the battle of Monte Casino.'

'Oh, sure.'

'She's happy at this school, that's the thing,' Caring said. Today, he would not take a brandy, and Ember did without, too. It looked better. Of course, Caring was flashing these school snaps to show prosperity, and to tell Ember loud and clear he was wasting his time in the Monty and had better get in with them – a snob giggle from this piece of tailoring over Venetia and Fay sunk in a day school.

'The school lawns give a sense of dignity,' Ember said. 'What you can't visualise is pissed teachers having it off together on this grass last day of term, like in the comprehensives.'

Oliver pointed to the money. 'You can see why we need someone we can super-trust, Ralphy. If our go-between cut loose, there's enough here for quite a few weeks in Florida with all the comforts.'

'You don't have to worry on that, Ollie.' Then he asked again: 'But, what do you mean, *first* part?'

'We don't worry, Ralph. Track record. And there's your family you have to consider. With Ian Aston, it was a bit different. Newish kid, really. No dependants. We could feel exposed?'

Ember grew suddenly slightly giddy. Not panicky, no, giddy.

Caring said: 'A bit of a map here I've had drawn for you.' He pulled a sheet of paper from the case. 'You'll be going by car, of course, because we want you to saunter on a little way afterwards.'

Suddenly, Caring seemed to see Ember was troubled. 'Oh, don't misunderstand what I said about Aston. What happened to him injury-wise was nothing to do with us, Pete or me. You know that? Cunt's always an incalculable element, but he was a bloody head-case to keep after her.' He laughed very briefly again. 'Yes, bloody head-case. Fact remains, we knew we were taking a risk.'

Aston tried to walk off with their cash? Still not clear in his head or stomach, Ember asked: 'What saunter are you talking about, Ollie? I thought just up and back.'

'Map's a bit primitive. This is Kew way, a really nice spot, they tell me. Not the kind of area you'd expect gun dealings at all, which is clever. Leafy, big old houses with yellow bricks, sanded drives, antique shops. They can afford it because of people like us, satisfied customers who keep coming back with cash.' He pointed. 'Here's Kew underground station. And here's the house where they'll be expecting you, just around the corner. You can pull right off the road, out of sight. Number eight. You all right for memory, Ralph? I'd like you to look at it and then I'll rip it up. The people up there could be bothered, otherwise.'

Ember gazed at the map. 'Fine.'

Caring Oliver tore it into small pieces and put them in an ashtray. Ember took a book of Monty matches from the bar and lit the pile of paper, something he had seen in a spy film. 'Good thinking, Ralph. That's what I mean about sensible habits from way back.' They watched the flames.

Ember waited anxiously for more about this added dimension of the job. Instead, Caring pointed to one of the school pictures. 'These lawns. Ever seen girls' cricket? To me, it seems all wrong, if I'm frank, a girl with big, wicketkeeper's gloves on, like deformed. I think I'll be able to stuff one of the mistresses, called Angeline, would you believe, but it's got to be a gradual approach. Physical Education and Computers. Sublime arse. Sports day – school against teachers – she really makes the high jump worth hanging about for. As we said, pack the guns and ammo that comes with them somewhere nice. One of the lads from Kew called Winston will come with you then.'

'What? Back here? Is this new? This is the other lad?'

'No, not back here. This is the second aspect of the trip, Ralph. Always has been.'

'Oh, now, look Caring, I—'

'Yes, the further element in this job is a drive to Cardiff, Ralph. I've got another map.'

'Christ, what? Cardiff? Bloody Wales? What for? This is more weaponry? Why two of us? Who is this guy, Winston?'

What kind of activity needed a pair? Jesus, should he ever have started all this again, even for seven hundred and fifty? Was this the stage when Aston tried to back out?

'This is what I meant – liaison, Ralph. You're more than a piffling messenger boy and transport man, I hope.'

'What? Well, yes, maybe.' A few years ago he could have eaten these two and all the rest of their lot. For a few seconds then the past made him feel strong, even pushy. He could take on anything dreamed up by this crew. 'So what second element, Ollie?'

'I knew you could see to it, Ralphy. Here's Lynette, the daughter, with some friends in this picture. Her teachers say university material, Colleges? It could be different now, but a few years ago, drugs, and non-stop, all-round shagging – Oxford, Kent, wherever. Condoms, yes, but will the upper classes? Sons of dukes, all they care about is the estate and bloodstock.'

'Cardiff's where you're doing the job? Whatever?'

'As a matter of fact, this is very handy from Kew. Right down the M4. No, the job's not Cardiff, but we have a contact there due to give some information. We want you to listen and bring that back with the armament, Ralph. So, get the guns in Kew, then Wales for the information.' He spread another hand-drawn map on the table. 'Where he lives at Cardiff. You'll have to keep this one. Not a memory job.'

'This is a contact in Wales? A different lad from Winston?'

He laughed. 'Oh, yes, very different from Winston. It might take two of you to handle this Cardiff lad. Why we're including the fee for Winston.'

'How come?'

'This lad, the one in Cardiff – Denzil? Damien? something like that, Winston's got the name – this Denzil promised information, which is crucial to a project, and then he started getting coy. But we can't do without these facts and I don't think I can expect you to go down there and shake such matters from him on your own. If Denzil sees two of you he's going to change his mind back again and feel easier about giving us what we need. That knife thing on your jaw is clearing up, Ralph, yet still shows you've heard of rough and tumble. Denzil will read the signs very quick. Winston's pretty and young, but people can see somehow that he's capable of giving exceptionally sharp stress.'

Caring picked out one of the pictures of the school and pointed to a first-floor window. 'This is where the teacher lives. I was in there once, only for a couple of minutes, though, just pleasantries. Framed certificates on the wall – physical fitness, life saving, A-levels – and a lot of netball photographs. I talk about her arse, but education, too, and culture. She loves Loudon Wainwright the Third's records.'

47

'This could turn violent with this Cardiff boy, Denzil, you mean, Ollie?' Ember gazed at the picture of Caring's daughter, a dark, fat thing, with a big, bath-sponge face, sad like her father's, who was not going to get cock trouble from duke's sons. Ember ran his finger along the jaw scar. 'Caring, I've got to say this straight out, I can't get involved in any brutality, I mean, beating talk out of someone. All that's very much another era. Maggie would quit me.'

'Shall I tell you what I regard it as when someone like this Denzil gives an assurance and then backs down, Ralphy? Unmanly. I'm going to leave now, as a matter of fact, before Maggie and the children arrive again, much as I'd like to see them.' He gathered the photographs up and put them back into the case. 'I don't want your wife thinking I'm up here all the time, Ralph. She might misinterpret that as leaning on you and the family.'

Chapter 11

'Forgiveness,' Sarah said. 'You spoke of it after the funeral. I didn't understand. Could I talk to you? Just for a few minutes.'

'My dear, you've come all that distance? Alone?'

'Alone, yes? Sort of alone. The baby's in the car.'

'Oh, you mustn't leave her there. Please, bring her in.'

'May I? I wasn't sure what you'd—'

'Please,' Mrs Aston said. 'And driving all that way to Bristol by yourself. And about forgiveness? Well. You poor girl. Your heart is exercised over a grave matter.' The words sounded like something Mrs Aston might have heard from a platform, unnatural and heavy, yet Sarah felt real sympathy in them, too. Mrs Aston walked out to the street with her to bring Fanny from the car.

It was a large, neat council estate built around three or four long, curving, identical streets, the sort of district where Sarah had been born, and as soon as she drove on to the estate today she felt comfortable and comforted. Here, she might learn something. She had it in her head that these sorts of people thought straight, because they couldn't afford not to. Of course, she had it in another part of her head that if these people could think straight they would not be stuck here. Her own parents had moved on. And also, of course, she knew that Desmond would take one glance at the streets and mutter, 'Bill Sykesville.'

Until now, this house had been only an address in her little book, somewhere Ian had suddenly fled to once in a while, or oftener, when urgently needing a bolt-hole. Yes, oftener. She would write to him here. He used to say it was a place to come back to and a place to escape from, and she had never disagreed. To escape from here he had done the sort of work he did and taken the kind of risks he did – the ones she had never asked about. So, why hadn't Ian realised he should disappear to

Bristol for a period this time? In case friends of Preston thought the acquittal was part of a police deal and came looking for him, he had moved from his flat immediately after the trial, but only as far as a bed-sit half a dozen streets away. How could he be so careless with his life?

With Fanny in the carry-cot they went inside. 'A friend of Ian's, Don,' Mrs Aston called.

'A friend? What sort of friend?'

'It's harsh to speak like that. The lady at Ian's funeral.'

'Came with the police?' the man said. 'I half remember. Only a few things I remember from that day.'

'About forgiveness,' Mrs Aston said.

'I don't forgive,' the man replied.

'We agree to differ on that, as well you know.'

They were in a small room which seemed to have been newly decorated with wallpaper showing bright foliage and plump, smiling brown birds. There was a long, stone fireplace, nearly big enough for a castle and occupying most of one wall, and a gleaming, modern sideboard with mock-brass fittings. The man was seated in an easy chair near it. Like Mrs Aston he was in his sixties and grey. Perhaps a long time ago one or both of them had been as fair-haired as Ian.

'No, I wouldn't say harsh,' he went on. 'But we're living with a tragedy, aren't we? Some questions I have to ask. He was my son.'

'I don't mind being asked,' Sarah said. 'I loved him.'

He waved a hand, maybe dismissing the word as fancy or womanish or a lie. Not signalling much of a welcome for it, anyway. 'Well, yes, I supposed you'd say so,' he replied. 'But are you sure? You're one with police connections? He was my son, but I still wouldn't have thought he was your sort.'

'Sort?'

He slowly looked around the room, searching for inspiration to give him a better word. 'Well, sort.'

'Yes, he was my sort. We were each other's sort. That's exactly what we were.'

'Tell me this, then, did you send him letters here?'

'Sometimes.'

'Those were the best of envelopes, very creamy and solid. And the way you write. We're not used to envelopes like that here.' He was round-faced and almost chubby, seemingly made to look cheerful, but his skin had barely any colour and his eyes were sad and defeated, as if he had come to expect only insolence from life.

'Was he pleased to get the letters?' she said. Sarah sat down on a mock-leather settee opposite him and struggled to imagine Ian in this room, lately or as a child.

'Don't ask me about pleased,' he replied. 'Ian wasn't a talker, recently. He seemed half frightened out of his skin. Peeping around the edge of the curtains, like something hunted. What had he done?'

'He had worries,' Mrs Aston said. 'Business worries, he called them. But, well. Of this world, anyway.' She had made tea and gave Sarah a cup with some biscuits.

'It's because of her beliefs at Jericho that May says forgiveness,' Don said.

'I thought so,' Sarah replied.

'Oh, guilt,' Mrs Aston said. 'We're all guilty, all sin through and through. Why point the finger?'

He moved to the front of the chair and leaned towards Sarah: 'What forgiveness? You want to forgive whoever did that to Ian? Why? Seven or eight blows. I know about the New Testament, via May and otherwise. In its way, Jericho is fair enough, but this is a boy, battered to death. That's got to be out of proportion.' For a second the eyes shone with grief and fight, then quietened into another collapse.

'Yes, but it's not the first murder, is it, Don, love? "Forgive them for they know not what they do." '

'That's what I don't understand, and I want to understand,' Sarah said. 'How you can feel like that.' Her voice came out weak and earnest and confused, like a student quizzing a teacher.

'Why do you worry over it so much – forgiveness?' Don asked. 'Are you thinking about someone particular?'

'I'm not sure,' Sarah replied.

Mrs Aston said: 'Of course, I don't feel forgiveness all the time. The flesh won't allow it. And I understand when the world and Don cannot forgive.'

'If I knew who killed Ian, or thought I knew, you still think I should be able to forgive him?' Sarah asked.

'This is police, yes?' Don said.

51

'Possibly.'

'Someone close?'

'Oh, you poor dear,' Mrs Aston said. Her big, hefty face creased for a moment, as if she might weep.

'I have to go on living,' Sarah replied.

'My feeling is this is to do with the baby as well,' Don said.

'Partly to do with the baby,' Sarah replied.

He sank back in his chair again. 'As I see it, this child could be family, May.'

'Well, obviously.'

'Let me give you the sort of rumour we heard,' he told Sarah. 'Ian with someone's wife. What you'd call love, I expect. The husband offended to such a point, especially after the child. And then the death. Can I be expected to make light of that?'

'Born in sin, yes,' Mrs Aston said. 'That's an old story. But not just this baby. All of us. In the eyes of God. So, you must be the Mrs Iles we've heard of. It's still lovely of you to have come.'

'And you go on living with such a man?' Don asked. He stared at her, uncomprehending.

'None of this that you're saying is at all certain,' Sarah replied, almost shouting. 'It's rumour. My God, it's crazy. We're talking about an assistant chief constable, for heaven's sake. Ian had dangerous friends and contacts through his work. You ask me what he was afraid of. He was afraid of most of them. All of them. Look, I'm sorry to have blasphemed.'

'You would like to forgive him – your husband?' Mrs Aston said.

'I would like to know how it's possible, if all this is true. To forgive the killing of your son.'

'We have a lesson about that, haven't we, Mrs Iles?' Mrs Aston replied.

Don said: 'What I mean about not being your sort: close to police, well, married to police, then the good stationery, thick as slices of toast.'

'Sort?' Mrs Aston said. 'We're all one sort. Sinners in the sight of God.' She pulled back the corner of the quilt on the carry-cot and looked at Fanny. 'Oh, she's so like you. She's like Mrs Iles, isn't she, Don?'

'Everyone says so,' Sarah replied.

Don Aston stood up and came to look at the child. 'Yes, very like her mother,' he said.

Chapter 12

Late one afternoon, Harpur drove the Chief down to where Aston's body had been found. For a while Harpur had known such an outing must be on the cards. Then, in his mild, edgy fashion, Lane had asked today whether he could look at some of the main areas of the case for himself. Occasionally, if he felt unhappy at the way an investigation was going, the Chief would do that, and about this one he would be unhappy and more. Tortured. Christ, he must fear the Force had begun to break apart. He had to do something.

They pulled up near a telephone booth and walked to a small rectangle of waste ground dotted with fly-tipped builder's debris, alongside the main rail lines north. Lane looked anything but police. It must be part of what made him a very useful detective before climbing higher: scruffy, sallow, flabby, he was also awkward on his feet, so that the hundred yards they walked seemed an effort, like someone exercising gently after a hernia operation. Lane took pride in radiant unsmartness: part of what Iles called his 'lowlier than thou' complex. But who, except police, would spend part of their day on an unofficial rubbish tip?

A covered footbridge over the lines started at the edge of the ground and came down on the other side at the end of a terrace of small houses with front doors direct on to the street. High, rusted iron railings cut off the waste ground and the street from the railway. 'About here, sir,' Harpur said. They were near the dumped remains of a couple of old beds, some empty paint pots, and the splintered glass and rotten woodwork of replaced, ancient window-frames. 'Lying face down, with his feet towards the footbridge. We think he might have crawled a little way. There were blood marks.' Harpur turned and pointed. 'A train was stuck on a red this side of the bridge for a few minutes and someone looking out thought he saw a man crawling, resting, forcing himself to crawl again, then finally sinking down. Night, of course. The train passenger assumed it was a drunk, until he read about Aston.'

Lane gazed around and Harpur could sense his distress. 'My God, Colin, what sort of place are we policing, and what sort of job do we make of it? The middle of a major English city, but at ten o'clock at night a man can be head clobbered so badly he has to drag himself away on his knees to die on a shit heap, with no help. And we know nothing of it for how many hours afterwards?'

'Seven and a half,' Harpur replied.

'They picked up corpses quicker in No Man's Land. All right, he was a would-be crook and a shagger of other men's wives, but he still did not deserve that death.'

The Chief enjoyed reflections. Certain crimes would strike Lane as emblematic of the state of Britain or Western civilisation or the world, and gloom of a respectable width came easily to him. Another of Iles's remarks was that the Chief ought to put 'grief' as his hobby in *Who's Who*. The actual entry was 'Gilbert and Sullivan'. Harpur said: 'The ground's been scoured and re-scoured for a weapon, sir. No luck.'

'Plenty of half house bricks.'

'None with blood or hair on.'

'If he took it away, it could be someone who knows how important to us the weapon is.'

'Sometimes it is, yes, sir. Not always.'

'A brick would hold prints?'

'Yes, but if it was someone as wise as you suggest he wouldn't be bare handing, would he?'

Lane was pretty new to his big job, and probably suspected that Iles, Garland, Harpur himself, and other old hands, might keep him in the dark when it suited them. Might? This was standard treatment for incoming Chiefs anywhere. Like every other new boy, they had to earn acceptance and trust. Lane's Catholicism hindered integration, too, in this Force, with its big Lodge contingent. To Harpur the Chief's religion might be immaterial, but for some it made him eternally dodgy, to be told nothing beyond what he had to be told. In Lane's eyes, this, above all, must look like a time when people would get together to curtain him off.

One of their own might be in bad trouble and Lane was outside the club.

Lane walked to the iron railings and took a grip on two of them like a prisoner looking out: maybe how he had come to feel about his job here. Or maybe something about all jobs anywhere. 'The stopped train would prevent people in those houses seeing what happened?' he asked.

'Yes, sir.'

'This sort of back-street crew would be glued to bloody television at that time, anyway. Which do you reckon is the wrong side of the tracks here, Colin? Both?'

These were untypically cruel judgements for Lane, possibly proving how troubled he felt. The Chief picked a path back through the heaps of junk and turned towards the footbridge.

Yes, Harpur liked him well enough, and perhaps better than he liked Iles – 'like' was a crazily unsuitable word for reactions to the ACC – but he had known Iles years longer and partnered him in all sorts of work; with him put God knew how many people away, and with him failed to put a few away, too. All that counted heavily when someone was in trouble, even if you were beginning to fancy his wife.

There was a phrase, hatched by some smart, wordsmith sociologist, to describe such absolute loyalty to one another in low rank police: 'canteen culture'. Harpur's wife, Megan, would often delightedly quote it at him when she wanted to stab, which was fairly often, and getting oftener. It did not stop with the troops, though. You could even say, the higher the stronger, though in this instance it shut the Chief right out, of course. One day, Lane might become tolerated and wriggle his way inside this mythical club. Nobody could really hate him, not even Iles, with all his laid down cellar of venom. The Chief might look like an abandoned breakfast, but he meant well, which God knew was rare enough in top police.

Lane said: 'This man was crawling? Like a drunk?'

'The passenger's description. We think dragged part of the way, then recovered enough to move again.'

Lane seemed to ponder this as they walked over the bridge. Was Lane thinking, as Harpur had thought, that this made it look unlike Iles's work: not tidy enough or ruthless enough? Surely, if jealous rage had finally driven the ACC to ambush Aston and leave him for dead, Aston would have been totally finished. Iles did not mess about: Harpur suspected that a couple of full-time villains, who briefly and stupidly thought they had got away with murdering a young detective not long ago, could have confirmed this. They would need a medium, now, though.

Harpur said: 'We have another witness from the next street, where Aston was living. He saw him come out and walk down towards the bridge just before ten p.m. This had happened on one or two previous evenings, apparently.'

'At the same time?'

'Pretty well.'

'Do we know how long he was out on these other occasions?'

'Half an hour or a little less.'

'I'll have a look at his bed-sit, shall I, Colin?' They walked on. 'So, we assume he was attacked on the bridge and then somehow staggered and crawled to the waste ground?'

'We think attacked near the phone booth. We found no blood or other signs of violence on the bridge.'

'Someone waiting for him?'

'Or more than one.'

'Of course. You're still determined to nail it on Pete Chitty and Oliver? I saw an account of what Chickenfeed Reid said.'

'I still believe they're in the frame, sir. Or people who think he'd grassed to get acquitted.'

'Have we talked to Chitty or Oliver, or to any of them?'

'I'd prefer they weren't alerted, yet. We're not even doing surveillance on them. These are experienced villains. They're wide awake and they know how to build barricades. Here we are.' The landlady who opened when Harpur rang showed them to Aston's small bed-sit and left. 'He abandoned his flat and came here immediately after the acquittal, sir,' Harpur said. 'Naturally scared. He'd think he might get callers.'

'No pictures of Sarah Iles,' Lane said. 'Or have they been removed?'

'This is as it was, sir.'

'Single bed.'

'The landlady says he brought no women in.'

'I take it we knew he'd hidden here?'

'We had a good idea, yes, sir.'

56

'Did the ACC know where he was?'

'I couldn't say.'

'But he'd only have to look at the notes.'

'I don't think there were notes, sir. There's no dossier. Aston's never been convicted.'

'You just had his new address in your head?'

'And Garland. Possibly one or two other people.'

'Including the ACC?'

'I couldn't say, sir. Not from me. The matter never arose.'

The Chief opened a few drawers and glanced from the window. 'Nothing helpful here at all?'

'Nothing, sir. A bit of a transit camp, I imagine. He would have gone back to something more spacious when things cooled down.'

'No phone.'

'One downstairs in the hall, sir.'

'Yes, I saw that. But if he were ringing a— If he wanted to make a very personal call, he might not wish to do it from there. I wonder if he was heading for that public booth near the other side of the bridge. Someone might have discovered it was a routine and lain in wait: your witness says he came out at ten p.m. on each occasion. Might be an agreed time for a call – so the right person is ready and picks up the receiver quickly at the other end. In clandestine arrangements, it's a basic ploy. Well, I don't have to tell you.' Almost at once, he put a hand on Harpur's shoulder, seeming suddenly afraid again that he had given offence: 'I mean, espionage drama, and so on.'

'It's possible. Bit of a gamble on the phone being unvandalised.'

'Were there incoming calls for him?'

'Some.'

'A woman?'

'Sometimes a woman, the landlady says.'

'Well-spoken? Rougement Place?'

'She couldn't help on that, sir.'

'But what sort of woman? Surely, she—'

'Just a woman, sir. Perhaps more than one.'

'Lover boy.'

'There's his mother, of course.'

'Yes. I'm glad you were able to get to his funeral. You

can see now, I expect, what a mistake it would have been to travel there with Mrs Iles, or be in her immediate company at the service.'

'Absolutely, sir.'

'Such a difficult woman to categorise. I'll never understand how she and Desmond come to be together.'

'These things start well and fade.'

'Yes, I suppose so.' He sounded genuinely baffled, as if his own marriage had never shown such decline. 'So, now we have someone who is in so many ways a fine man driven to taking the—'

'We're still without any sort of clinching evidence, sir.'

'Are we? But, yes, of course you're right, Colin.'

'You're still considering bringing in another Force to look at this, sir?'

'What else can I do?'

Harpur drove the Chief back to headquarters, waited around for a while and then, as the evening set in, went down to the streets around Valencia Esplanade where most of the prostitutes had their beat. He hoped to find the girl Iles said he had been with on the night of Aston's death. The chances had to be low, but he owed Iles the effort. Time could be getting short.

After three hours, he had learned nothing. Most of the girls and their pimps disappeared, anyway, once Harpur entered the area. The rest did not want to talk. Harpur was too easily spotted and too well known. About to return to his car and abandon the attempt at around eleven o'clock, he thought he saw someone he knew walking slowly ahead. Increasing his pace, he found he was right.

Iles turned his head swiftly, ready for trouble, when Harpur spoke his name. 'Col,' he said cheerfully, 'looking for a night out?'

'Looking for *your* night out. Your alibi.'

'Tireless. You're good to me.'

'And you, sir? You're searching for her, too, for the same reason?'

'Not especially her. Just a girl. Just pussy.'

'I don't know whether that's wise, sir.'

'Wise? Oh, fuck wise. Necessary. Now I realise why things are so barren down here tonight: I suppose you realise you're ruining business, sniffing about, you great, ugly lump of law?'

Chapter 13

'So what happened to the usual one, Ralph? I can call you Ralph?'

Leopold, this bright-looking little character, probably knew the answer inside out, but you could never tell, so Ember said: 'He couldn't get here. No untowardness, though. Peter Chitty and Caring Oliver – I've known them from way, way back. They asked me to kindly fill in. Lovely boys.'

'Well, I know. Oliver came on the phone. But this other one called Aston, who was here once or twice. It's not too good, is it? Frankly, we heard dead.'

That 'frankly' – so thoughtful and cocktail-party.

'And not quite natural causes, Ralph,' he said.

So, if he knew, he knew. 'Nothing to do with this job, trust me, Leopold,' Ember said. The room was full of quite decent pieces of old furniture, even antiques, with dark green velvet curtains nearly heavy enough to bring the wall down, and Ember felt it was not really right to be here at all on villainy, let alone mentioning someone with a head destroyed on a Nowheresville dump. Maybe when you'd been out of this work a while you grew sensitive. It was not helpful.

'We're at a distance here, Ralph. We hear all sorts. It leads to confusion.' Although it was afternoon, Leopold had the lights on. He certainly deserved some display.

'This was a lad who messed about in all directions,' Ember explained. Jesus, this was billed as a nice straight deal, money in, guns and ammo out, then a trip to Wales. Why all the preliminaries?

'So police everywhere, fuzzing, quizzing, from now on, Ralph? This was a lad who suffered heavy, unignorable violence?'

'He took a beating.' Ember used to think he'd never have to deal with scrotes like this again, except taking their crooked money at the Monty, and now here he was working at being sweet and communicative.

'They came on the phone with a glittering c.v. for you, Ralph. No better reference for Lord Hailsham, but—'

'This lad was giving it twice or more a week to an important police wife.' Ember would prefer not have people talking his career on an open phone, but dip your toe into the old business again and that was bound to happen. If you wanted secrecy, work for MI5.

'You're telling me hit by a big cop? In person?' Leopold asked. 'How big?'

'They're pretending to look everywhere, of course.'

Leopold tightened up all his tiny, bag-of-bones body and the bare scalp. 'So, are we a bit of the everywhere? Chitty, Caring, you, me, my activity here. You say what you say, but did the police know this lad worked for Peter and Oliver?'

'Aston was clever about the basics, keeping always right out on the edge, Leopold, no come-back. Why people queued to use him.'

And he did look like a bloody Leopold. He had on a cravat. Ember sometimes wore one himself, so that was all right as far as it went, but then a black, shapeless jacket with it, hanging off the scraps of shoulder, probably some exciting new mode or other, and built-up shoes with chunks of yellow metal all over, making you think it was a Morse message every time the electric light caught him. Even without the platforms, he would not be a total dwarf, but his face was skimpy, like a school kid's, and it seemed all wrong with his baldness and the teeth that had a long life-time of neglect to tell you about, in green and black. These did not stop him smiling a lot, such a good, friendly style, which Ember gave him back in full, because everything in this transaction had to run sweetly and be based on absolute, warm-hearted respect for each other. What was known as mutuality.

Leopold went to the window walking how they did on built-ups – stiff, like tin legs – and stared out towards Kew Gardens, keeping himself half concealed by the curtains. He was very still and could have been a tailor's dummy in a shop fond of jokes. 'Relax, Leopold. I had no tail,' Ember told him. 'I can spot them a mile off. Shall we do the business, then? And afterwards meet this Winston I'm supposed to take to Wales.'

For a couple of seconds he did not answer, then suddenly turned around, with one of the messy smiles. 'You don't hang about. They said it had been a loss, you opting out, and I can see why.' He clumped back across the room, the black jacket flapping like a ship's plague flag, and went to what seemed to be a cabin chest, one of the Victorian pieces in the room. When he bent down and opened it, Ember spotted a very modern safe inside, probably bolted to the wall through the wooden back of the chest. Leopold worked the combination and produced two white shoe boxes, with no lids, and now Ember saw the blue Smith and Wesson K-frames. From where he sat, they looked new enough. Christ, he wished he was back at the flat, talking homework to the kids. Talking to the kids did not pay for the school that gave the homework, though.

Ember had an executive-style, black attaché case with him, and he opened this now and brought out the plastic bag of fifties. Of course, it was a peril coming into an unknown place like this carrying extensive cash. Charming area, Kew Gardens, but it could be Fuck You Gardens, too: Leopold looked like a minor wet dream, but one of those revolvers loaded in advance and he's Jesse James. And then, he might have other people in the house.

'And this is all you do?' Ember asked. 'Guns? Ammo?'

Leopold put the boxes on the table.

'Receiving as well? Fencing?' Ember persisted. 'Look, you dragged me through enough questions. Why not you?' He said this in a loud, chummy voice. All of it was to do with getting equality in this sodding, classy room.

Leopold jacked up the smile to a laugh. 'I do like your pace, Ralphy. Did you count the money?'

'Haven't opened it.'

'Possibly best.'

'I don't even know how much is supposed to be there.'

'Possibly best. You familiar with guns? Well, of course. Gather round then, gather round.'

Carefully, as though they were special Sunday cream cakes, he put three revolvers one at a time on the table and then three from the second box.

Ember crossed the room. 'I can handle?' It would feel like committing himself, but he was up to his neck already.

61

Ember picked up a gun and gazed at the hammer, then down the barrel, screwing up his eyes for wisdom. Leopold grinned and nodded, as if it was a wine tasting and he knew Ember was enjoying the special fruitiness. Ember nodded, too. He could not tell if the revolver showed wear, but Leopold might not spot it.

'How do we bring them into this country for you?' Leopold said. 'That's what you're dying to ask?' He threw himself on to a dinky blue moquette settee and stretched out, like Bette Davis being tempestuous in a telly film, or kid's clothes slung down for collection by the Salvation Army.

'Your trade secret, Leopold. You're entitled.'

'I don't mind you asking, Ralphy.' No answer came, though. 'I'll take the packet, shall I?'

Ember passed him the money and Leopold balanced it on his palm. 'Feels about right,' he said, and, without getting up, lobbed it into the safe, everything so big city cool. 'Never had a light one yet from Caring and Pete. Continuance.'

'They speak well of you, too.'

Leopold reached into a corner of the settee under him and brought out a duster. He gave it to Ember to wipe the gun he was handling then use for putting the consignment into his case. 'I'll find you a box of shells before you go. But, look, I don't know if Caring and Peter made this clear: you mustn't use any of those weapons today on the job in Wales. Absolutely *verboten*.'

For a second, Ember could not speak. Then he said: 'God, of course not. I'm not into that sort of stuff, and never have been.'

'Things can take a sudden turn for the worse. Study history. If I were you, I'd leave any crises to Winston. He's handy. And I expect he'll be carrying something of his own. What Caring and Peter would hate is shells from any of those K-frames picked up forensic-wise before their job, whatever.'

'There's going to be no shooting in Wales,' Ember told him. 'Not that kind of outing.'

'They asked for Winston by name, so it just might involve muscle. This Cardiff boy, Denzil, must be a real hindrance. Oliver and Pete are not jungle savage, but they take people out. Well, same way they dealt with Aston.' He spoke very quietly, as if this last bit was obvious, and no argument.

So Ember jumped in fast. 'No. Haven't I told you?'

'Well, yes you have, you have, Ralphy. You say Aston's dead by an angry husband, not Pete and Caring at all.' He was lying on his back, eyes closed, still so relaxed. Any minute he might yoga himself.

'Right.'

'A police officer.' Without opening his eyes, he did one of the smiles and then offered a cheery shrug of those little-boy shoulders, not too noticeable when he was flat. 'It's possible.'

'You don't understand about Iles. This one thinks he can get away with—'

'Murder.'

'Anything. There's a lot of talk about something he did quite lately. Worse than this, if it's true. He's the law and he's lawless.' Hell, he should have said no right away, not let Oliver get where he could shove.

'So, suppose you were right about this officer – I still ask, are they going to look in this direction?'

'Not at all. Nobody ever saw Pete and Caring with Aston. You know those two. Tracks get covered.'

'Well, I know them, and then I don't. They didn't even tell me this lad had death on account of a high-level wife, if that's really it. How high-level?'

'ACC. Where's Winston? Black? That name.'

'Assistant Chief Constable. Assistant Chief? Oh, lovely. So, say you've got it right – if you were up there, an ACC, wouldn't you expect your boys to look around and find someone else for it? This is a sought-after neighbourhood, Ralph. Cachet. I don't want heavies crashing in here, fixing something on us because some long-cock's been raising G-spot gasps from My Lady Cop Brass. We hold all sorts of materials in this house.' Leopold swung his feet and shoes off the furniture, drew himself up to what had to be called his full height, and went to lock the safe. 'Well, whoever did the head job, I'm sure you yourself will be all right handling work for Peter and Oliver now. Christ, you, a club owner, and around with good status for decades – those two couldn't risk something like that with you, Ralph.'

'You just don't listen, do you, Leopold? These boys had nothing to do with Aston's—'

'Here's Winston now,' Leopold said. A door slammed somewhere. 'Winston's into décor and so on. He's been over Putney giving a friend advice on the whole spectrum of ochres. Don't get him talking about it. He'll bore the arse off you.'

'Does he live here, too?'

'Like fuck. Am I going to have his sort permanently in my home? I'm not accepting blood-stained toe caps and shirt cuffs. This house has a history going back to a friend of William Wilberforce.' Leopold smoothed his little face, like someone polishing a medal.

A few hours later, just as it was growing dark, Ember reached the outskirts of Cardiff, with Winston folded up asleep in the passenger seat. Ember had an address and a map from Caring Oliver and drove across the city towards a decent cathedral that stood on the edge, above some big open park. From what he could make out at this time of night, the buildings around the church, known as Llandaff village, looked extremely weighty and religious: a nice little green with proper ruins and the spire behind, and the houses tall, some in grey stone, with genuine old windows.

Sometimes Ember thought he must have missed out on a lot, stuck in a dud street at the Monty, serving drinks to mostly horse shit, while Leopold had a nest in the middle of all that great Kew leafiness, and now this boy, here with his own flat. Ember liked church and would go with the family now and then, and always at Christmas and Easter. It gave a flavour to things, and all those buggering vicars did not bother him. Tolerance. Gays, estate agents, Labour, blacks, you had to make allowances.

He stopped the stolen Carlton in front of the ruins, near a big stone cross, and Winston woke up.

'On the ground floor of the big one there,' Ember said. 'It's showing a light, so we could be in luck.'

'So bloody quiet here.'

'For meditation.'

'If we get yelling from Denzil.'

'I never saw a cross like that,' Ember said.

'Celtic. But they all count.' He stared across the road at the lighted windows. 'It's all bloody loose. Let's go, anyway.'

Ember did not move. 'Loose?'

'This Denzil knows someone who knows someone who knows about the bank's cash movements for half of Britain. That's too many people involved. Then bringing in me, you, plus Leopold told what's what. Is this security?'

Winston was not black. Gingerish. He had long red hair done in a neat little pony-tail with a rubber band at the back, like some sixties dropout, and a thick red moustache. For this sort of work he seemed very young, about twenty, and you could not believe he had experience. He was built more like an athlete than a dropout, thin and with long arms and legs, and he would look right with a tall pole in his hands at the Commonwealth Games. Ember would not have picked him out for someone who was supposed to be frightening.

'Caring thinks this Denzil might be selling his information to someone for a better price,' Winston said. 'That's our problem.' He had opened the door of the Carlton and was half out.

'Christ, that could mean he's being looked after here. Protection.'

'Of course it does. Why there's two of us. Lock the car good. Don't forget you've got a precious cargo. If you go back without the weaponry you're— Well, think of Aston.'

Ember, checking the doors, said again: 'No, it wasn't like—'

'Oh, I know. Some cop, yes? All right. It makes you happy.' They crossed the road quickly. 'We'll try the back,' this kid said.

The garden had a stone wall, with a smart, wrought-iron gate, and beyond it Ember could see light reaching out to a bit of a patio. They went through the gate and stood together at the side of some french windows, looking in. Ember had heard that people with class never pulled the curtains over, as though living in the midst of their acres with only deer about.

The first thing he noticed was how very old this Denzil was, if it was Denzil. Maybe you did not get to know people who knew people at the top of banks until you had been around for a lifetime and looked worn out, but it still came as a shaker. He was sitting in a big armchair with wings, holding a magazine close to his glasses. Ember could make out the title of the article, Anne, The Princess Who Found Herself, so you would know even if you could not see whose hands they were that it must be someone old or half-baked or a woman or the lot. Jesus, it chilled him to think of getting rough with this poor faded sod. Yes, that was what it did if you dropped out of this work – it took away your zest. You started feeling the way other people could feel and you would never get to be Leopold in Kew like that.

They pulled back from the window. 'You go to the front and ring the bell,' Winston said. 'If there's a guard he'll answer.'

'Thanks.'

'I'll do a little bit of glass breaking this end and let myself in while you're there. Take him front and back. Our job just to clobber him a bit. We don't want noise and police. We need time to talk to Denzil here afterwards.'

Ember went out of the garden and made for the front door. This boy in his rubber band threw the orders around. But another thing about this boy was he had Chitty and Oliver behind him, besides the rubber band, so it was best to give a heed to what he said.

He rang the bell and stepped back and to the side in case they had a spy hole, and in case a guard came out hard, expecting trouble. Nothing happened and he rang again. He was sweating a little, but nothing too bad yet. He thought he heard someone stir far back in the house and in a moment a woman as old as Denzil opened the door and peered into the darkness. Not far behind her in the nice, big hall, Denzil himself appeared and called out: 'No, Alice. He said not to open.'

'Not open my own front door?' she snarled.

'Is he here now?' Ember said.

'Who are you?' Alice replied.

'Is he here now?' Ember pushed into the house past her. He was shouting. Occasionally he understood why people called him Panicking Ralph.

'He soon will be,' Denzil said, and turned towards a telephone on a table under a genuine countryside painting.

Winston came out from the room behind and stood between Denzil and the table. 'Close the door, Alice,' he said. 'You're mentioned very favourably in my briefing notes, love. Contain them, Ralphy, will you, while I have a swift look around upstairs et cetera in case? Close the door, Alice.'

She did. Winston had a definite way with him.

Chapter 14

Sarah Iles said: 'Colin, I'm so glad you've phoned. I was going to call you, as a matter of fact. But it's difficult: if I ring the nick, people know it's Mrs Rougement Place. And then at your home – that's not easy, either.'

'I'll come out there now. He's going to be tied up the whole evening in a traffic seminar.'

'Yes, now's fine. The babe's asleep.' She put the receiver down feeling puzzled. What sort of conversation had it been? Was Harpur calling as a detective, needing to talk privately about a case that might involve herself and her husband? Or was he coming as something else: a friend, the man who had comforted her at Ian's funeral, a bit more than a friend? Both of them had spoken just now as if the need for secrecy were assumed. She found herself analysing the words. 'He's going to be tied up the whole evening in a traffic seminar.' That no-naming, distancing way of referring to Desmond reminded her of how Ian used to talk – as any lover might have talked – treating her husband as someone to be sliced out of their lives.

Up to a point, she tidied the downstairs rooms. Up to a point would do for Colin. Harpur had visited often enough with her husband to know she did not run the cleanest house in the West, even before Fanny. She picked up some baby clothes from the floor and a half-full biscuit packet, squirted air freshener about, then went upstairs to tidy herself rather more thoroughly than the rooms. So, was that necessary for a business call by a cop?

Opening the door to him, she noticed that his car was not in the drive. Had he parked a distance from the house and walked? Perhaps he did not know what kind of visit it was, either. Always when she looked at Harpur she felt safer. It was something she did not altogether understand. Safer than what? She had experienced it from way back, from long before she had any reason to believe herself threatened, and almost since she had first known him. He seemed to radiate a determination to help. There were few men like that, but plenty who radiated a determination to help themselves. Yet it wasn't sexless what she felt about him, was it? And what about what he felt?

'Are you still in charge of it, Colin? I heard Lane might bring in power from outside.'

'He still might.'

'And you want that.'

'Why would I?'

'Get you out of a spot. You wouldn't have the job of covering up.'

He seemed to think about it for a little while. 'I don't want strangers sniffing about on my ground – people building their careers by digging dirt here.'

'Sometimes I think you're as obsessive as the rest of them.' She took him into the lounge and made up one of those foul, youth drinks he was fond of, a pint of mixed cider and gin. For herself she liked her gin neat and poured a decent one now. He sat opposite her, unrelaxed, massive, as carefully dressed as Desmond always was, his black lace-ups very superior. Almost anyone would pick him out as police, and certainly any half-experienced crook would. Lately, Harpur's fair hair had started to thin, and she thought he looked a bit worn, slightly faded now for a whizz kid. His face had always had a rather battered air, but it seemed tense and weary today. Despite what he said, perhaps this case and its strains had begun to get to him. And the story was he had those other strains, too – the sergeant's wife. That might be over now, though.

'I need to know when you saw Aston last, Sarah.'

'Of course.'

'I've held back from bothering you.'

'Yes, I know.'

'It's painful. And I don't think it's got much bearing. But if I neglect the basics Lane could see it as shielding Desmond and you – the sort of thing to make him seek help from outside.'

'And is it?'

'What?'

'Shielding Desmond.'

'I've been following other lines of inquiry.'

'Oh, so official. Why, Colin?'

'They look promising.'

She stared at him for a few seconds. 'That's what I mean about the stress of covering up. You have to look after Desmond?'

He stared back, his face not really saying much, except for the fatigue. 'So when did you see Aston last, Sarah?'

'The day he was killed.'

That probably shook him, but he did not show it.

'The afternoon,' she said.

'Where?'

'Some forestry commission land, up towards Dobecross. In my car.'

He nodded and stayed silent.

She assumed he had read the full meaning of that, but she spelled it out just in case, feeling forced to shake that bloody impassiveness. 'I had the baby with me in the carry-cot,' she said. 'We moved her off the back seat into the front and—'

He held up a hand. 'Sarah, I don't need to know all that. Only that it was still strong then, the relationship with Aston?'

She would stick at it now, she decided. 'Of course. Would I be fucking someone with the baby present if not? That's why I gave you the details, Colin. I'm not boasting.'

'Did Desmond know?'

'That I'd been making love with Ian the same day? Hardly.'

'No. Did he know it was continuing regardless, you and Aston, even after the child?'

'I didn't tell him.'

'Did he know?'

'I'm not sure. I'd go out sometimes without much of an explanation. As ever. He would probably read the signs.' Yes, Desmond had read the signs.

'Lane thinks Aston might have been on his way to phone you when he was attacked. Was there some arrangement of that sort?'

'Yes, Ian would ring me sometimes.'

'In the evenings?'

'Yes.'

'Even though you'd seen each other during the day?'

'It was that sort of thing. We liked talking – liked talking ·

even more if we'd had a grand day. You understand about lovers, surely. They like to savour, make the most of things.'

He ignored that. 'On the hour?'

'The telephoning? Yes, that's right. So I could be ready and grab it. Mark Lane guessed this? He's not such a fool, then.'

'Who said he's a fool?'

'Desmond.'

'Well, yes. Could Desmond have noticed these calls, the same time every evening?'

'Not every evening.'

'A lot of evenings.'

'He might have. He's not a fool, either.'

'But you risked it?'

'Some risks there have to be in that sort of thing. Again, as you know.'

He ignored this, too. 'Were you actually expecting a call that evening? Had Aston said he would definitely ring?'

'He never said he would as a certainty. Things could get in the way. I hoped he would.'

'And he didn't?'

'No.' Her voice wavered.

'Sorry. What did you do? Were you anxious?'

'No. I hoped he would ring the next night.'

He nodded again.

She said: 'But you haven't asked whether Desmond was in the house at the time. Surely that's the important thing?'

'He's told us he wasn't.'

'Has he said where he was?'

He seemed to hesitate for a moment. 'I've got a note somewhere,' Harpur replied. 'On his way home from another police function, I think.'

'He's all right, then, isn't he? People must have seen him.'

'Probably.'

'What function?'

'I'll check the note.'

'Yes, do. Check the note. So, what other promising inquiries, Colin?'

'Oh, Aston was into all sorts. Some of it hazardous. You probably know.'

'No.'

70

'Oh, yes.'

Up to now she had tried to keep it all brisk and crisp. This was not going to be the funeral again, no break-down. She had given only that one sign of pain, she hoped. Then, suddenly, she feared the tears might come, as she thought of Ian out of his depth, probably big-talking the way he always did, but mixing with people he could not even remotely manage. Sarah recalled that doomed wish to protect him which she had always felt, and which he had always laughed at. She did not try to speak for a moment. Sodding gin gloom. She would fight her way out of that. 'So why haven't you taken anyone in?'

'We'll get there.'

'Does the Chief believe you will?'

'Lane's afraid.'

'Afraid—'

'That the whole outfit is coming to pieces. People at the top of any organisation suffer from it all the time. Like God with Lucifer.'

'Afraid his ACC did it? I'm afraid of that, too. I have to live here. And the baby.'

He seemed to listen, as if trying to pick up the sound of a car in the road. 'So it's you who'd lie to see someone brought in from outside to deal with it? You don't trust me?'

She looked at him, his big body filling the easy chair, his eyes friendly, and she felt again that lovely sense of safety in his presence. 'I don't know whether I trust you. I think I'm like Lane. I see an alliance, a club – you, Desmond, a couple of others – that I'm not part of and never can be. It's notorious and strong, isn't it, Colin? Absolute. Built in. It would lie and lie again to me, and probably has.'

'I'd better go soon. He'll be here.'

Perhaps this was an attempt to rebut the charge and say they had an alliance, too. She did not know whether she could believe it. And she was still not sure what kind of talk this had been. One minute she thought he was trying to exclude Desmond, and the next she felt horribly excluded herself.

'You really think he didn't do it, Colin?'

'We're talking about an Assistant Chief Constable, for heaven's sake.'

'And that's the only argument? This is the alliance speaking.'

'And because I know him inside out.'

'That's the alliance speaking, too.' There was a yell from upstairs. She almost said, 'Fanny's stirring', but amended that: 'The baby's stirring.'

Chapter 15

'It's a task really well done, Ralphy. As expected, if I may say,' Caring Oliver remarked. Ember had noticed before how good Caring could be at sounding humble and warm and intimate. For somebody youngish, Caring had such a range.

'That fucking maniac, Winston,' Ember replied.

'I know, I know. It's always a heart-search whether to use him.'

'I don't work with him again.' As soon as he said it, Ember knew he had made a mistake. What they would hear was he did not mind other work for them.

Peter Chitty said: 'Yet people tell us he's nice as pie usually. Debased by the job? It can happen to anyone. Thatcher. Pierrepoint. And Denzil's not going to have to see a doctor, or the wife. That's correct? No stitches?'

'They'll be all right, probably,' Ember replied. 'Because I was able to keep him within bounds. Just.'

Oliver had the Smith and Wesson K-frames in front of him on the leather-top desk, still in the shoe boxes. 'All beautifully virgin,' he said. 'Would they try to fool an old hand like you, Ralphy?'

They were in Caring Oliver's house. Ember preferred it like that. These two looked a credit, Oliver in one of the suits and Chitty with his Rolex and haircut of tomorrow, but they were known, and he did not want them in and out of the Monty. This was Caring's library. That was his word, and Pete Chitty had not giggled or made a face when it came up, so Ember took it very straight, too. There were definite, long shelves and hardbacks, quite a handful, some in old, leather bindings, and perhaps it really was a library of sorts. A library was calibre, and would be a necessity for Oliver.

'So now you know our little project, Ralph,' he said. 'Obviously.

You've supplied good, clear notes on Denzil's information.'

'Easy. He wasn't talking very fast by then.'

'So, what do you think of it?'

'God, I'm no judge, Oliver. Especially not now, having been out of things so long.'

'It's quite a catch, if we can do it, yes, Ralphy? This is real information, real timing,' Chitty said.

'The money? Honestly I forgot the figures as soon as I handed the notes over to you. This sort of assignment, I forget everything.'

Caring and Pete had a thorough laugh. 'Oh, I'm sure,' Chitty said, still chuckling. 'A figure like that, and all the noughts! It doesn't get to you at all, does it, Ralph? Oh, no! You could buy ten Montys.' Ember could see Pete had picked up that this meeting should be amiable right the way through, or Oliver had briefed him on it direct. Pete's laughter stayed very kindly, like an uncle.

'Let's put it this way, Ralph: this is money worth travelling for, yes?' Caring said. 'Kew, Wales, and now the job itself, Exeter.'

'That was always your way, you two. Sites a long way from home. Exeter? Really that sort of money down there?'

'Distant locations sow confusion,' Chitty replied.

Ember began to feel anxious. He wanted to put a stop on discussing these things. He had the fee. They had the guns and the report on Denzil and his wife, and that was it, finished: he had burned the stained Leach suede boots in the Monty incinerator, which knocked £95 off the £750, but never mind. Today, these two talked to him like an equal and a partner. He did not want it, would have liked to run. He had built a life that kept pretty much on the unindictable side. Back to the club and the girls' homework now, thanks very much. Ralph W. Ember was beginning to create a sort of upbeat status.

'Obviously we wouldn't be taking Winston with us on this Exeter jaunt,' Oliver remarked.

Chitty gave a very big laugh. 'Winston? Jesus, I don't want to be in the same street with him.'

'We value you, Ralphy. We want to cater for you.'

Ember said: 'Well, as long as he's up there in Kew and I'm—'

'Exactly,' Oliver remarked.

'I ought to be moving,' Ember said. 'Thanks for this.' He patted his jacket and wallet.

'That's not going to last long, if you've got a serious slump at the club, Ralph,' Caring remarked.

'It will help.'

'I want to help more,' Oliver replied. 'What I'd very much like to think, Ralph, is that you and your family are always going to be really safe. Margaret, Venetia, Fay. I mean, safe financially, of course. Seven-fifty's not going to do that.' That sad face blazed in a total, considerate smile. It made Caring look nearly boyish, and in a way inspiring, like a young saint with a vision.

Oliver had a place on a hill, old but done up more or less all right by the people he bought it from, exposed stone-work and beams, all that peasant mode, and looking out over country and eventually the sea. There were paddocks, which Ember thought they might be hearing about. The daughter would have to get aboard a horse as soon as she arrived from that school on holiday, so her image did not take a fade through being with Caring.

'Denzil said two big ones,' Ember remarked. 'His mouth and lips, after Winston – I could hardly make out if he was saying million or trillion.' He still did not want a part in the job, or increased closeness to these sods. But nor did he want people thinking he was scared of any prospect, or any amount just because it was heavy, and he needed to show he could apply his brain and know-how to it, and pick out the weaknesses. He would not have this pair, or anyone, think of him as Panicking Ralph.

'At least,' Chitty remarked. 'This is a headquarters bank holding its own cash and main funds of two branches while they have their safes and security modernised. Possibly even up to 2.5 million, we hear unofficially from elsewhere. Twenty-four hours only. Mostly large bills, so not impossible bulk.'

'You can see why Denzil was crucial, Ralph,' Oliver said. 'The date. Plus a minimum estimate of the amount, to be sure it's worth the travel.'

'Money on that scale sets up tremors,' Ember said. 'The world will be interested.' God, now it was he who sounded like an uncle, all wisdom, all warnings. 'Who says he hasn't told it elsewhere? That's what you were afraid of, yes? And he was in contact with someone. When he saw me, he was going for the phone. It's in the report.'

'Fair point,' Oliver replied. 'But he eventually did say clearly to you two that he hadn't disclosed, didn't he?'

'Yes, he said it. And clearly. But eventually is too bloody right. Winston had the old duck stripped by then and— Oh, Jesus, I'm not going to talk about that. Denzil would have told us anything to stop him.'

'Winston's impression was it was the truth. I really third-degreed him about this on the phone,' Oliver replied.

Ember groaned. 'Impression? What's Winston? What's his judgement? Some things he might be great at. Well, go with him some day and listen to the screaming. But impression? So, he's sensitive now?' He was scared of these two, but they respected his brain and career, and he knew they would put up with rough tongue from him. They expected it. It showed he was serious.

Chitty said: 'You know he got the name of the protection out of him, too? The one he was trying to phone. Well, that boy, the protection, is a total nobody. He's in a little local fart-arse crew down there in Wales, antiques, general burglary, bloody semi-detacheds, that level. They couldn't come within ten miles of handling something like Exeter.'

'We've put out some feelers, and the way we see it, Denzil was in touch with this lot near him, with the idea of bidding us up, that's all. It would serve him right if he got nothing, but I'll see him OK, I expect, the greedy old sod. Just this time. He hadn't told anyone anything. Only promises. We don't expect competition, Ralph, though I totally sympathise with your caution. We're listening to a pro, we both realise that.'

'Too true,' Chitty said. 'Two and a half million plus, there's got to be certain caution, but don't overdo. We're talking about four hundred thousand in your little pouch, Ralph, minimum. Maybe half a million. This would be recognition coming at long, long last. Only what you deserve, but it won't arrive through the mail like a pools win. It's got to be taken.'

Oliver stood up and walked past the books to the big window, gazing rather nobly out over fields towards the coast, as if it was all his, including the sea. He was side-face on and Ember saw him smile again, in pleasant harmony with it all outside. 'Well, I expect Ralphy knows it has to be taken, Pete,' he remarked. 'He's not just starting in this game. Ralphy's temperate, not impotent.'

One day he would tell Caring to call him Ralph or Ember,

76

not Ralphy. Ralphy sounded like a goldfish. Not now, though. 'Exeter,' Ember said. 'New industries, tourism, West Country squires. Yes, I suppose there could be money about.'

The Monty was no busier that night than it had been any time lately and at around 11 o'clock, when the children would be in bed, Ember left the barman in charge and went up to the flat to talk about Caring and Chitty to Margaret. He was frightened and excited. Margaret had a good, clear head and he liked to discuss problems with her, and often listened to her advice.

'It's the same as before, Maggie, except I've got figures now.'

'The same – meaning you don't think there's any choice?' She was sitting opposite him with a cup of tea in her hand, small, neat, bright-looking, full of loyalty and suspicion.

'I've been in on some messy work already for them. I'll tell you about it, if you like. But I'd rather not. That trip to Wales.'

'So now they won't let go of you?' The tone of voice said Maggie could have told him that from the beginning, but she did not speak the words. She had consideration.

'Caring talks about wanting my family to be safe.'

'What?' Her eyes went hard. 'My God, he spells it out like that? The kids?' She had the cup to her mouth, so the words came towards him in little puffs of steam, and he almost smiled because it was like a tv dragon.

'You know Caring,' he replied. 'So oblique and gentle. He says he wants you and them safe, gives your names nice and slowly, and then when I'm digesting that, he says what he means is safe financially, of course. Well, of bloody course. And he knows I've got what happened to Aston in my mind.' He did what he could to keep his own voice level and stop the dread from the memory of it drying up his spit.

'But I thought the Aston thing was nothing to do with Oliver and Chitty.'

Ember nodded. 'I don't know. It depends who you're listening to.'

'You mean police won't say it's police? You thought they would?'

'All right. But Caring and Pete charter a Londoner who would have ended Aston for them and thought nothing of it if he got out of line, and Ian was the sort who would get out of line. Very freelance.' He saw she was staring at him. 'You're trying to work out whether this jumpiness adds up or is just Panicking Ralph going into frantic orbit again?'

She leaned forward and smiled. 'No, that Panicking stuff is nuts. I was thinking you seem really thrilled, better than I've seen you for ages, regardless of what you're saying. Ten years younger. Would you be glad to go back to that work, then, Ralph?'

It was because she could read him like this that he valued her so much. 'You don't mind? It's flattering, yes, that they want me. My age, and the rustiness, nor the Panicking – Caring doesn't worry.'

'Age, my backside.'

'And Caring's no idiot. If he wants me it's because he thinks – he knows – I could do it. That place of his. He didn't get it by picking the wrong people.'

'Five bathrooms? Was she there?'

'No.'

'Out buying up half of Philemon Fashion. Whenever I see Patsy, something new, and spot-on.'

'There's supposed to be a quarter of a million in this for me, Maggie.' You had to be sensible about disclosing figures. 'That's what I mean, flattered. They won't be short of takers for a quarter of a million. But Caring says it's got to be Ralph.'

She stood up, ready for bed. He would have another two or three hours in the club in case a few drifted in after the boozer. 'Well, no real problem, is there, Ralph? You want it – good for the ego and the image. Plus the pay sounds delightful. And there's no way out, in any case. No safe way out, for you or us. That's what you're saying?'

'You were right. I shouldn't have started.'

'Late for that. And I'm not too sure. Look, I like to see self-respect bubbling in you again, Ralph, not thinking of yourself as a fucking pot boy.'

He went and kissed her on the forehead. 'We could get out of this dump. I fancy something Kew way. Plenty of quality girls schools up there.' He felt strong, dominant. 'Don't fret about the children. Caring knows I won't let him down. And he's got a daughter in school himself.'

'Oh, yes, that would make a hell of a difference if he thought you— But you can cope with them, Ralph.'

'That Aston was just a stupid kid. They see they're dealing with something else now.'

He went to the bathroom to throw water over his face and cool down. Big sweats had always been a problem. They said Ron Preston, one of the people Harpur sent away not long ago, was the same. Margaret had swallowed it all too bloody easily. He had wanted her to protest and argue, so he could have his change of mind tested. But perhaps she was just clever and honest. Right away she had seen what had taken him a lot longer – that he had no real choice. And the silly cow would love the idea of being able to keep going to Philemon and giving almost new stuff to Oxfam, like Caring's Patsy.

When he went back into the living room he found she had waited there, to kiss him goodnight before he returned to the club. He said: 'I don't know whether you'll think this is Panicking taking over once more, but I'd like to pop down to Wales again tomorrow and see the old couple I visited are all right.'

'Oh, why?'

'There was some trauma. I worry about them. At their age.'

'Ralph, you're a darling. No, that's not panic. That's feelings. But would you want to be seen there again?'

'I'll just hang about for a while near their house, and hope they come out. It's all right. I had a stolen Carlton last time. I'll go in my Montego, so no one's going to make any link. I can just check the two old bodies are in fair shape.'

'The Montego? Registration tracing, Ralph? Are you sure it will be all right?'

'Absolutely. It will simply be a parked car.'

'Why don't I come? I could knock the door, pretend to be looking for somebody in the area.'

'No,' he said. 'Better not.'

'Why?'

'Better not.'

'Something I shouldn't see? They're badly scarred?'

'So old. So greedy. He shouldn't be into this sort of thing. Did he realise what he was starting?' But, then, who the hell anywhere, at any time, knew what he was starting.

Chapter 16

Iles said: 'Look, I know exactly what you've been wanting to ask me, Col: don't I worry about bringing back something very nasty to Sarah through having whores?'

'Three ways, sir.'

'I know, I know. High risk. Yes, I suppose there were safer things about President Kennedy I could have chosen to emulate.' Wearing civilian clothes today, Iles was in front of the long mirror used for checking his uniform, apparently preoccupied by his mouth and teeth.

'We still haven't found the girl you say you were with, sir,' Harpur told him. He softened that immediately: 'The girl you were with, sir.'

'It's a mystery. Usually, having had me, they turn up at the same spot again, hoping.' For a few seconds, he had put a hand over the buttoned crutch of his grand, old-style, grey, three-piece suit, as if to confirm that, whatever was happening to his teeth, no general rot had set in. Then his mind swung back to Lane: 'I hear you took him down to Aston's place, Col.'

'He insisted, sir.'

'Thanks, friend Harpur.'

Francis Garland knocked and came in, obviously with something important to say, his eyes full of urgency. Iles ignored him. Still in front of the mirror, the ACC said: 'Do you think Lane's turning this thing into a personal mission against me, Col?' He glared at himself. 'And one used to have such a dinky, wholesome smile.'

Garland said: 'We've had a call, sir, from down near where Aston had his bed-sit. A neighbour tells us—'

'So, speaking for yourself now, Col, do you think I did Aston?'

'That's not the question, sir. I have to—'

'Of course it's the fucking question. The Chief thinks I did it?'

'Probably, sir. He's come to believe he's inherited hell here.'

Iles, pulling again at his mouth before the mirror, asked: 'But you do both believe I'm capable of it, Col? Garland?'

'Of course, sir,' Harpur replied.

'Certainly,' Francis Garland said.

'Well, that's something. I wouldn't want to be thought of as an eternally happy cuckold. None of these diseases show themselves in the dentation first, do they?' He put his head on one side, mouth open, for a different perspective. 'The Chief's got a theory?'

Harpur replied: 'He suspects you tumbled to the fact that Aston rang Sarah most nights at a specific time, waited for him to come out on his way to the pay-phone and did him when that train was stuck there, screening everything. He regards that as typically professional.'

Iles nodded. 'Yes, Aston did ring her regularly. At ten p.m. She'd be ready to grab it on the bedroom extension.'

'Didn't you ever pick up the other receiver and listen in, sir?' Harpur asked.

In the glass, Harpur saw him register nausea. 'One doesn't, surely.' He returned Harpur's gaze in the mirror. 'Yes, looking at you, I suppose you would. A wife's entitled to her own life. Was I interested enough in that babble?' He went and sat at his desk and picked up some papers.

Garland said: 'This neighbour tells us a man has been down there knocking doors and asking questions. He's gone into the Aston house. He's there now.'

'Lane?' Iles snarled.

'The neighbour wasn't too hot on the description,' Garland told them.

'Holy bastard, questioning, digging. He thinks he's a detective still,' Iles said.

'I'll get down and find out, sir,' Harpur replied. 'This just could be useful.' He was glad of any chance to end the meeting with Iles, even a wait in that shabby street.

Although away from the mirror now, Iles began probing his gums with a finger, grunting occasionally with effort. Then, for a moment, he took his hand out of this mouth: 'People like us, who lived and formed our life-style in the sixties, we're supposed now to tie a knot in it or do research into previous experience every time? Ask Lane how he manages, will you?'

Harpur and Garland went down quickly to Coss Street, where Aston had had his bed-sitter, and watched from the car; but the man who came out of the house eventually was certainly not Lane. At least sixty, he walked away towards the railway footbridge, wearing a long raincoat of a style from around the Harold Wilson period and a nice old navy homburg hat. Harpur and Garland left the car and followed on foot. The man looked even less athletic than the Chief, yet dogged, imperturbable. He went laboriously over the bridge and on to the piece of ground where Aston's body was found. For a moment he stopped and pulled on spectacles, then moved around slowly among the rubbish, as if searching. A few minutes later, he paused, his body crouched forward, and seemed to be weeping, holding his head in his hands. He took the glasses off, wiped his eyes with the sleeve of his coat, put the glasses back on and resumed his scrutiny of the filthy terrain.

'Who is he?' Garland said. 'Someone's private snoop?'

'Aston's father, maybe?'

'How do you know, sir? Doing what?'

'Oh, looking for answers. He thinks he can do better than us.'

'Can he?'

'Ah.'

So as not to alert the man on the waste tip, Harpur and Garland would have walked on, then turned and observed him without being seen, but, as they passed he suddenly called out loudly: 'You police? Perchance.'

They joined him on the waste ground. He was chubby-faced and ought to have appeared jolly, but his cheeks lacked all colour and the eyes behind the glasses were bloodshot and defeated. He did not look as if he took much out of life.

Garland said: 'Trawling? Found anything interesting, old gentleman?'

'On the contrary, if I may say, have you lot found anything? That's more to the point. Are you really looking for who killed my boy? A nasty bout of inertia? Inoperable?'

'Mr Aston, it will distress you to come here, sir,' Harpur replied. 'And all that distance. There's no point. It's been covered.'

'Somebody has to do something. I'm on a day trip. Senior citizen's special rail fare.'

'You came alone?' Harpur asked.

'My wife, May, is into turn the other cheek. Jericho. It's

admirable, but some take advantage. I'm retired. Time's no problem. I wanted to see, not just read in the papers.'

'We're doing all we can,' Garland told him. 'Closing in. Believe me.'

'No. Are you the famed Mr Iles?' he asked Francis. 'Perchance. Too young? It's one called Desmond Iles I wanted to talk to. Full of himself, I gather. Fashion piece. Is that why you hang about here, because you're him? They say people do that, don't they?'

'Which people? Why do you want Mr Iles?' Garland asked.

'I think he'd know. I think you know. As for you, you were at the funeral, weren't you?' he asked Harpur. 'Anyone would remember that haircut.'

'We can imagine how you feel,' Harpur replied.

'I'm not going to get to meet this Iles?'

'Oh, I can't see why not,' Harpur said. 'He's very accessible. Today?'

The reply seemed to put him off balance. His eyes grew even more worried. 'Today? Oh, well. Next time I visit, perhaps? Prepare my questions. If you could facilitate it.'

'You'll come again?' Garland asked. 'Have you found out anything? Perchance.'

'One or two matters.'

'Oh?' Garland said. 'What sort? You could help us.'

'I could? But I thought everything was covered here. Or covered-up, do you mean?' He turned his utterly blank face towards them both. 'Do you mind if I don't say what I've discovered? At this juncture. These matters point in a certain direction.'

'You sound like a policeman,' Garland said.

'Don't get insulting, please. I wouldn't know, anyway. I never hear police saying a dicky bird about this death. Why I would like to see Mr Iles. In due course.'

'I'll be in touch,' Harpur replied.

Aston ambled away and began turning over piles of heavy refuse with his foot, even though he was wearing sandals. Harpur and Garland walked back to the car.

'You know, sir, despite everything, I felt pleased to be mistaken for Iles,' Garland said. 'When I go into a room and he's there I feel I'm in the presence of greatness, even now.'

'Yes, he's got that.' For Garland to see greatness in anyone but himself was a move forward.

'So where does the aura come from, sir? Only that he's uncontrollable? We assume madness is genius?'

'God knows.'

'I used to be aware of it even when I was tied up with his wife. Possibly what gave Sarah some of her attraction, in fact. Does that make sense?'

'Oh, yes.'

'You feel it? About Sarah?'

Harpur unlocked the car.

Garland said: 'So, you'll protect him now. I mean, *we'll* protect him?'

'Greatness or not—'

'Doesn't come into?' Garland asked. 'You'll say he's part of us. Of course he is.'

Chapter 17

Ralph Ember walked through the customer area of the bank at Exeter, trying to appear loaded and troublefree, and helped himself to a meaty handful of leaflets about special deposit account interest rates. His hands shook a little and he dropped a couple. They dived and carried like paper darts and he left them on the floor. He wanted no long scene here. If banks had any sense at all they would do sneak pictures of everybody who came in to collect investment brochures: no better way to get a nice view of the interior, and bank robbers' cars and houses were waist-deep in the things. Ember went through his hurried quota of gazing, not too obviously, he hoped. Jesus, but it looked a tough one. Outside in the street he rejoined Peter Chitty. For today, Chitty had on one of those squire class, dirty green, waxed, waterproof coats and a Land-Rover cap, not his youth ensemble, knowing he must chameleon into the local West Country scene. What he managed to look like was even more of a prick than usual.

'All right?' Chitty asked. He sounded surprised.

'Fine.'

'You were quick.'

'Time on reconnaissance is never wasted, but don't take too much of it. People behind the counter remember things.'

'Jumpy? But you've got a good, working picture of it all in your head, Ralphy?' Disbelief rang like a fire bell in his voice. Chitty never seemed to bother with all the reverence for Ember and his skills when Caring Oliver was absent. Chitty might be only an assistant, but now and then he seemed to spot more than Caring and think quicker, the sod.

'I saw enough and what's germane sticks,' Ember said. 'A knack from the old days.' A week or two ago he had watched a film on television called *Atlantic City*, with Burt Lancaster as a retired hood, always drooling about the past. Sometimes, with Pete and Caring, he felt like that.

'Not far for a look at the manager's house. We can walk,' Chitty said.

'Lead on.' Ember made it sound clipped and very eager. That was important with this all-seeing mastermind. For the past few days Ember had found himself sliding very fast into panic about the job, and longing to get out, whatever the money. In a day or two Caring was going to issue him with one of the K-frames, and when that happened he would be really sealed in. Well, if he wasn't already. Of course he was.

He did not know how it had happened, this breakdown, but he did know the symptoms, from way back. He had felt them like a disease as he forced himself to stroll through that bank, and felt them now, as they went towards the manager's house: sweat, plus the clamp-like ache across his shoulders and chest, a loony suspicion that the knife scar on his jaw had opened up and was trailing nerve ends, and then double or triple vision, so everything looked like trick photography. It was a bloody total guffaw to think he had observed anything at all worth seeing in the bank, or would remember one useful fragment.

At home, he had felt too ashamed to tell Maggie what was sweeping over him again, and was too scared to tell anyone else, or give them enough evidence to guess, like Chitty now. Ember walked beside him, head up and cocky, as if he could not wait to get this whole performance under way next week, preferably with himself out in front, mopping up all the flak, like a pathfinder plane in the war. 'Nice, pretty town,' he told Chitty. 'For a heist.' He had a good, hard-voiced laugh. Chitty didn't.

He was looking at the traffic as they made their way out of one of the main streets. 'We'll be operating earlier in the morning. Not the rush hour, and before it builds up to this again. We should be all right.'

'Traffic's one of those imponderables. We make the best of it,' Ember grunted, feeling like a book of useful phrases.

Yes, the abrupt slip into dread had come from nowhere, just like the change when he decided he would do the job. Sometimes he wondered about his mind. The stinking, sudden way his morale could rise and drop meant he never really knew who he was supposed to be: Ralph the Rock of Ages one minute,

Panicking Ralph the next. Was everybody's psyche like that? No wonder the asylums complained about under-funding. What about the people who ran the asylums? Did they know who they were? For a time, the thrill at being valued and wanted by Caring and Pete had given him rich delight. 'Call it a come-back, call it a renaissance,' he had told Maggie, full of himself, when they went out to dinner to celebrate. Even pouring drinks into the offal at the Monty had become tolerable, because he felt he would be away from there for keeps soon.

Chitty said: 'I've got a bit of bad news for you. Trust Caring to let me break it.'

Ember almost stumbled but recovered and forced himself to show no fright, simply went on striding and staring happily about at the shops like some soft tourist.

'I'll tell you in a minute. When we've seen this guy's house,' Chitty said.

'Please yourself.'

'But at least the job's still on.'

Fuck. 'I should hope so. Why are we trekking otherwise?'

It was all travel lately. Two days ago, Ember had made that second run to Wales which he had promised himself: the alarm about damage to Denzil and his old dear gave him no peace. He had hung about near their place and then, as soon as he saw them and realised they could still walk, almost every one of his anxieties trickled easily away. Facially, as far as he could tell, they had nothing too bad showing, though that afternoon each was wrapped up in a scarf and wore dark glasses. At that moment, watching from the car, he had felt he would have been an idiot to turn down the job, even if turning it down was a possibility. In fact, he became so pleased and confident about the future he had decided to make the most of his visit and went into the cathedral for a while. He sat up the front, quietly admiring the layout, and meditating about Venetia and Fay and other pleasant family matters, plus the likelihood of huge gain. It was only decent to pay respects to a cathedral if you were in the area. Ignorance he loathed. Just the same, Ember did not go much on a big, modern-looking statue of Christ, which had been placed high in the church, gazing out over everything. It gave him a bit of a freeze for a while. Too intense. Too deep. People needed a leg-up from a church, not that. A plaque said *Majestas* by Epstein, which was all very well.

He and Chitty crossed the street now. 'It's a bank and a half, yes?' Pete said. 'Definitely not one to take head-on. That's why the hostage bit, holding the manager's family. It's an old gambit now, but can still work a treat.'

'Sure it can,' Ember snapped.

Naturally, he had not mentioned to Caring or Pete that he had been to Wales again, and he had asked Margaret to keep quiet about it, too. Caring was caring but with Caring caring had sharp limits. He and Chitty might regard a welfare trip as stupid: there was a chance the Montego would get noticed and traced, and a chance he would get noticed himself. Denzil might be under watch, either by the other team mentioned, or even the police, if he had made the injuries official. Ember had been careful and took a good look around outside Denzil's place while he waited, but some of these people were very, very clever. Perhaps it was the worry that Caring and Chitty would find out that had kick-started his panic this time, and the thoughts about Winston, and maybe Aston.

They turned into a nice road of Victorian houses. 'Oliver says he would have come today. He asked me to tell you there was nothing he wanted more, Ralphy. It's just he's got some big property deal on the go, and today of all days the lawyers need him on call in case of queries.'

'It's all right.'

Chitty turned towards him and grinned. 'Don't believe it? You know Caring, don't you? Yes, bullshit, of course. Now and then Ollie's just got to talk like straight business. It makes him feel honest. And it's supposed to help people working for us feel good, too. Such as you. Caring's trying to prove villainy is only something on the side. Two and a half million on the side? This is the house. We keep walking. Caring's got drawings, anyway, and of the bank, but he thought you ought to see the actual. Called field-work.'

It was a big, three-storey semi, with a garden half visible behind the garage. Ember glimpsed the children's clothes on a washing line. A doll sat on a ground-floor window-sill.

'Caring's not sure about entry yet. He likes the way you did it at Cardiff – one knock the front door, the rest in at the back while they're distracted. Of course, Caring thinks everything you do is touched with twenty-four-carat gold.'

They walked past the house and out of the other end of the street. Ember decided to show iron, in case this smart arse, Chitty, had started picking up how sick he felt. 'Let's go back, Pete,' he said. 'I'd like another look.'

'You sure?'

'If you don't fancy it, find another way to the car, I'll see you there.' He gave it a very gentle voice, like someone who would never mock yellow in a novice.

'No, I'll come.'

Ember kept about half a pace in front, as if he was in charge. His legs felt like wet cardboard and he wanted to keep looking down to make sure his feet were still there. They passed the house again and saw nobody. As they turned back towards the centre of the town, Chitty said: 'As a matter of fact, Oliver's seeing Winston today. Why he couldn't come.'

'I thought you and he never met the London end. Policy.'

'We didn't.'

'So?'

'Crisis. It looks as if we'll have to include Winston in. That's the bad news I mentioned, Ralphy.'

Ember stopped. 'Include him in the job?'

'Keep going. We're noticeable.' They walked on. 'I don't want him. Well, you know. Nor does Caring.'

'A hostage job with Winston? Kids. Jesus Christ.'

'I know. Caring said you'd feel bad about it.'

'Oh, did he?' Ember snarled. 'Feel bad? Feel bad? This is a different bloody job, Pete.'

Chitty pointed. 'There's a cathedral down there.'

'Bugger cathedrals. Who needs them?'

'Caring took me in there last time. Drunks and druggies on the grass all round. Our trouble with Winston is this – we should have thought, of course – he knows the figures now. He's got a whiff. Clearly. From when you saw Denzil. He says he's got to be in – that sort of money. He can handle armament. Well, as you'd expect. Leopold's backing him, that's the point. He'd be on a cut from Winston. They've all got costs, Ralph. Mortgage rates up. Above all, we don't want to upset Leopold.'

They reached the car. 'I'm going to have to really think about this,' Ember said. He felt suddenly very cheerful and strong. Christ, this could be it, the way out. Absolutely. They must know he had a reasonable right to turn it down now. They were the ones breaking terms. Even this sort of game had rules.

Chitty said: 'This job, it's beautiful but stuffed with snags from the start. Well, it's the rush. And just one day to do it. Pressures.' He shook his head sadly. 'Then Aston getting it. That was a tragedy and a set-back.'

Ember felt his spirits start falling again and was glad to sit down in the car.

'I know I don't have to go on about Aston. You've thought about him quite a bit, Ralphy.'

'So, what the fuck does that mean?' He really let go with a bit of rage. Didn't he have Irish on his mother's side?

'Because he was a friend.'

'He was a customer, that's all, a member of the Monty.'

'Well, either way, it doesn't matter. You've thought about him, I'm sure of that.'

Ember made himself turn to face Chitty in the passenger seat. 'So, if I've thought about him? What are you telling me?'

'Only that he got very hit, Ralphy. I'm not doing any forecasting, obviously. Look, I hate dwelling on this. Only that when Iles took him out the way he did it left us in a real, acute difficulty, the first of what I've called snags on this job. Aston was important to us, and for a moment or two things looked disastrous. This was someone built-in to our system and suddenly he's missing. But then we got lucky again and thought of you, that's all. I give Ollie the credit. You seemed lost and forgotten up there at the Monty, but you've done us proud, Ralph. That's unquestionable. Coming out from behind a bar and acting like a real soldier. The upshot is we couldn't face losing you now. I speak for Caring. The Winston situation's a tangle, everyone agrees, Ralph, but Caring won't think of letting you go. Well, even less now. He says we need your coolness. This is four hundred thousand plus, Ralphy. He really wants to think your children are secure. For the future.'

Ember left the car keys in his pocket. 'Keep my children out of it. I'm not talking about counting cash, am I, for Christ's sake? I'm talking about this Himmler, Winston. Are you trying to tell me now he wasn't in this from the start? You're trying to tell me you didn't know he would want some of the big cake as soon as he heard about it from Denzil? I've been strung a-fucking-long here.' He let himself shout. He reckoned he could have this boy

90

on the run, and Caring, too, if he had had the nerve to show.

'We'd better get moving, Ralphy. We don't want to hang about here longer than we have to. Your car could take a place in someone's mind.' He did up his belt, like trying to will Ember into driving away. 'Listen, you've got my sympathy, if that's any help. I'll tell you something for nothing, shall I: myself, I don't think you look or sound too good. I've thought so for a while, not just the stress today. No, Ralphy, it's your famous old rubber legs trouble. If it was me, I'd let you go, like a shot. I don't see the plus, carrying someone on a job this size who's got high anxieties.' He put a hand on Ember's arm for a second, but Ember pulled away. 'Anxieties, even panic, Ralph. I'll say it. But Caring sees you as something else. He gave me a real briefing on how I must talk to you today, and persuade you, despite everything.'

'Caring told you to speak about Aston?'

'That was no death for anyone, even a mad shagger-around. A head in that state. But think of it as water under the bridge, Ralph. Nothing like that's likely to happen again. Now is it?'

'What? Again? No,' Ember said. He started the car. 'A pity we've got to move. I do like looking at cathedrals.'

'There won't be a chance next time we're here, either.'

Ember laughed. Chitty joined in.

'Hogwash.' Her voice crackled with certainty, but she felt sick. Once or twice Ian had put the receiver down because Desmond answered.

'I think so. I'm sure I could have made a bright go of ballet or possibly professional darts if I hadn't drifted into the police. You might have been happier married to a different job.'

'I have been happy.'

'When?'

'Des, I can definitely remember it.'

He waited, perhaps waiting for her to specify, but it would be too much of an effort to check back at the moment. After a minute, he added: 'I think I've got flexibility: needed for ballet or darts, you see.'

'Or police.'

Next night, Desmond had a Lodge meeting and she was alone in the house, except for the child. As the time approached 10 she found herself growing tense and breathless and lurking on her feet near the telephone. This had to be ridiculous. Ian Aston was not Constant Lambert and Constant Lambert had never called from the Beyond, anyway. But then, at a minute before the hour, the ringing started and she moved quickly the couple of steps to the receiver. Her hand was actually on the instrument when she decided against lifting it. Decided? Not really: simply, she found herself too terrified. Instead, she ran upstairs and unplugged the extension, hoping the baby would not be disturbed, and pretending to herself that this was her chief worry. Below, the bell continued to call her. For a minute she stood in the bedroom listening to it buzzing through the floor, hardly aware of whether Fanny had cried or not. She felt half-paralysed with fright. Then she forced herself to go downstairs and unplug the instrument there, too. Leaning against the bookcase, she watched the receiver, as if it might somehow rush her like a savage animal and do her damage even now. It had always been a treat in the past when Desmond was out and Ian rang at 10 or one of their other agreed times: no need to whisper into the receiver then or listen for footsteps. Now, the loneliness fiercely magnified her fear.

She had not been quick enough to prevent the bell waking the child again, and the sound of crying came from upstairs. Sarah went to settle her again. It took longer than last night, and Sarah grew irritated. Sometimes, in moments of pressure like this one, now, this evening, she felt – Oh, Christ, she did not want to define what she felt. But it was a kind of hatred of the child, wasn't it, a kind of wish to blame the baby for her suffering? That was so stupid, so malevolent. She knew it, yet the feeling still gnawed at her. Absurd, absurd, especially as she had been afraid that it might be Desmond, never herself, who turned against Fanny.

When she came down again, she hesitated for a second, then plugged in the telephone. To her horror it was still ringing. The endless din seemed as deeply menacing as before, yet plaintive and desperate, too, like someone yearning to be heard and to hear and hanging on and on. Violently, she disconnected again, went into the kitchen and sat down on the floor in the corner in the dark, like a child herself, an autistic child or one banished as punishment, knees up under her chin and her arms around her legs. The cold of the tiles got through to her after ten minutes and she stood and folded a *Financial Times* into four to sit on. She remained there for another half an hour, simply waiting, with her mind as empty as she could make it, then returned to the living room and this time without a pause connected the phone again. It was silent. She smiled, as if she had won some great victory, or been liberated in a wonderful deliverance. Catching sight of herself in a mirror, she thought, Jesus, what a stupid smirk: I've triumphed over a bell: some big deal. For a little while she sat and watched the receiver again, then climbed the stairs and reconnected the extension. Feeling strong once more, and loving and protective, she went and sat with the baby, and gazed at the crumpled, sleeping face. It had to be admitted, the child was not pretty, and not really like any one of them, herself, Desmond or Ian. But entirely loveable, surely: again unlike all of them.

Desmond arrived home not long afterwards. 'Fanny behaving herself?' he asked.

'All quiet.'

On the next night, they had some people in for dinner: Mark Lane and his wife, Sally, and a couple of neighbours who ran a string of fashion shops. It was a good evening, though Lane seemed tense. The talk swung about between music, politics, antiques, graffiti. As it grew near to 10 o'clock, Sarah found herself participating in the conversation with almost manic energy and commitment. She wanted to become so caught up that she would forget her anxieties, and perhaps even discover eventually that the time had slipped past and the crisis point gone. Desmond, sitting diagonally opposite, seemed to sense what she was doing, and he fed her the kind of topics he knew she liked discussing, and started anecdotes which he insisted she finish, saying she told them better. But when it came to 10 o'clock she knew very well it was 10 o'clock: had never been more precisely certain of anything in her life. Her powers of talking and of listening disappeared suddenly. She stood: 'I thought I heard the baby.'

'Oh?' Sally Lane moved her head to listen better.

'Yes, I think so,' Iles said. 'We parents, we're ever tuned in to the cry of our young. Like animals, you know.'

'Excuse me.' Sarah made for the door. It was another of those times when she had to get out of the room. Going quickly upstairs, she looked in on Fanny's silent cot, and then went and stood near the bedroom telephone, not knowing what she would do if it rang. That previous rigmarole would not be possible. Tonight, though, there was no call. She felt her body slowly begin to relax. At 10.20 she went back downstairs and animatedly rejoined the talk.

'Mark's going to sing for us, aren't you, sir?' Desmond said. 'A little of your favourite?'

Lane had a nice voice. The fashion shops man played something from *The Pirates of Penzance* on the piano. It was a pleasant and wholesome evening again. Desmond stood beaming near Lane as he sang, as if the Chief were one of his zappiest protégés. Sally Lane murmured to her: 'I'm sure everything will come out well.'

'Are you?'

At exactly 10 o'clock next night, when Sarah and Iles were doing the crossword together, the telephone rang. He must have been ready and stood at once.

'No, I'll get it.' She had begun to despise herself and had to crack this mad, disabling dread. Picking up the receiver, she held the wrist of one hand with the other, to stop it shaking. 'Sarah Iles.'

'Ah, I've been trying before.'

'Who's speaking?' It was a man, probably elderly, and she almost recognised the voice.

'You see, I knew Ian used to ring at ten o'clock sometimes, when he was staying here, and the number's written down on the blotter. You'd be expecting it. Well, not expecting it now, of course, but—'

'Mr Aston? From Bristol?'

Across the room, Desmond frowned and sat down again.

'I've been up to see the place. The place where Ian— Near the railway.'

'Oh, dear. That would be upsetting for you.'

'It could be so necessary.'

'If you think so, Mr Aston.'

'They were about. One of them said I could meet your husband. The big, yob-looking one who came with you to the funeral.'

'Oh, yes.'

'I wanted to. I asked. That seemed necessary, too. Look, I suppose he might be with you now. In the room?'

'Yes.'

'I had to put the phone down first time.'

'Yes.'

'I don't know now if I do want to see him. Perhaps I'm afraid to, a bit. And May says forgive and forget. As you know.'

'Yes.'

'Why I'm ringing, Mrs Iles, is to come right out with it. To ask you straight, did he do it? That's the point. If he did it, well, I've got to see him, haven't I? This is my son. If you know he did it— What I mean is, can I just walk into a police station, one of the top people, and ask him straight out did he murder my boy if I don't know for sure he did? You see what I'm getting at? And yet, if you know he did it, could you still be living there with him? That's another point for consideration. None of it's very clear.'

'No.'

'When you say, No—'

'I mean not very clear.'

He did not speak for a long while. 'You mean nothing at all's very clear?'

'Nothing.'

'Maybe you'd have to say that, in the circs. Your husband. In the room.'

'Nothing.'

Again there was a pause. 'So, in your opinion, what should I do? Should I go and see your husband and ask him?'

'I think it's up to you, Mr Aston.'

'Have you asked him, yourself? If I may inquire.'

'It's not the kind of question people always answer with the truth, is it?'

'Asking it could be important, though. Asking is sort of putting it on the record?'

'Yes, it could be. Yes, perhaps you had better see him and ask.'

When she rang off, Sarah sat down again. 'Nothing much. Old Aston wants to come and ask you if you killed his son and he wants me to ask you as well. Now.'

'Of course he can come.'

It was her turn to wait.

'What do you want me to say?' he asked.

'Want?'

'That I'd kill to keep you for myself? You'd like that?'

'No. My God, no.' She felt certain that answer was right, wasn't it?

'Some women might,' he replied. 'You might ask, how else could I deal with him – with the situation he presented?'

'Yes, I might.'

He gazed at her. 'No, I didn't kill him, Sarah.'

She waited a moment, in case he added to that. 'So, how else could you have dealt with it, the situation, supposing you wanted to deal with it?'

'Yes, I wanted to. I wanted it to end. How? Oh, I thought the baby might do it.'

'Does Lane think you killed Ian?'

'The Chief? Yes, I'd say so. He believes he's come to live in a swamp. He's a game one, I'll admit that. Could still give us a song.'

'Harpur? What does he think?'

'Half and half. But haven't you talked to him?'

'There's a wall around you people. Who do I believe?'

'Harpur's straight. Pretty straight.'

'And the wall's high.'

Chapter 19

Ralph Ember returned at near dawn from what he had told Margaret was a late night stag function for club owners put on by the brewery. She might believe it. The moment he closed the Monty's outer door quietly behind him he sensed there was someone standing in the dark at the end of the bar, a man. For a second, the shock hit him so hard he could not move. He had forgotten how to deal with moments like this, if he had ever known. His memory raced back to another night a long time ago when he had walked unsuspecting into the blackness of a room and found people waiting. The scar on his jaw dated from then: the kind of hellish encounter he had thought was from another, eternally closed part of his life.

Now, he reached suddenly for the switches alongside the door, but when he pressed them no lights came on. He was wearing a white shirt and the light, beige suit, which the girl he had been with tonight considered full of distinction, like an ambassador's on TV News, she always said. He knew he gleamed. Anyone used to the darkness in here would pick him out like the burning bush.

Also from far back in his mind, a survival trick surfaced, and he dropped to a crouch, while moving quickly to his right. His first instinct had been to pull the door open again and get out into the yard. Retreat was his nature. But he knew that in the doorway he would be beautifully framed and on show for a second against the outside half light, half dark, and a second might be far too long.

Behind the bar counter he had a piece of piping and a knife, but he would not be trying to get to them now. He did not know what he would be trying to do, except steer clear. But then he thought he heard someone shift in a different part of the room altogether, nowhere near the bar counter. So, steer clear of where? Oh, Christ, what was he doing in this sort of situation again? He was too old, had become too soft. What he was these days, no question, was non-confrontational.

There was a small sound and all the lights went on. He felt like a betrayed escaper in a Stalag movie. Caring Oliver was at the fuse box near the bar, smiling a welcome. 'Sorry, Ralphy, but we didn't know who might come in, did we? We've had a hell of a wait, you know. Could have drunk you dry. Still dipping it all hours? What about fitness? There's dodgy work coming.'

'How did you get in?'

'Winston's with me.' Caring pointed, and in a moment Winston came out from the lavatories corridor.

'Winston? Winston down here?'

'There've been developments, Ralph. We needed certain talents on the spot very presto.'

'Ralphy, you should be watching your back. Get her pubes out of your eyes. They can cause cataract.'

'What developments?' Jesus, Winston in the Monty. Ember felt everything was running away from him. Once you started, that's how it always turned out.

'They've traced you. You had to be told,' Caring said. 'But you know my ways, Ralph. I don't like the phone for anything sensitive. And you wouldn't want me coming up here making an entrance in one of my ensembles, nor Winston, when there are people about, eyes open. No good to any of us, frankly. It's like an announcement. So, a night call. We saw the Montego was away and knew you must be making a woman enduringly happy somewhere and that we were in for a wait. The fact is, I've been in a fret. I don't like your name being around. That's why I needed Winston. You've got to have some immediately insulation.'

'Traced me? Who? My name around where?'

Caring moved away from the bar towards the switches. 'Listen, those window blackouts: they 100 per cent? We're not going to get a police patrol here because they've spotted lights?' He worked the switches until only the bulbs behind the bar remained on.

'That's all right,' Ember said. 'Those stay at night, anyway.'

'Come and sit, Ralph. You need to know,' Caring said.

'It's all in hand, Ralph.'

They took a booth in the shadows at the end of the room. It was behind one of the pool tables and near a framed photograph of last year's Monty outing to Paris on the wall, the people in it looking really respectable and pro-Europe for that moment, or Ember would have banned the picture. Caring said: 'Leopold was in touch. He hears stuff from everywhere, Ralph. These are real contacts he's built up over a hell of a time. So, his information is that your name's been mentioned about that heavy inquiry visit to Denzil and his lady in Wales.'

'Mentioned? How do you mean, mentioned?' Ember asked, his voice high. 'Where?'

Caring said: 'There's another outfit involved, buttering Denzil, also looking for inside material. Well, I don't have to tell you.'

'They've got my name? Jesus.'

'That's the information.'

'I thought Peter said they were nobodies. How do nobodies bring off something like that? That's not nobodies, that's top-class skill.' In this sort of business, when you were dealing with someone like Caring, at his sort of plush level, you never knew when they were lying. Ember realised all this could be to give him more pressure. Or it could be true. He was not sure which would be better.

'I can't say if they're nobodies, Ralph,' Caring went on. 'We might have to revise views. Anyway, they've noted you.'

'And Winston?'

'Not that we've heard. Only you they've got marked.'

'You're famous, aren't you, Ralph? That past. I'm nobody. Denzil or the woman might have recognised you.'

Caring said: 'What makes it a mystery is you used a stolen car, so they couldn't have got to you that way. Obviously, if it was your Montego, that would be easy through the police computer. They dangle a handful of twenties to someone in Traffic, and up comes the trace. I'll tell you, Ralph, when I heard they had you listed, I thought for a minute you must have been sloppy and taken your own vehicle, even you, an old pro. But, of course, Winston assures me it was a nicked Carlton. Its registration leads nowhere we have to worry about. You ditched it afterwards? Yet they still come up with your name, Ralph.'

Winston said: 'And address.'

'Exactly. What I meant about not knowing who was going to come in through that door just now, Ralphy. It could have been a seek and find party.'

Ember had a second to decide whether to tell them he had been back down to Wales in his own car and doing quite a long lurk at Denzil's place on the green. What he had to think was that tomorrow or some day soon they might find out this was how he had been identified, and, if he had kept quiet about it, even Caring Oliver would get recriminatory. Think of Aston. All the same, Ember did keep quiet. He was not sure the words would have come if he had tried to speak, anyway. Old pro? Old fart, old fool, worrying about the health of people of no account, like Denzil and the woman. Who the fuck had he thought he was, the St John's Ambulance Brigade? 'I'm going to have a drink.'

'It's nearly four-thirty a.m., Ralph,' Caring said. 'This is a new day.'

Ember poured an armagnac for himself all the same. He was taking a good sip when the door from upstairs to the flat began to open slowly. The other two had seen it as well and became very quiet and taut.

'Who's there?' Ember called.

'Daddy? I heard a noise.'

'Venetia, love.' Ember walked quickly towards the door, hoping he could turn his daughter around and send her back to bed before she saw into the bar. He was too late, though. She came hesitantly forward, blinking in the bit of light, wearing only some white, see-through thing that she had kept on about for her thirteenth birthday. She was a child, but not entirely a child. Didn't she realise how visible she was?

'Daddy, is it nearly morning?'

'Yes. I'm just back from working very late somewhere.'

'Your best suit.'

'A dress-up function. But now off you go, back to sleep, love. You'll be like a rag at school.'

'You were talking? I heard voices.' She stared over towards the pool tables.

'Some friends came back with me. A little business conclave. Venetia, you're not at all dressed, darling.'

'Hello,' she said.

'Hello, dear,' Caring replied.

'You come to the club, don't you?'

'That's it.'

'But not your friend.'

101

Winston waved: 'Perhaps I will be in the future. It looks nice.'

'It's not too bad, is it, Daddy?'

'Won't you be catching cold?' Winston said. 'It's brave of you to come down and investigate like that in the dark, Venetia.'

'I was a bit scared.'

'That's what bravery is – being a bit scared, but doing it all the same,' Winston told her.

Ember took Venetia by the shoulder and moved her back towards the stairs, standing between the two men and her, so they would see as little as possible of her body. She turned and waved to Winston and then, as if remembering her politeness, to Caring. Ember closed the door behind her and went to rejoin the others.

'Smashing, friendly kid,' Winston said. 'Venetia? That's quite a name, too. How old exactly?'

'Anyone can tell that's a proper school she goes to,' Caring remarked. 'Poise. Middle of the night, it doesn't matter.'

'Does she have any idea what a big wheel her dad was – well, still is?'

Caring Oliver said: 'A really nice interlude, a meaningful interlude. But, look, Ralph, I feel responsible for what's happened, obviously. You being put on the line. After all, I sent you down to Cardiff, threw you a tough one right after a lay off. You did it fine, top to bottom, but still they've got you in the sights. I have to look after you. That's what I was saying about bringing Winston down in a bit of a hurry.'

'We've had a good look around outside tonight and I don't see any trouble. Not yet,' Winston said.

'What I suggest is Winston ought to move in here until after the job, Ralph. There's a lot that's precious on these premises – Venetia et cetera, as well as you yourself. What I meant by meaningful. I expect you've got plenty of room, a big place like this. If they know he's here, they'll think twice, Ralph, I can assure you, and then think twice more.'

Appalled, Ember said: 'Winston move in? But, you've seen, I've got d—' He had been going to say 'daughters', but changed it quickly to, 'I've got dubious people in and out of the Monty all the time. They could spot Winston, start thinking and pondering at a dangerous level, then take to talking around. And, going back to what Pete said – that these other people don't rate. Are they going to have the bottle to come after me? Off their home ground. And what for? What do they want with Ralph Ember?'

Winston leaned forward, laughing a bit, and punched Ember in gentle, friendly style on the shoulder. 'Now, come on Ralph Ember, don't be modest. What for! They assume you're in charge, don't they? They think you'll be leading the raid. They'll think if they knock you off they've got it clear for themselves, supposing Denzil has talked to them as well about the time and the spot, and I'd bet the bugger has. That's how they'll think.'

'Exactly,' Caring said.

'In charge?' Ember was scared and deliriously thrilled.

'Of course,' Winston declared. 'You've got a quality history. People hear Ralph Ember's working seriously again and they think straight away this is one who's used to big stuff, made for leadership.'

The door from the flat opened again. Venetia reappeared. She had put a dressing-gown on and slippers.

'Oh, now this really won't do, Venetia,' Ember said.

'Daddy, I'm sorry. I just wanted to tell your friend, if he wanted to come to the Monty, when is the best night.'

'That's sweet of you, Ven,' Winston said.

'It's Friday, because of the raffle. All sorts of good prizes. Malt whisky not winos' sherry.'

'Sounds great,' Winston told her. 'Friday. Yes, I might be here then.'

'Every Friday.'

'Right,' Winston said.

'There. Now I'll go again, daddy.'

'Yes, you must.'

'Bye again.' She closed the door.

'A charmer,' Caring said. 'Ralph, we can't leave her or you exposed.'

'But if you put it around that Winston's living here it's the kind of thing that could reach the police, not just this other outfit. The law might start wondering, wanting to know who he is, and why. Then where are we?'

'Fair enough,' Caring replied. 'You spot real difficulties, Ralph, which is only what I'd expect, and why we need your know-how. But we won't go spreading this news just anyhow. This can be distributed through Leopold and his contacts. This will be a leak.

It will reach these other people, like its been sneaked out, but not anyone else. Not police.'

'Winston moving in when?' Ember asked.

'I'll get my gear together. Day after tomorrow?'

'At the latest,' Caring remarked. 'Things could start happening.' He stood and walked back to the bar. 'I brought your pistol and some shells, Ralph. You should have them now.' He bent down and picked up an old style, leather Gladstone bag. Opening the case, he produced a newspaper parcel, brought it over and laid it carefully on Ember's lap. 'You're twice the man with a .357 handy.'

Winston said: 'You know, Ralph, I get the idea you don't really want me here at all. I'm the perfect lodger. Take no notice of Leopold. Look, you see me do a roughish job with Denzil and think I'm pure vandal. I can understand that. Not true. I can have a look around, if you like, and offer an idea or two about giving the club a bit of a refurbish, though tasteful and preserving all the grand old features. Only if you want, mind. You're the boss.'

Chapter 20

Ember was sleeping late on the morning after Caring and Winston's visit when his wife woke him. 'Someone to see you, Ralph. I would have left you, but he's agitated.'

It had been a fine, blank, total sleep without dreams, not the sort he managed very often lately, and somehow Winston-free, Denzil-and-his-woman-free, Caring-free, K-frame-free, panic-free. Being pulled back like this to the now and sticky sent his heart banging fast and kicked his brain almost numb again, as it loitered its way out of slumber. He had a very cheerful hard-on. This was usual when he awoke, regardless of the night before, but what sort of genuine comfort could that give if someone said the kind of things Maggie was saying?

'Who?' he grunted.

'He wouldn't tell me. He says he always has to deal direct, or not at all. "That's already been my policy in this matter." Those are his words. He sounds like President Bush.'

'Deal direct? How many?'

'What?'

'How many there?'

'One.'

'You let him in? He's through the door?' Ember sat up. All his instincts were to pick up the phone and scream for Winston to get here. Jesus, but fright was a foul master. A few hours ago, he had been struggling to keep Winston out of this place, and to keep the lout's eyes and plans off his daughter's bright, readying flesh. Now, all he wanted was protection for himself, and protection meant Winston. Ember had the K-frame in a dressing-table drawer, but for a couple of seconds did not even think of it. He needed help, someone to take over and do it all for him. 'Shut the door,' he said. They could have followed her up the stairs. 'Have you looked outside?'

'In the street?' she asked.

'The street, the yard. Are there more?'

'Who? Ralph, what the hell's it about? This is an old man. Apologetic.'

'Old? Scarred?'

'The man from Wales?' she asked.

'Is it?'

'Ralph, how would I know?'

'Marked around the mouth, and eyes discoloured?'

She stayed silent for a moment, taking this in. Then she said: 'I wouldn't have thought he'd travel so far for more, would you?'

'It wasn't me, for heaven's sake.'

'No, I don't think he's marked.'

Ember feared he had delivered his life over to a grim, recurring pattern – constant invasions of what used to be the safety of the panelled Monty and his home. He felt like a boxed-in animal. Once, he had been on a badger dig, when men put Jack Russells down the set. Perhaps in the old days, when he was still looking for a future, and ready to grab it wherever, he saw himself like one of the terriers. Now, was he the poor old badger? He left the bed, pulled on some clothes and then went to the drawer and took out the K-frame. Thank God the gun had been already loaded when Caring brought it. He was shaking too much to have handled bullets now. Margaret watched him.

He muttered: 'OK, make judgements, but I told you we were into something with no choices left.'

'Judgements? Not me. Accept it. Try not to look so destroyed, Ralph, love.' She put an arm around his shoulders and pressed herself to him for half a second. The scent she had on was something cheap bought by the children, which she had to wear. He admired her for it. This was consideration.

'Yes, sorry, Maggie.' There must be times when she felt ashamed of him and the way he went to fragments, yet always she could be relied on to offer strength. Whatever he did, he never forgot he depended on her, and never would. Just the same, he wished Winston was here. Ember went to the window. The curtains were still across and he stood at one side and peered down around the edge. His view was restricted to a corner of the yard and he saw nobody. He had been holding the pistol at arm's length at his side and he put on a jacket now, so he could have a pocket big enough for concealment and easy to pull it from.

'He seems so harmless, Ralph. But you think—'

'If they're smart enough to find me they're up to anything. Him first to lull, the rest ready.'

'I'll say you're not here?'

'They know I'm here.'

She sat on the bed. 'Well, call the cops?'

It was a joke. He even managed to smile. She smiled herself and leaned out and touched him again. 'Right, let's go,' he said.

'Good boy.'

A snarl almost broke from him at the words but he doused it somehow. He would have liked to turn on her and say he was no tame, quivering kid in need of a mother – that there were all sorts who thought he could be leader of a huge and gorgeous up-coming operation. But she most likely meant no harm and he smiled at her again, and found it easier this time, his face muscles less paralysed.

'Do your hair, Ralph.'

In front of the swing mirror he put himself right. It always amazed him how little his terrors registered in his face. He saw craggy, intelligent yet kindly features and even his eyes seemed unflinching and resourceful. This was a man with stature and durability, wasn't it?

He led the way down to the bar, his right arm savouring the outline of the gun in his pocket. He was shaking, but not anything like as much now he was dressed and on his feet, he felt almost sure of that. Wasn't anyone woken so suddenly bound to be jinxed for a minute?

Maggie had given the visitor coffee and he was sitting at a table, the cup empty in front of him, staring towards the door to the flat. He stood up at once, the clothes dismal, his grey hair straggling. 'Mr Ember,' he said, 'I didn't mean to be mysterious, but I have to be careful in this matter – ringing off on phone calls, just rolling up on people's doorsteps. I've done both. I'm Ian Aston's father. What I understood is, you identified my boy's body. Excuse me, but I'm trying to talk to everyone concerned.'

Ember's anxieties changed. 'Please, sit down, Mr Aston,' he said. 'Such a tragic business.'

But Aston remained standing. He was round-faced and chubby,

like someone born to be jolly, yet to Ember he seemed full of defeat. The shirt and tie had been through a lot together.

'Looking into the death,' Aston said. 'Just asking around at various points of contact. I hope you don't mind. But the police – I'm not sure what they're supposed to be doing. And such stories.'

Maggie went and sat at the table. 'Please,' she said, pointing to the chair. Aston sat, too. 'Which stories?' she asked.

'My idea was to ask you about that, or rather, Mr Ember, as a matter of fact. Looking at you now, Mr Ember, I see someone I can trust. I'm not used to that in this inquiry. Also looking at you, I'd say you have children. It's something I sort of sense? So, you must know how I feel.'

'Thank you. You're very kind. But we know so little,' Ember told him. 'Nothing.' He wished Maggie would not press this interfering fool in that bloody pointed way of hers. Sometimes she failed to see hazard. He remained standing himself, hoping that Aston would not settle and soon go.

'Few seem able to tell me much,' Aston said. 'Well, the police – involved in all sorts of ways, apparently. You can understand why people don't want to discuss it and get mixed up in things.'

Maggie said: 'Yes, a mess.'

He turned to Ember. 'I wanted to ask what sort of work Ian did. He'd say "in business" if you asked. But no details. Perhaps he had some connections you know, Mr Ember. People I could inquire of.'

Ember said: 'I don't think I can help you there, much as I'd like. I've nothing germane. I knew Ian as a good member of this club. About as far as it goes.'

'He was very private, I'll admit it. Even with us, he was close. If I could be frank, I'll tell you I wasn't always happy about what sort of work he might be in.'

'Why do you say that?' Maggie asked.

'And if it was something, something – well, off colour, it might help explain what happened. If I could get to the people he worked with. That's really why I called, Mr Ember. People you could direct me to.'

'I wouldn't say close or secretive,' Ember replied. 'It's just that in the club people came to relax, not talk about their work. I couldn't tell you what nine-tenths of my members do for a living, as a matter of fact.'

'If he'd crossed someone. It's a terrible idea, but it's a factor I've thought about.'

'My only task was identification, Mr Aston, and a sad task. I didn't go deeper. Couldn't. It might be best if you didn't, either.' The gun against his side felt preposterous now, and yet he was still conscious of peril.

Aston said: 'And then, eventually – very eventually, I'm thinking – I might be able to go and see one of the big police. Assistant Chief Constable Iles? Does the name mean anything to you?'

'I think I have heard of him,' Ember stated.

Aston picked up the empty cup and then replaced it, without taking it to his mouth. Ember glanced at his wife, telling her not to offer more. Aston said: 'Ian wasn't an angel.'

'I always found him a gentleman,' Ember declared.

'He could have offended all sorts. There are very difficult people around, some in big jobs and big houses. What chance for someone like Ian, so sure of himself, but such a child? On the other hand, you might say, What chance someone like self to find out the truth?'

'We've thought a lot about his death, my wife and I, but we make no sense of it.'

'Or others in the club might be able to help,' Aston said.

'I doubt that,' Ember replied. 'As I say, a social club. I'd honestly call it a day, if I were you, especially as far as the Monty goes.' It would do him no good at all to be sniffing around here once Winston had moved in.

Aston said: 'Excuse me, but you don't feel in danger yourself – I mean knowing him so well, if there are such vicious enemies about? I don't say this to disturb. But whenever I come into this town – well, I sense there's something dark, something evil. No offence.'

'Now, I'm afraid I must start getting the club up to scratch for a new day, Mr Aston,' Ember replied.

When he had gone, Ember said: 'Caring wants one of his people to move in for a few days. It's just a matter of accommodation. I said we had the space. A nice enough lad.'

'Which lad?'

'From near Kew Gardens, a great spot.'

'To do with the Welsh trip?'

'I told you – Kew. London.'

Chapter 21

Sarah Iles grew increasingly sure her husband had killed Ian Aston. In one of her cooler moments she muttered to herself that it was no joke to be living in the same house as the man who murdered your lover, and going to Mothercare and sherry parties with him. In some of her less cool moments, and these increased in frequency, she came to fear the strain was driving her out of her mind.

Perhaps it was the contact with Ian's father that helped make her certain Desmond had done it. Or it might be the unwillingness of Harpur and his people to stage even a show of proper investigation into one of their own. Wherever it sprang from, this conviction started to produce in Sarah sharp bouts of uncontrollable resentment, confusion and hatred. She knew she was over the top, but could do nothing about it. In the spells of rationality that came between, such dark fits appalled her. Appalled her because they were directed not at Desmond, but at the baby.

This afternoon, terrified by the power of one of these spasms, she rushed to pick up Fanny from where she lay naked on the hearthrug and ran sobbing with her from the house. The child was slung over her shoulder and seemed to think it a delightful new game, chortling in Sarah's ear. They kept a carry-cot on the back seat of the Panda and Sarah threw the quilt over Fanny and drove out at once into Rougement Place, not knowing where she was going nor caring, except that it must be some busy place, not the countryside or the coast, so that she would see people and people would be able to watch over her and the child, like guardians. Above all, she had to get away from the awful privacy and opportunities of the house.

Gratefully, she sat in an immobile traffic jam. Old women passengers on a bus in the adjoining lane beamed down on the baby, and Sarah beamed back, as proud mothers should. Three minutes earlier she had almost attacked the child, using a fragment of that huge, ugly, glass fruit dish given them by Sarah's parents one Christmas. Desmond's mother and father were monstrous in all sorts of ways, but would never be guilty of something like that. With care and forethought, Sarah had just now smashed this eyesore on a corner of the fireplace to make a horribly sharp, wide, curved weapon.

She saw that Desmond had killed Ian because of the child, not because of her. It astonished Sarah to find how much this hurt. Did she care about his motives? Since the birth, family had become crucially precious to Desmond, almost – this comparison would enrage him – like a Catholic. Before that, he had seemed prepared to let time take care of Ian Aston. She believed now that to preserve the family he would be capable of anything. Didn't some say he had always been capable of anything, and had proved it on a couple of crooks?

'Oh, sod off,' she called to the ugly, soft women in the bus, while still gazing happily towards them. They could not possibly hear her above the traffic din and through the closed windows. She had wanted people to keep an eye on her and the baby, but those people? 'Ever had your lover's head banged open by hubby?' she yelled, smiling amiably. Fanny, hearing the words, responded as if they must be for her, and waved her arms and blew a bubble in pleasure. The women enjoyed that and pointed and grew even softer looking, as if they had just seen royalty after an all-night wait.

She went on monologuing to the happy women in the bus. One of them saw Sarah was talking to them, but pointed to her ear and shook her head to show words would not carry. Really? 'The only person I trust and would ask for help is the one who's protecting my husband by a chronic case of blind eye. I even think this man might like me, I mean really like me – yes, it's possible, now something's happened to another part of his love-life – but there's a stronger factor working: the bloody club. You know that Thatcher phrase, "Is he one of us?" The self-serving clique. Well, the police were there a long time before her. Any idea how it is belonging to a group like that, yet not belonging?'

The bus began to move and the women waved. Sarah grinned a goodbye. She crept around the main streets of the town for another hour in more jams, loving the slowness and proximity and freedom from temptation, and then went home, reasonably calm now and still shaken that she could feel so jealous of the baby. She cleared up the glass fragments and, when Desmond came in late, said: 'I broke that fruit dish today.'

He laughed, knowing what she thought of it, and eager to endorse any insult to her parents, however oblique. 'Some breakages can't be helped. It was an accident, of course.'

'But of course.' She laughed, too. 'Any developments?'

'Harpur has some promising moves in mind, I hear.'

'Great.'

'He plays things very close.'

'Yes? Which means he could be doing nothing at all.'

'Sure. Detection's that kind of game. Fanny?'

'Fine. Sleeping now. We had a little drive out this afternoon.'

'I think I'll go and have a look at her,' he said. He was in uniform after some function, still with his cap on, and went out of the room as if on an official visit.

A minute or two later, at just before 10 o'clock, while Desmond was still upstairs with Fanny, the telephone rang and through the floor she heard him walk quickly to the extension in their bedroom. When she lifted the receiver she knew he was listening.

'Sarah, dear,' her mother said. 'How are you, darling?'

'Well, great.' She heard the extension put down and Desmond go back to Fanny's room.

'Are you sure, darling? I had such an odd experience, Sarah,' her mother said. 'This afternoon. I felt there was something terribly wrong, something to do with you and the child.' She would never use Fanny's name. 'This would be at about three-thirty.'

'Fanny's safely asleep. Des is up with her now, as a matter of fact. Admiring.'

'Thank heaven. This was so strong. I'm afraid I've been going on about it a bit here. Daddy said I should ring – for peace of mind.'

'Well, I did break that lovely fruit dish you bought for us. That might have been about three-thirty.'

Her mother giggled. 'I hope I'm not wasting telepathy on a fruit dish! We can soon get you another one of those, can't we, darling, if you're upset about it?'

'Oh, mother, you mustn't. So careless of me.'

'It's nothing. As long as you and our baby are all right.'

'Couldn't be better.'

'My mother's getting premonitions,' she said, when Desmond came back down.

'I love to hear of people extending their range. I think I'll have an early night, Sarah. Coming?'

'I'll hang on a while.'

Chapter 22

Harpur sat down on an easy chair in the dark, his legs stretched out. Always when he broke into someone's property he wanted to take things slowly and savour the fullness of the joy. It was a part of his work he prized above all, this private contact with the quiet intimacies of a target's life. He loved the revelations. They were usually small, but full of interest and charm and newness, sometimes interlocking with what was already known, sometimes forcing all that into breathtakingly different shape. Often he thought of this illicit poking about as comparable only with the techniques of psychiatry. His wife, Megan, had once told him that Sigmund Freud said psychoanalysis was like excavating an ancient city. Harpur reckoned that scouring some villain's place was a better comparison: the same crafty, ruthless ferreting for the hidden essences of an identity. Psychiatrists talked of the furniture of the mind, didn't they, but charged a lot more than Pickfords to move it about? Megan had also told Harpur, but more than once, that he was a born burglar, 'respectabalised into coppery only by the accident of a decent working-class upbringing.' Megan did pride herself on insight.

He was in Pete Chitty's place, a long shot, based on what Chickenfeed Reid had said. Normally, Harpur handled this sort of work strictly alone. Only then could he take the deepest pleasure from it: one-to-one was how the gear in these flats and houses and bed-sits talked best to him. He did not want heavies around. They would speak of a house-search as 'spinning someone's drum', a phrase without even minimal delicacy. Tonight, though, the hazards in looking over Chitty's flat were too sharp, and he had Garland keeping an eye open outside, as at Urbanmiraclestrasse when they picked up Reid. Harpur would never have let Francis any nearer the rummage; especially not Francis, because his ego

114

set up such static that when he came close you heard nothing else. Garland certainly had a brain, but could not stop letting you know, like jeans tailored to spotlight the cock.

Harpur stood and did a quick tour of the whole flat, still without showing any light. It was a mess, though not a total mess, as if Chitty employed a woman to come in and clean, but one who had a drink problem, or who dreaded above everything being called houseproud. The grubbiness certainly fell below the level of Desmond and Sarah Iles's home, and glass jars with perfumed bits in did a fair job here in keeping the atmosphere reasonably sweet. Harpur picked his way about very carefully. Even in a general shambles, people would remember exactly where certain special objects had been. This visit must remain undetected, another reason for acting alone. He had come in using a plastic card, which would leave no trace.

When he had checked that the flat was empty, he went straight to the little, all-in bathroom. The only invariable rule he had on house-searches was always to examine the lavatory cistern first because of the hundred spy and crime movies where this had been the brilliant, unthought-of hiding place for secret items. He found nothing there tonight and felt he had insulted Chitty. Returning to the living room, he switched on his flashlight, shaded the beam with a handkerchief, and began a systematic trawl. Garland called on the handset to confirm they were still in touch. He did not know how to remain quiet for more than ten minutes, and a big career had to lie ahead.

Despite the muck, one thing his living quarters made clear about Chitty was that he had powerful ideas on ambience. There were bold Habitat Cherokee rugs and some modernistic prints with plenty of pink and blue and yellow in metal frames on the white walls. Both Harpur's daughters went for this sort of art, and he had come to feel fond of it himself under their badgering. He thought Chitty's might be Jackson Pollocks. The chair where Harpur had sat first was of soft, genuine, pale green leather and there was a three-seater chesterfield to match. No question, if someone chic in, say, an angora stole lay out on that chesterfield to watch television or eat chocolates it would make a perfect, life-style tableau, a real piece of class. Chitty would probably look all right himself on it, even in one of his denim outfits. Despite everything, Pete had genuine touches of refinement to his features, and could quite likely stand pale green as background. Harpur also lay on the chesterfield to try to get the feel of the room from there and see things as Chitty might see them when at ease. The leather felt warm and soft against his hands and the side of his face, a natural for serene meditation. Perhaps it was here Pete worked out how Aston should end up on a tip with his skull clubbed in.

He had put the flashlight on the floor, and noticed now that the beam was reflected over near the far wall on a wide scatter of mysterious small particles about the floor. In a moment he stood, picked up the flashlight and crossed the room. He saw then that the particles were pieces of glass which had fallen from a picture hanging above: what looked in the poor light like a blue, white and yellow horse with a noughts and crosses face, and in some sort of animal crisis even without that. A black slip-on shoe lay among the fragments of glass and it seemed to Harpur as if it might have been flung at the work by someone on the chesterfield. Had Chitty tired of Pollock? Or had he grown enraged because he could still afford only prints? Was he dreaming of something better as he idled there one evening? It might be his spot for promoting breakages of all sorts.

Harpur finished in the living room and moved on. A flying shoe did not mean much and he began to fear that this intrusion could turn out a dud. Would he be here at all, risking his career, if he did not feel the unavoidable obligation to try everything he could to help Iles? That was policing. You did it by instinct, even while anguishing over whether the sex chain his wife had been in reached Africa and might one day, or night, make Africa reach one's self. He took the kitchen next and went quickly through the smart pine units until he came to what seemed to be a locked drawer under the empty, built-in wine rack. Perhaps Chitty had learned his lesson and kept the scotch in there so the charwoman could not help herself. All the same, the drawer excited Harpur and he sat down on the floor and brought out the thick bunch of all-purpose keys he carried on these expeditions. He began to work through them, without any luck.

Garland spoke again on the handset, more urgently this time, and said Chitty had arrived back and was putting his car away in the basement. 'Time to get out.'

'Right. Will do.'

He thought of retreating, but remained fascinated by the

drawer. Hurriedly now, he tried some more likely-looking keys, and after a few minutes to his delight felt the lock move. He pulled open the drawer and found at the top about twenty or thirty snapshots of children. Beneath them in the drawer lay something solid in a white cardboard box, perhaps intentionally concealed. The photographs intrigued Harpur. Chitty lived alone in this private flat block and his dossier had no information about a family elsewhere. Perhaps there was one, all the same. There were two girls and a boy in the pictures, the girls older, all three smartly dressed and happy-looking. The collection of pictures seemed to show the children from babyhood up until the girls were about twelve and ten, the boy seven. One of the girls resembled Chitty. There was no sign of the mother.

Garland spoke again. 'Get out, sir.'

Now, from under the photographs, Harpur lifted the heavy, oblong cardboard box and set it on the floor. He opened it quickly and realised suddenly that he was expecting to find either something that would connect with Aston, or conceivably, because of the box's shape, a handgun. Instead, it contained a red toy fire-engine and silver and purple combine harvester, plus a children's book called *Uncle And The Treacle Trouble*, with a dust jacket which showed an elephant in a purple dressing-gown getting drenched under a bucket of tar. Harpur seemed to remember his daughters laughing over these Uncle books. Prints, the book – he was always coming across odd affinities with villains.

Placing the items from the box alongside one another on the tiled floor, he had a disappointed groan. So, did the girls and boy from a previous liaison come to see him here sometimes, and did Chitty offer to read them a story? Why give all this a security rating and keep kids' stuff locked up? To guard it from the eyes of any jealous and possessive bird he might invite to live in like a wife for a spell? Harpur had heard Caring Oliver was an earnest father, too. Well, why not? There was more to the lives even of people like these two than . . . than what? Than whatever it was he had hoped to find here, and hadn't. He replaced everything and locked the drawer. Of course, he would have preferred to run through Oliver's place tonight, the top man's nest, but the dangers there were too high: Caring had a bit of a mansion, with alarms and maybe dogs, and Chitty's looked an easier touch. Easier and a dead loss.

117

He stood and switched off his flashlight. If he did not hurry, Garland would be up here to pull him out physically. For a few moments he stood still, listening, and then made his way to the flat's front door. It was on the first floor in a quite smart building: Pete might be a sidekick, but he obviously made fair money. Harpur went out on to the landing and closed the door quietly behind him. Again he stood and listened. He heard the street door open and shut and then footsteps on the carpeted stair. He turned and went quietly up a floor and waited. After a few minutes, he called the lift and descended.

In the car he said: 'Absolutely nothing, Francis.'

'Surprised, sir?'

Harpur realised that, normally, neither Garland nor any other detective would have accepted his nil report on the search as gospel – would assume he must be sitting on something – but this was different. Garland knew very well how desperately he had wanted to unearth something to move the focus off Iles.

'I hope the Assistant Chief is aware what we do to save his skin, sir. What you do for him. Regardless.'

'Not for the ACC. We're investigating a killing, Francis.'

'Investigating it in all directions but one.'

'We're entitled to look at Chitty as a potential source of interest.'

'It's the one we're not entitled to look at who interests some of us, sir.'

'Us?'

'A few.'

'Which few?'

'Well, me.'

'You're vindictive, Francis. But I understand. Still a soft spot for Sarah?'

'Don't you ever look that way these days, yourself, sir? I had that idea somehow.'

'Sarah Iles? Is that what you meant, "regardless"?'

'She'll be needing big help, sir.'

Chapter 23

'This is Mr Don Aston, sir,' Harpur declared.

'Well, I'm glad. And welcome,' Iles replied, standing and coming forward from behind his desk, hand outstretched, smiling in a warm, comradely style. He had on one of his navy blazers.

'I would the occasion could be different,' Aston said. Harpur thought his voice sounded jumpy, and why not?

'The Chief has heard you're coming in, Mr Aston, of course, and will probably join us later,' Iles continued. 'We're all very aware of your distress.'

Harpur saw Aston gaze at the ACC, trying to sort something out before sitting down. Iles took a perch on the edge of the desk.

'Distress, true, but more it's frustration,' Aston said.

'Exactly,' Iles replied. 'The word. Sadness has settled into a permanent state, but now you want redress. This was a foul crime, the kind that strikes at the very nub of law and order. It's on this account that we're pursuing our investigations with all energy. Why I asked Mr Harpur to be with us. It's his direct responsibility, and I don't think you'll find a better man.'

'Mr Aston has been making his own inquiries,' Harpur said.

'Yes? I'm not at all surprised. Good for you, Don. I thought immediately you walked in here just now that you certainly weren't the sort to let the grass grow under your feet.'

Aston sat silent for a few seconds, his chubby, blanched face empty. Iles's soaring friendliness probably baffled him. He was not the first person to be baffled by the ACC. He should look out for violent changes, though. 'There are embarrassing elements, Mr Iles,' Aston said, lowering his head for a moment. He looked weary and timid, yet was obviously forcing himself to go on. Harpur found the doggedness grand.

119

'Don't feel in any way inhibited, Mr Aston,' Iles told him. 'Your son, my wife. Yes, it happened. I've had to face up to that. More than once. There are flexibilities in most marriages. This isn't something new.'

'She's a great girl,' Aston replied. 'If I may say so.'

Momentarily, Iles paused, as if considering whether Aston might. He slid off the desk and went and sat more formally behind it. 'She is.'

'Would you still be together otherwise? Such a way with her.'

'I think so. Always have.' The ACC nodded: 'I worry about her now, but, yes, she's tops.'

'What worry?' Aston asked.

'She's disturbed, as you'd expect, Mr Aston. A result of all this.'

'Disturbed?' The word obviously had some special, dark meaning for him, even frightened him. 'You mean off balance?'

Iles laughed for a moment and made a tent shape with his hands under his chin, like a mischievous professor. 'If any of us are in a constant state of balance, which I doubt, yes, I'd say she's off balance. The stress she's under is pretty exceptional, isn't it?'

Still anxious, Aston said: 'I don't know if I ought to say this . . .'

'Whatever you like, please,' Iles told him. 'Frank's my middle name.'

'But Mrs Iles came to see us.'

Iles made his eyes large with surprised delight. 'I'm glad. It's the kind of wholesome thing Sarah would do. Personal relations are supreme to her.'

'She seemed sad, but, all right. Not at all disturbed. I mean, not, well, sick.' He produced the word very slowly, like something evil crawling from a pit.

Iles nodded. 'To be specific, I worry about the very safety of our child, Mr Aston,' he said gently.

Harpur, standing near the fireplace, felt a tremor go through his body. He watched the ACC with fascination. Was this part of the show?

'But she seemed to love that baby beyond anything,' Aston replied.

Iles frowned and nodded again. 'Yes, perhaps. Beyond anything. I think there are terrible, ungovernable moments when she sees things quite differently, that's all. But I mustn't trouble you with all this, Don. Not why you're here at all.'

'I didn't realise.'

'Fanny's mine, of course.'

'Of course. Of course,' Aston said. 'My wife and I both commented.'

Iles ruminated. 'I suppose people worried that it would be I who might turn against the baby. Cliché is a powerful master. But no. Fanny's taken on a kind of malign symbolism for Sarah. The child diminishes her, pushes her to one side. Can you understand, Don?'

Harpur, himself unable to understand, thought Aston would need some aid: 'I'm sure Mr Aston is here only to—'

Iles said: 'I'm sure he's here only to, also. I think it's admirable, an oldie like this, making the journey and strolling into the Lubianka as bold as you like to quiz one of the top, tainted men. Let me put it this way, Aston, may I? We had a glass fruit dish at home, so ugly it was kept out of sight in a cupboard and therefore wholly unlikely to suffer damage.'

'Obviously, Mr Iles, my main concern is not really with your wife, but with what happened to Ian.'

Harpur said: 'We all have the same deep concern. The Chief will make that very apparent in due course.'

Aston suddenly turned away from staring at Iles: 'My trouble is, I don't know if I can believe you, you see, Mr Harpur. I've got to mention it. You look like someone to be believed, but there's no certainty.'

'Are we going to take a murder lightly?' Harpur replied.

'I don't say that. I say there could be – could be, well, private concerns involved. Can I put it clearer?'

'This dish,' Iles continued, 'it's the sort of monstrosity that, as a gift, can invade any home, no matter how otherwise tasteful that home might be. Don, I'm quite sure you have such objects in your own place in . . . Yes. But a day or two ago the dish somehow got itself out of the cupboard and was smashed. Now, there could be an acceptable explanation – a lot of fruit around, or out of season spring-cleaning – but this was not a casual thing. This breakage was craftsmanship, Aston. I found a piece of glass in the waste bin afterwards fashioned like something from the Zulu war. All right, nothing happened. The baby's fine, not a mark.

But we're getting a replacement dish. Now, do you see what I mean: disturbed? Am I putting it rather tamely?'

The ACC's voice fell, as it sometimes did when he was being hurried into despair or rage or the two. 'Take a look at yourself in the big mirror there, will you, Aston? What do you make of it? You traipse over to see me from . . . elsewhere, in your three quid sandals and those mesmeric clothes, but have you any fucking idea of the kind of woman we're discussing? This is not the Samaritans. Do you know what you're messing with?'

'What I'm trying to find out.' It was as if politeness forced him to do what Iles said, and he stared for a while into the ACC's full-length mirror.

'That's enough,' Iles said. 'You'll make yourself puke. I do it myself, daily.'

Aston leaned forward and put an elbow on the desk. He gazed at Iles, almost fondly now, almost sympathetically: 'Once I read a bit of a letter she wrote to my son when he was holed up with us. I couldn't help it. He left stuff around. You're police, so you're reading other people's intimacies all the time, and you won't understand why I felt funny. You'll say I should have known what it was, the heavy-weight stationery, but I'd given it a glance before I realised. Know what she wrote?' To Harpur he said: 'I told you I had information.'

Iles leaned forward to examine his profile in the mirror.

Aston went on: 'These were the words: "Ian, you make me feel so beautiful." '

Iles's head jerked towards Aston and the ACC seemed about to lean across and grab him around the greyish, old neck above the whitish, old shirt. Iles somehow kept himself restrained though. '*Feel*, for God's sake? Feel beautiful? She *was* beautiful, *is* beautiful,' he said. 'She didn't need some recidivists' baggage-handler to tell her that. I look at Sarah sometimes when she's walking naked about the bedroom, the small of her back, the lie of her belly button and so on, and, Aston, do you know what I think? It's banal: I think to myself, This is mine, and to quite a degree, she is. Well, to some degree.'

'Mr Iles, I feel as if I know her a little, you see. There's that letter, and coming to visit us in Bristol. That's a link. It's these links I'm following, Mr Iles. I can't do other.' He sat back again.

similar?' Iles asked. He turned to Lane. 'His point, sir, of course, is that since his son was banging Sarah, even in my own bed, I might finally have turned rough, and now there's a cover-up.'

Lane frowned. It would be in part because Iles had expressed the Chief's own thoughts, and not only the Chief's.

The ACC went on: 'Some people do regard adultery as grave and a motive for all sorts. It's not beyond comprehension. I know you set great store on the sanctity of marriage yourself, Chief. So admirable.' He switched back to Aston. 'All the same, I'm shocked that you compare your son with two pieces of contemptible dross like Jamieson and Favard. They deserved all they got. Not only a gifted boy detective done to death but a very lovely woman probably cindered by them in a fire, as I understand it.' He paused and looked away briefly, his face heavy with grief. 'Really lovely. Had you heard that too, Aston? Yes or no?' Momentarily, he was shouting. Harpur had seen him go wild once or twice before over the death of Celia Mars, his mistress in those days, who had become somehow caught up in the violence. Then Iles turned back and grew conversational again. 'They should have been allowed to live? That your benign theme, Donald?'

Harpur said: 'The file is still very much open on that case.'

'Of course it is,' Iles commented. 'Do we ever give up looking for the killer or more likely killers? Could one person have brought that off alone? I'd like to meet him, if so. Gifted. Those two – garrotting, which was how they happened to die – garrotting was too good for them, if you ask me. But, clearly, on the other hand, it was against the law, and not to be tolerated in an ordered society.'

'Never,' Lane said.

'And the death of your son obviously cannot be tolerated, either,' Harpur added.

'I would like to say, Mr Aston, that we are as much bound by the rules as anyone in the land,' Iles remarked.

'If anything, more so,' Lane commented.

'That's what I mean, Don, about the over-view. The Chief can set all these things into their full perspective. In some ways, this sort of remarkable vision comes with office, but there are also elements in it entirely personal and unique to Mr Lane.'

Chapter 24

For security, Winston did not roll up direct to the Monty with his luggage but reported to Chitty's place, and, driving across to collect him from there now, Ember suddenly decided he had a blue van on his tail, an old Citroën. The sweat gushed at once, running cold down his back and spreading like freezing wires half-way around his body when it reached the waistband of his trousers. It was ten years since he last drove watching the mirror more than the road, trying to identify over his shoulder. You needed to be young and fight-mad to get kicks from this. How the hell had he been sucked back to it? Well, the cost of living.

And, as an extra, something inside felt hot pride at being singled out, even by a palsied Citroën – especially if they truly had him down as El Mastermindo. Flunkeying at the Monty and pissing about with all that family stuff and the school could be a grim drag now and then for a man who had seen contention and known full-scale people. The van occasionally edged quite close and occasionally fell out of sight altogether. As far as he could tell in the dark, the man driving was alone: thin, quite small and nobody he knew. Maybe glasses, maybe a small moustache, but those might be shadows. President Truman? He felt proud of that, the bonny ability despite everything to get wry. Wryness he revered as part of polished living and was an item he tried to alert his daughters to. They should encounter quality wryness in the people he hoped they would marry into after that school, or it was more a waste than he suspected already.

Of course, it could be imagination, possibly just a van on the same route. His sweat kept pumping though, and best respect sweat because it was nature giving utterance. This lousy Montego. It labelled him. Caring Oliver must be right, and they had worked a trace through the registration. Christ, he might be a brilliant display every time he went on the road, like a coffin in a lillied hearse.

Perhaps the jerk in the Citroën was not so small, just keeping right down so as to hide his face. And what about in the back? Vans were an enigma. Was it low on the rear suspension? Now and then, he let himself believe the boys when they said Panicking as a name did him wrong. At this moment, though, with the van sneaking forward and breathing close again, its sodding headlights badgering him, he recognised the label couldn't be fairer. When he hit this condition he would feel his mind lock on to a single worry so it could not cope with anything else. His hands were so wet he had trouble holding the wheel. His eyes had misted.

Luckily, they were driving through a bit of the city he knew, up behind Marl View school, where half the villains in the region had learned to count and decided that they didn't have enough. He turned off suddenly into a side-street and put his foot down hard, then slowed marginally and turned off again. The brakes squealed like *Bullitt* and he found himself almost grinning as he recalled ancient chases and crises and triumphs he had been part of. As then, the excitement gave him an instant, tumultuous hard-on. That was nature talking, too. He still had juice. So, perhaps he was not past it, after all. Never. Looking in the mirror as he made this second turn, he saw that the Citroën had followed from Stipend Road and seemed to be trying to keep up. He accelerated again towards a T-junction that could take him deeper into the web of small streets around the school or back to the main drag. Until he found whether the Citroën made the turn after him in time he would keep his options open. He liked that dim phrase. Didn't it signify a return to cool? Whatever this van was, instinct told him he must avoid giving a lead to Chitty's flat. They might have only him marked. Oliver, Pete himself, Winston and some new boy called Harry were all going to be at Chitty's, so it could be highly non-forgivable to bring a spectator. Besides, he wanted no possibility of Oliver getting his suspicions about the Montego confirmed. Ember meant to lose this Citroën and say nothing. He might not know the real tale about Ian Aston, but he did not forget about him, either.

At the junction he glanced in the mirror again and saw nothing behind. He went right, back towards Stipend Road, but, instead of continuing on the route to Chitty's place, joined the opposite flow and fitted the Montego into a nice line of night-on-the-town traffic. Even if the Citroën did take the right at the T-junction all the little driver would see when he reached the main road would be a string of anonymous rear lights. And he would probably be looking the opposite way, in any case.

Now Ember felt good. It might be kiddish, but chucking a car around like that was still fun. To be able to get back to the skills of pre-Monty days so fast showed that although his brain was nearly blacked out by fear something else would take over – memory, old habits. Why Caring wanted him, of course. Veteran's stock. His clothes stuck to him still, but he thought the sweating had stopped, and he had no trouble turning the wheel. In fact, his driving just now had been up to an expert's. Yes, he could panic. But, yes, he could beat panic as soon as it surfaced. That was what counted, surely to God.

He drove another mile, then pulled off Stipend Road and did a big circle through back streets again to Pete's place near Grant Hill, a quite decent area, with new flats and some older, stone houses, properly looked after, where school teachers and that sort lived because of repair grants. There was no trace of the Citroën. All the same, from the glove compartment he slipped into his jacket pocket the heavy wrench he always carried, then did a roundabout walk to the flat and kept his eyes moving. When he arrived about half an hour late Oliver looked evil, but Ember could not explain, not with the truth anyway. The new man, Harry, seemed to be dozing in an armchair.

Caring said: 'I wanted to see people here, not in my own place or Ralph's, because Pete's got something to show us. It's sombre.'

'My idea is someone's been having a quiet look around this place,' Chitty explained.

'Why the picture's broken, and the shoe underneath among the glass bits?' Ember asked.

'That's not to do with it,' Chitty replied. 'Just normal wear and tear. Isn't that obvious?'

'He got fed up with Pollock,' Winston said.

'With what?' Ember asked.

Winston said: 'A flat done out like this – mode of Tasteville, New England, circa 1957. Wouldn't you go to pieces and want to get violent, Ralph?'

'In here,' Chitty announced, and led them to the kitchen.

Winston had a chuckle. 'Tale of the loathsome pine.'

Pete bent down and unlocked a drawer in one of the units. 'I keep some cherished photographs in here – kids by my first – and toys and things. Nothing valuable, but sensitive. I'm pretty sure someone's been browsing.'

'Only pretty sure?' Ember asked. 'We're getting nervy?' One thing he loved was to go one up. Always grab any chance to sound knee-deep in equanimity.

'I thought someone was on the stairs when I came in the other night. Then the lift goes down. Why I had a sharp look around in here,' Chitty replied.

'So where did they get in?' Ember asked.

Caring said: 'Maybe a key. Maybe a credit card. Think of Access. Oh, this is Harry. Ralph goes way, way back, Harry.'

'I heard that,' Harry replied. He had trooped into the kitchen with the rest, still looking half-asleep. 'That's something, Ralph. History's got its strong points.'

'So would they find anything in here, anything problematical?' Ember asked.

'No. I just don't go for it, that's all,' Chitty said.

'Why are they searching, anyway?' Ember asked.

'Exactly,' Caring said. 'You always get right to it, Ralph. Well, these people might be the ones trying to reach Denzil down in Wales for the bank date and money figures, and maybe they've failed. They think we didn't fail, which is right. So they come looking, in case Pete's got some fine information hidden here.'

'This could be good news, then,' Winston argued. 'They're in the dark.'

'Spot on,' Ember said. He saw all sorts of possibilities he did not like.

'Let's all go back to the leather, shall we?' Caring said. They followed him into the lounge and sat down, Ember on the chesterfield with Winston. He had started thinking of him not as fangs out on a saunter but as an ally. Winston could be right about this flat. The place was loud but said bugger all, except that Chitty had heard the word style once or twice and would never discover what it meant. Denim and white socks were Pete at full stretch.

'They're in the dark? Well, maybe,' Caring remarked. He

always looked worried and tonight worse than ever. 'In the dark but they found Pete's pad. And we think they know about Ralphy. You seen any signs at all, Ralph? Any menace?'

'Not a thing.'

'You're sure? Not a suspicion?'

'Nothing.'

'That's a relief, anyway.'

'This could all be a bit of a panic, couldn't it, Caring?' Ember suggested. Turn that bloody word on them for a change.

'My feeling,' Winston said.

'You'll ask me what's the connection. How do they bring together Ralph and Pete?' Caring went on. It was as if he had not heard Ember or Winston. Often when he talked there was this step by step thing, little thoughts climbing slowly one on top of the other like locusts in a glass jar, but determined to get there. Perhaps he was learning logic by correspondence course. 'Ralphy, I'm afraid it's got to be that bloody car of yours again.' He shook his head, sad and baffled.

'This I don't get at all,' Ember replied instantly. He put a snarl into it. Didn't he have the right? Maybe not, so snarl more. 'My poor bloody car. Always that. Honestly, sometimes I wish I'd bought Jap. Am I some scapegoat here?'

Harry, sitting now on a black canvas thing with thick chrome arms, said: 'These discussions. What we farting about for, Ollie? Is Exeter on or isn't it? All this yesterday stuff. Next week is what we should be thinking about, trying the weapons, going over the ground plan.' He was young, in a green track suit, perhaps even younger than Winston, with a dreamer's face, all sleepy eyes and half smiles. But the voice bit in like Adolf's piano wire.

'This is important, Harry,' Caring replied. 'This could be about next week, or I wouldn't have started it.' Ember was surprised at the respect and patience Caring gave this half-doped looking youngster. 'When I say the Montego gets the two of them known, what I'm thinking of is the trip to Cardiff, then the jaunt Pete and Ralph had together to Exeter, to the bank, in that car. You see what I mean, the obvious link?'

'Except we didn't go to Cardiff in the Montego,' Winston told him.

'That's what I hear,' Caring replied.

'And what's true,' Winston said.

130

Pete Chitty said: 'This sweet, family-man side of you, Ralphy – really great qualities, don't mistake me – but, look, you didn't get worried about those folk who live near the cathedral and hop down there by yourself on a sick visit, did you?'

Winston yelled a laugh. 'Sick visit? After all the trouble getting an anon, nicked car, first instance? And what sickness, anyway? A few grazes. Definitely nothing intensive care.'

Ember held up his hands to show no offence, and laughing a careful quantity himself. He gazed at Chitty and Oliver and thought he kept his face just right: calm and amused, but not a crazy state, not someone obviously working flat-out on a merry cover-up. When he had his hands up like that he realised they might notice the wrench bulking in his pocket and soon lowered them. 'No, Pete, no welfare trips, though I don't regard your inquiry as untoward, not at all. Ralph Ember doesn't mind being accused of humanity, however wrongly.'

'So that's settled,' Harry grunted. He stood up and went and had a closer gaze at that thousand-to-one-against blue horse in the blitzed frame. 'Art's got a way of seeing things, though, hasn't it? What about your Smith and W., Pete? Did this breaker-in find that, take it? Are we down on fire power?'

'I don't keep the gun here, obviously,' Chitty replied. 'I—'

'That's all right then,' Harry said. 'We're equipped.' You could tell he wouldn't wear another load of talk. All that bothered him was getting the job done.

Pete Chitty said: 'Montego maybe. Winston and Harry are right, though. It makes no odds how it happened, but it's happened. I'm moving out until after the job.'

'You've got personal anxieties?' Winston asked.

'I like privacy.'

'It's not nice to think of a stranger playing with your toys, is it?' Harry said. He made a voice like some fussy, soft woman and shivered his tits.

Winston had a smile and then, eventually, Caring and Chitty. At this stage, Ember let himself smile, too. That was not impertinent.

Caring said: 'All right, all right. We can worry too much, I know that.' He seemed to be letting his hair grow longer, so it bushed at the back, very thick and grey in curls, and you could have thought he was media or wholesale fruit and veg. That grey

131

hair would be great for juries, but you never mentioned juries or anything similar to Caring. 'Maybe Pete's nervy, like Ralph said, and there was no intruder.'

'The photos in the drawer were out of order, Caring, and the combine harvester not put back right, either, like someone getting out in a hurry,' Chitty declared.

'I can't stand a combine harvester looking wrong,' Harry muttered.

'I don't know if we're going to arrive for this job and find another team trying it at the same time,' Caring said. 'It sounds a laugh, but it's no laugh. We'd have to see them off as well as handle all the other problems, such as guards. Pete's going to move into a boarding house with Harry and the other lad, Fritzy, who's arriving tomorrow. Winston will be at Ralph's place. Ralphy, or any of you, I want to know the first time you see the slightest thing that could mean trouble. Even a hint. The point is, if we could hit these people now, before the job, it leaves a clear run. I used to think, no outfit from down there could give us any serious worry, but they might be showing they can reach out. This could be a different situation.'

'But still manageable,' Winston said.

'Nothing,' Ember replied.

For the rest of the time they talked about the way the job would go, with all the details. Harry really woke up. He must have been down to Exeter, too: everything you could observe in that bank he had clear in his head, even the height of the door handles from the floor and the names of the clerks, which he saw on the grill boards they put up. He had looked at the manager's house, as well. 'There's a side room, the study, not overlooked by anything. Herd them into there.'

For a kid like this, with a mind like this, really into scientific method, you had to give total admiration. Listening to Harry, Ember grew suddenly convinced the job at the bank would be a disaster, and convinced just as much that he had to be there. This lad, Harry Lighterman, had all the planning to perfection. But these things were never about planning. Among all the lessons Ember had learned from experience and age, the top one was that an operation like this depended first on guts and second on luck. The planning came third. And he knew as a golden certainty that his guts would fail on the day and he could mess up the whole enterprise. Habit and instinct might take over when it was a basic routine like dropping a tail car such as the Citroën. Cracking a loaded bank was different. He would be what cracked. He had done it before. Thank God, the job then had been such an all-round shambles, nobody had time to see his collapse, and no blame had ever come his way, though there were men from it still doing time, and one in a wheelchair with some of the best bits of his central nervous system marksmanned. There would be no chance of dodging out of responsibility like that again.

But because the planning sounded so fine and thorough now, and the people so bright and brave, he would never be able to argue his way free. If he had spotted some stupid risk, or a streak of weakness in one of the team, he could have said, even now, that he didn't work with Mickey Mouse gangs and pull out no bother, because they respected him and could still respect him, even then. Or not too much bother, anyway: nothing on the Aston scale of skull damage.

These boys were not Mickey Mouse and he could spot no exit. If he tried it now, they could rightly think of him as an Aston re-run. Take Caring and Pete, on about the Montego just now: it gave a hint of how touchy they could be, and how well they knew him and how they watched him. So, next week, he would be back-packing his terror and sweat and paralysis and taking them along with him to Exeter, and also taking with him, very likely, full bloody catastrophe. If he tried to get out now and save himself, and maybe save them, also, they would kill him. And if he stayed in, he would probably get himself taken or blasted on the raid, and some of them, too, or all. He wanted to hear Caring, with his big flair for logic, work this one out, though he did not want it enough to ask him.

Winston had very calibre luggage and a ton of it, like Zsa Zsa Gabor at the airport – lightweight, grey with crimson trim, and some truly redolent destination labels: none of that package tour Acapulco or Rio stuff, but Vladivostok, Zanzibar and Lucknow. Perhaps you could buy new cases with them already on. There were five, all full size, plus a holdall. How long did he think he would stay at the Monty, for God's sake? The job was next week. But probably he carried a big supply of rubber bands for his ginger pony tail. He was in quite a quality suit today, modern-style loose, like that black jacket of Leopold, shoulders wide enough to grab a whole television screen: people did not realise this new fashion came in for cameras in the House of Commons. He might be going on to stay somewhere dressy after the job and had packed all his suits. Lucknow was fussy? They loaded the luggage and set out for the Monty, Winston slewed around towards him in the front seat of the Montego to talk like an old friend.

Or possibly not just to talk. Before they were out of Pete's road, Winston said: 'How about this blue Citroën van behind us, Ralphy? Like a French baker's. Mousy-looking guy driving.'

'Where?' Ember asked.

'He's slotted in after the Senator for a minute. Could know we've spotted him.'

'You sure?'

'Not, not sure. But I'm thoughtful.'

'I'll soon lose him – suppose he really is a tail.'

'You haven't seen him before?'

'No. And I don't see him now.'

'Turn somewhere.'

These kids. You had Harry, a creative thinker and researcher, and pretty good at it, too. And Winston, an organiser and second-string boss, and pretty good at it, too. Harry looked like an absent-minded teenager, and Winston, with all that red whiskering, like one of those dawns that gave sailors warnings. But underneath they were similar: both as sharp as you could get and pushy, both able to focus the whole lot on a job.

'Yes, I'll drift into the side-streets,' Ember said. 'He'll never keep up.'

'We don't want to lose him, do we? This little fellow is information.' For that moment, he sounded as know-all as when they did the Denzil trip, but perhaps something had reached him at last from the mentions of Ember's track-record: 'Hark at me, explaining the obvious to someone of your standing, Ralph! I mean turn so we can see if he's definitely with us.'

Ember went right, his hands sliding around the wheel again, and did not even bother to watch the mirror.

'Here he comes,' Winston said. 'Cheeky.'

'I don't want to take him home.'

'Home's on his map already, Ralph. So is Pete Chitty's. He's the sort who'd get a lot of fun out of a combine harvester.'

'Who the hell is it?' Ember heard his voice crackle a bit with nerves and noticed Winston glance at him for a moment before concentrating on the van again.

In a while he asked: 'So has Caring got it right, after all? This car spotted?'

'How?'

'Yes, of course, how? You're bound to be one hundred per cent fireproof, Ralphy, whatever Pete said. So, what you're suggesting is we drive to somewhere quiet and then stop suddenly and try to draw this companion into talks? Not too quiet, or he'll see what's up and refuse to follow.'

'This is a van.'

'More in the back? We're going to have to deal with them at some stage. So let's do it on ground we pick, you say? Fine.'

They were driving through the same streets as Ember had used before in the attempt to lose him. This time, though, he could not move past the sweat stage and into excitement. That's how life often turned out these days. He knew things were getting worse. Is this what finale looked like – the lights and bonnet of a doddery croissant van in a Montego mirror? Christ, he thought he had worked up to something better. A turbo Saab mirror wouldn't have been so bad.

'That's not the K-frame, is it?' Winston asked. He leaned over and put his hand into Ember's pocket. 'A wrench. Why? You knew there'd be trouble and you'd need a club? How, Ralph? The famous educated instinct, yes? Myself, nothing. Sometimes I think I'm a bloody innocent.'

So true. Just the word for Winston. 'I'd still rather lose him,' Ember said.

'We wouldn't lose him. He knows where we're going and where we've been.'

'So what's he want.'

'We need to ask him. Do I see ships? Looks promising.'

Ember turned again, past the lock-gates and then drove up towards Young's Dock, hoping to God the Citroën would spot this was terribly wrong and not enter the trap. Only a couple of vessels stood at the quays, and those were on the far side. Ember saw nobody about. Now there was no other traffic he did not need to look in the mirror to know the Citroën had followed. He could hear it grinding away.

'Swing us broadside on in a minute or two, Ralph, so if he

tries to get around he's into the dock. Nice shadows up near this big warehouse.'

'He can't be solo. He wouldn't risk it.'

'He's got orders to stick with the Montego, Ralph. He might be scared not to. Especially if he's already had trouble keeping track of you.'

'What trouble? What are you—'

'Don't crack him open with that wrench, will you, Ralph?' Suddenly, he sounded very anxious. 'Jesus, it wasn't you who clubbed Aston, was it? But, now listen, please, no instant damage, Ralph. This boy in the van's got to talk to us. Caring will want that. Here. This'll do.' Suddenly, he was yelling.

Ember pulled the wheel over hard and braked. Winston, the innocent, had it exactly right and the bit of road was ideal, made narrow by the big warehouse on one side and a dockside crane on the other. Ember heard the Citroën brake and skid, and then the groan of gears as the little man tried to get too fast into reverse and make a turn. So he must be alone. If he had support in the back why bolt?

Before Winston had moved, Ember was out of the Montego and running to the van. Fear held him as hard as it ever had, but for once it did not take the strength from his legs and body, nor wipe out all his mind. He was left with a single, overwhelming thought: the man in the Citroën must not talk, because his talk could be about how they had fixed on the Montego during that second, feeble-minded visit to Wales, and then made the link to Chitty, as Caring had seen. No, it was not true Ember had room for only one thought. There was another. It centred on what had happened to Aston for his mistakes.

As he ran, Ember pulled out the wrench. He had to get there before Winston, even if Winston did have youth and drive and those long legs and the build of an athlete. Ember's panic was filling in pretty well for all those tonight, especially drive. As he tugged open the door of the van, the wrench raised in his other hand, he found himself once more almost grinning, part amusement, but a bigger part pleasure, this time at the notion that he might be the one who saw off Ian Aston. The name Ralph Ember did still mean something, regardless. It was formidable. It told a bloody big tale, even to such a hard, London whizz-kid as Winston, and even if it was only a tale.

Chapter 25

Harpur heard it first from Jack Lamb, the world's greatest informant, though he would never get an award. Jack picked up things early, picked them up right, and picked them up from more or less everywhere. Jack knew people, substantial people. Living in a manor house and trafficking in fine art, Jack was a substantial person himself, and always would be unless caught; which went for all substantial people. Although like most informants he feared the telephone and its open lines, Lamb did enjoy occasionally ringing Harpur with items that would bring him outstanding pain, and especially loved delaying such calls until dead of night, so the shock went right through to the bone. This time, he rang Harpur's house at about 3 a.m. and Megan, who had just come in from London and was undressing, answered before Harpur had woken properly. She loathed Jack and especially what she called 'the grateful blind-eye' Harpur gave his business. Sitting on the side of the bed now, she chatted to him for a minute in a hostile whisper. Then she passed the receiver over.

'Colin, old acquaintance,' Lamb declared, 'here's a gorgeous treat. The chance to speak to both of you. But what the hell's your wife doing out until this time of night? Are you still *mari complaisanting*? Still living in a different era, the two of you? Still so positive – oops! – that it can't hit heteros? But is that my affair? Haven't I got my own problems?'

'What *is* your affair, Jack?'

'To tell you you're all right. The Force's pride and comradeship intact. Lane won't bring in an outside officer on the Aston death, regardless.'

Harpur tried to keep the relief from his voice. 'Why should he? We've got matters in hand. But thanks for the good news. So why are you so happy?'

'Because you're going on air. I look forward to the show. Midlands TV. No more than you deserve.'

'What's it about, Jack?' As Megan finished undressing, Harpur thought he glimpsed a red-blue suck or bite blur on her inner thigh. Newish. She climbed into bed naked, kissed him on the forehead, then resolutely turned away to sleep.

Lamb said: 'You and the Aston case, to be the first on ITV's new version of that BBC thing, *Crimewatch*. You know the one? Where they re-enact a crime and invite viewers to ring in with information. I hear Midlands regard the Aston affair as very meaty – quite big enough for the series launch. Their programme will do a lot more independent research than the BBC's. "Less police-based" is the formula, I think. And "wider ranging" is another phrase I read in *TV Times*. It means a lot of investigative poking about. You'll like that – genuine public scrutiny, won't you? Give the lie to that rubbish about the police being a closed club.'

Christ almighty. 'Could be extremely helpful, Jack. I can understand why you'd want to let me know about it right away.'

'Exactly. You always see the plus. Obviously Lane can't disclose that he's so worried about the case he'd like a stranger to take over. Midlands would immediately want to know all the ins and outs – not to mention the watching millions.'

'Obviously.'

'My acquaintances tell me the meeting with the Chief's at noon.'

'What meeting?'

'To finalise arrangements for the programme.'

'Noon tomorrow?'

'Today, Col. You're invited. Midlands researchers have already talked to old Aston. Tell me, Col, have you heard something about a lump of fruit bowl – as a dagger?'

'He was hit over the head, Jack.'

'No, I don't mean him.'

'What fruit bowl, for God's sake?'

'Something along those lines. They'll mock up the murder of Aston on the tip. I don't know who's playing the killer. Tricky one. Not Mia Farrow. Oh, the series is to be called *Where Is Truth?* Might you regard that as offensive, Col? Police get proprietorial about the word truth, don't they?'

'Sounds spot on.'

'Fruit bowl?' Megan muttered, when he had ended the call and lay down again, his arm around her.

'Possibly Jack's going to pieces. It's always been on the cards.'

'A fruit-bowl fruit-cake?' she said and giggled for a while, before beginning to snore gently. Megan had a gift for relaxation, not to mention that she must be played out.

The Chief called the meeting in his suite, so Harpur would have deduced in any case it was special. For routine discussions, Lane liked to drift into people's rooms and chat as if spontaneously, without agenda, jacket or shoes, furthering the image he had of himself as easy-going and consensual. Still pretty new here, he had chosen informality as his way of getting inside the barriers. It was too flagrant to help him much, and it did not help at all with Iles.

Instead of Lane, it was Iles who arrived in Harpur's office this morning, about half an hour before the meeting. He seemed to have shed a little weight recently and looked vehemently athletic, even for him, in another navy blazer with some small, classy-looking sporting club badge on the breast. He refereed rugby and had boxed and fenced, or so he said. He could certainly head-butt consummately, but no badges were given for that.

'You've heard?' the ACC asked.

'These programmes can sometimes . . .'

Iles beamed. 'You'll get on screen, Col. I doubt whether they'll invite me.' He ran an auditioning hand over his face. 'They want police who look like nothing but police – features homely-to-crude and worthy clothes – or the viewers get confused. I adore the excitement these programmes build up: banks of telephones visible, blurting away with calls from loonies in the great outside.'

'Now and then they stir a useful recollection.'

'Unquestionably. Lane didn't want to have anything to do with it, of course. He loves huddling around his dear, little secrets. Well, I suppose it's the essence of high command, that and a stop-at-home wife with a body like a life-boat. Midlands know how to put the pressure on, though. I'm certain I'm going to take to their people, the collarless shirts. Spare clipboard pussy? They'll talk to Aston's father. Perhaps already. Did I say too much there?'

'Sir, is it—?'

139

'Is it safe to leave Sarah alone with Fanny?' Iles sat down under a multi-coloured breaking-and-entering by district graph. For a moment he held his face in his hands, as if hopelessly baffled. Then he shrugged, dropped his hands and said: 'I agree. It was a problem, Col. I saw no solution, no safety for the child. So what to do? Well, I told Sarah I've just been for a test and am unquestionably sterile. Congenitally. You see, Harpur, I have a sickening certainty she wouldn't hurt anything of Aston's.'

'That's—'

'You're absolutely right. Piquant: to keep the baby intact and to keep her mine I have to swear she's someone else's, and jack in all my previous claims. Col, you've heard of *Life's Little Ironies*?'

'I was going to say *Catch-22*.'

'Were you? Well, of course you were. I hoped you weren't, but of course you were, Col.'

'Sir, your behaviour has been—'

'Noble? Yes, I'm afraid one must put it as high as that. I've had the operation now – obviously had to. But you'll be bursting to ask if I really was sterile before. Was macho swordsman Des Iles an unseeded entrant, incapable of putting Sarah in the club, so the baby's Aston's?'

Another club. 'No, sir, I wouldn't. Never.'

'I don't know whether I was or not.'

'At times ignorance is best.'

'The family motto from your escutcheon, Col?'

'Noble? Yes, I'd put it as high, too, sir.'

Iles made a loud, farting raspberry. 'Bollocks, Harpur. What else could I do? We're talking about the life of my daughter, and something like peace of mind for a terrific woman.'

'Sarah is, sir.'

His grey head whipped around: 'You sniffing there now? Jesus, the permutations.'

Entering Lane's conference room a few minutes later, Iles declared: 'This is a corking idea of yours, Chief. There may be difficulties between police and public just at present, but nothing brings the two sides together more readily than the recognised need to solve a foul crime. Brilliant of you to co-opt that great, gross medium of the people, television, to summon the mob's all-thumbs aid, and effect some elements of this reconciliation.'

140

'Here's Mike Yare-Gosse from Midlands TV, Desmond,' Lane replied.

'Any connection with the Yare-Gosses of Cheadle Hulme?' Iles asked. 'Cooperation aplenty is what you can count on here, Mike,' he went on, shaking the television man's hand. 'I know I speak for the Chief and for Colin Harpur, who has notched up such remarkable progress on an extremely messy case. Think of the impact that lumpy face and the honest eyes are going to make on the cameras.'

'As I understand it,' Lane said, 'Mike wants to use this particular investigation as a means of examining the sociology of crime in its more general aspects, plus the organisation and background of the Force.'

'Wise,' Iles replied.

'It's to be in-depth,' the Chief continued.

'Ah!' Iles cried, and felt about in his blazer, as if seeking pencil and notebook before these words escaped his memory.

'I hope I can avoid sounding pompous, but we feel we should give a wider context to each of the crimes we're going to feature in this series,' Yare-Gosse explained. 'Find some pattern, some meaning, in these seemingly isolated acts of lawlessness. Ask questions about Britain's current *mores*, as thrown into dramatic relief by this or that offence. This is our brief. We must do what actuality television always seeks to do: pose and possibly answer the people's basic questions; but also look deeper.'

Iles exclaimed: 'Pompous? Pompous!' He glanced at Lane and Harpur, seeking their support in denial of the preposterous charge. 'No, indeed, Mike. I love the sound of this. I hear the voice of real seriousness, not exploitation. I hear synthesis instead of sensationalism.'

Yare-Gosse was about thirty, not in a collarless shirt but what could be a custom-made dark-striped job, with a silver tie. His beige-to-white light-weight jacket was free from flashiness, and would not have been out of place in a decent casino. He was slight, soft-voiced, small-featured, much less shifty and cocky-looking than standard middle-rank media people: Midlands had clearly picked him carefully for police programmes. 'With some questions possibly aimed at very sensitive areas,' Yare-Gosse remarked gently.

Iles laughed for quite a while. 'All sensitive areas here are spruce

141

and open to inspection, aren't they, Chief? Aren't they, Col? No lice or crabs. Mike, I think you'll find a unique atmosphere in this Force, in some sense indefinable, yet which I hope you'll be able to capture in the programme. It's one of our prime assets, second only to the quality of the man at the top – though he'll skin me for saying this. It is our Chief who is largely responsible for the creation of all special strengths here. Please, please, don't be deceived, Mike, by the lowness of his profile.'

They sat down at Lane's long conference table, the Chief democratically in a side-seat, with Yare-Gosse at the head. At once he began to explain how they would re-stage the crime, interview witnesses and consider other unsolved local murders, especially those with a gang background. 'One of our problems is to cut through a mass of competing rumour,' he said.

'That I can believe,' Iles replied.

'Like how hard can we go in comparing the death of Aston with the garrotting of those two villains a while ago, Jamieson and Favard?' Yare-Gosse continued.

'These are names that do keep coming up,' Iles conceded.

'Not at all, I wouldn't have thought,' Lane said. 'Entirely different circumstances, aren't they, Colin?'

'I'll be frank: we hear appalling links made between the two crimes,' Yare-Gosse went on.

'Myself, you mean?' Iles asked.

'Any policeman who does his job properly can expect attempts to smear and frame him,' the Chief remarked. 'They target Desmond because he's our Assistant Chief, Operations, and a thorn in their side. Criminal families, friends, seek revenge.'

'And, in addition, you're bothered about my wife?' Iles asked Yare-Gosse.

'Obviously none of this could conceivably be used on screen, but we do need to know the background in full,' he replied. 'Then the programme will have authority between the lines, as it were – feel mature and well-informed. The public sense such things.'

'Isn't it a straightforward matter of asking people to ring and say whether they saw anything?' Lane asked. 'Passengers on the stopped train and so on.'

'This isn't simple *Crimewatch*, Chief,' Yare-Gosse said.

'In-depth, sir,' Iles reminded him. 'They're looking for a theme.'

'Precisely,' Yare-Gosse said. 'That is our, so to speak, *raison d'être*: to give a shape.' He looked down at the table for a moment. 'I'm afraid that does sound like jargon on the march. But believe me I'm very conscious I'm talking to the sharp end. And then, yes, there is the matter of Mrs Iles. If I may say.'

Lane frowned: 'This isn't at all the kind of programme I had in mind.' He was in one of his High Street suits today, waistcoat thrown in, and quite a new-looking brown tie: really doing his decent best to give out tone.

'I fear Sarah is bound to be seen as relevant, sir,' Iles replied. 'I mean, she was taking it from Aston right up until he was broken into.'

Yare-Gosse sat apparently dazed for a second by Iles's way with a phrase and then, perhaps still off balance, cried out: 'Mrs Iles relevant? For God's sake, we heard she tried to kill the child.'

'Kill?' Lane whispered. 'Fanny? This is so absurd, so vicious. Listen, Yare-Gosse, why have you picked us? Is this some sort of anti-police exposure disguised as help, a pretext to pry into personal lives? Does the Broadcasting Authority know about this series?' His skin showed faint lines of red.

'Sarah hasn't been altogether well, sir,' Iles said.

'Why don't we just stick to what TV can reasonably touch on, without danger of libel or speculation?' Harpur suggested.

Yare-Gosse declared: 'With respect, may I remind you, Mr Harpur, gentlemen, that our programme is called *Where Is Truth?* Our obligations are inescapable.'

'We have a maxim here: truth is what the jury says,' Harpur replied.

In the corridor afterwards, Iles snarled quietly: 'Since when have you been up to epigrams, Harpur? You got that stuff about truth and the jury from me.'

'Well, it's true, isn't it?'

'True about truth? Are we moving into philosophy?'

'It's a philosophical show he's trying to put on, yes?'

'Oh, yes, he's fucking dangerous all right. He believes he's the people. All media do. Yet most of them are hardly even persons.'

Chapter 26

There was still no mention on local radio News of any incident at Young's Dock. 'That's thirty-six hours,' Ember said. 'We're clear, Winston. Didn't I tell you?'

'Maybe.'

'No maybe. Anything untoward would be headlines. A while ago they fished some villain out of Young's in a car and the show was huge.' Although Ember's sweat torrent had started again while he waited for the radio bulletin, his voice was all right, could not be jauntier. A bit of will-power still went a long way.

Winston looked unhappy.

Ember stood up. 'Now. Right now. I'll take you to a spot where we can see the dock. Binoculars. If they've found anything, there'll be lifting gear and a posse.'

Winston stared at him and did not move. 'No, I'll buy it. You've got to be right.'

'I don't want you miserying around here day in day out. It's a dead loss with the customers. Come on.'

'Christ, no. Not in the Montego. That's more risk.'

'We'll stay off the dock. Nobody will see. This is from a hill behind the marina.'

Make it sound as if he was determined to go for Winston's sake only, to calm him: taking a wimp child to see there were no dragons in the woods. In fact, Ember was in terror and desperate to check Young's himself. Whenever he had a fear on him, he felt the urge to make a move somewhere. That was how all this had started – the second trip to Wales – and he realised he might be rushing into a repeat. Still, he could not resist it. Even without the worry of the Citroën, just having Winston in the Monty was all the pain and bottled-up rage he had expected.

Of course, both his daughters – one not much more than a

144

baby, for Christ's sake – both had started making their sickening fuss of Winston as soon as he moved in. Venetia was thirteen and Ember knew first-hand that the sexual thing in some girls warmed up very early. Anyone could tell she was forward for her age in all sorts of ways. The night she came down to the bar when Caring and Winston were there would have made that obvious, even if Ember had not spotted it already. Nature.

In the car, Winston said: 'We should have told Caring about that guy under the water. Jesus if—'

'He won't find out. Not now.' Why bother to argue, though? It was too late to tell Oliver, and Winston knew it. He had made himself part of the silence. The thing was, if Ollie heard of that tail, he was going to put two and two together, and it would add up to the Montego again. But Ember could not explain that to Winston. Again he wished to God he had never agreed to have him so close.

As they made for the docks area now, Winston said: 'That boy's people are bound to come looking for him and the van.'

'That boy's people are bound to be scared green when they don't hear anything more from him. They'll know now what sort of a pro team they're bumping against, and they'll go back to robbing gas meters on the home patch. If they do come, they'll find nothing.'

'You think so, Ralph?'

Joyfully, Ember saw it was a real question, not sarcasm. He could tell this young genius longed to believe him. He could also tell that Winston thought somebody with Ember's past and know-how might have things right. Winston was whimpering for comfort. All at once, matters had changed and he would not be giving encores of the leadership act for a while. Schoolgirls might think him ritzy stuff, but Winston himself knew he was only a jumpy kid with a flair for gouging the elderly. Ember felt the turn-around do him a lot of deep good. Now and then everybody was entitled to believe his own advertising. It brought a tingle.

'Why I dealt with that lad was to do us all a favour – you, me, Caring, the whole operation,' he told Winston. 'They won't be turning up at the bank now. He could have been their main man. Don't think because it's a rough, old van this character had no status. A cover.'

'Ralph, I hope you're right.'

145

He sounded feeble. What the hell did those girls see in him? Yes, girls, not girl. Although Ember might understand why the thirteen-year-old carried on like that, to watch Fay pampering this jerk, too, really shook him. This was a child of just eleven, flirting and fussing around Winston, making a big deal of spreading marmalade on his toast at breakfast today, like Leonardo doing that ceiling, and giving a long, careful feel to his cup, really fondling it, to check the tea was still nice and hot. To get herself ahead again, Venetia had taken Winston by the hand as soon as they had finished breakfast and tugged him into the other room to listen to tapes. He had smiled at Ember and Margaret, signalling he was helpless and just had to humour her. Oh, so tough. Ember had felt damn glad when the girls left for school with Maggie. He and Winston had sat down in the bar and waited for the 8 a.m. News on the portable.

They were driving now through some of the expensive, mock-brick new housing and flats that had come with the marina. Winston spoke straight ahead, out through the windscreen, not looking at him: 'Ralph, I saw you clubbing with that wrench and I couldn't believe it. Well, it didn't seem the way, and it didn't seem like you, not at all. I had you marked down as cool, and so did Leopold. OK, we'd heard about Panicking but that wasn't how it seemed to us. Then this.'

Ember tried to avoid re-running the details in his mind: that wrench skidding uselessly down the side of the driver's forehead and face in the first blows, not making properly square-on contact, not cracking anything really germane because the man was struggling for his life, and it was hard to get a finishing whack in at him under the roof of the Citroën. He chuckled: 'Not like me? So, what am I like? Cool? You could say that. I do what's necessary, Winston.' He kept his voice gentle, not like some mouthing heavy. Winston would have heard plenty of that. He would see through it. 'That's my training, and one thing I've learned above all is to sum up options fast. This was something other than a free-choice situation. He'd have had me if I hadn't had him. I've landed in situations like that before.'

They passed the school the girls went to. Normally, he would have pointed it out, sort of casually, but today he did not even turn his head to look. You tipped the earnings down the chute year after year in fees, dressed them like bits of young *Vogue*, plus the riding and foreign trips, and, first chance, they went for some ginger offal, as if he was peaches. Why give them the best if all they'd ever want was scum? Some distinction and fucking wryness they were going to get out of Winston! All the luggage and the moustache were 'wonderful', and probably the rubber band on his pig-tail. That school could do one thing all right – teach them how to say 'wonderful' in a loud, oozy, half-asleep way, like some lush, has-been actress on Wogan. They argued about the colour of his eyes, were they grey or blue or grey-blue or blue-grey? Ember almost said he'd ring Criminal Records. But it could just be true what Winston claimed and he had no form. Although he watched like mad, Ember could not make up his mind whether Winston was patting the girls along, with something obvious in mind. That brave little smile: oh, you put-upon bloody sufferer.

Ember pulled the car on to a special viewing space for car passengers to look down over the marina and docks, now the whole area had been given the treatment. These days, every town with a bit of coast had a marina. Marinas were the de luxe future. He put the glasses on Young's Dock and the spot where the Citroën went in. In a moment he handed the glasses to Winston. 'Give yourself a treat.'

Winston took them, watched and said: 'Looks OK.'

'Of course. Didn't I say, nothing problematical? Good depth and fine, filthy water. Same two boats. One mothballed, I'd guess, and deserted. The other too small to run to a watchman. No witnesses. They'll find him and the van one day, certainly, but how do they make connections? That one boat will be in Samoa by then, anyway. A stranger in town drives off the edge of the dock, weeks earlier, possibly even months. So what? The windows part open, so fish will help with anonymity. We've done this just right, Winston. Count on Ralph.'

Quite often he used to bring Margaret and the children up here to admire the development. It was pretty, it was spacious. Ember had felt pride sitting there with the family, like part of the respectable energy that had done this transformation. So he was, or had been. He and the Monty paid their taxes. Twice he had written to the local paper about planning, and one letter had been printed. These last years, he had turned himself into somebody with solid standing, a citizen, R. W. Ember. Initials had more punch: a shift away from Ralph or Ralphy and, above all, from Panicking Ralph.

Now, though, angsting alongside London dregs like Winston, he had no room for big community attitudes and hopes. He had come here to see whether a stupid dead and his crumbling old van were being winched out of the muck by police. He started the drive back to the Monty.

'Yes, it was a good idea to come, Ralphy. I should listen to you more.' He gave Ember a friendly little punch on the shoulder.

Such cosy charm. No wonder the girls were bowled over. Ember knew very well the way it could go, which was why he watched them non-stop. A year or two back there had been a girl of fourteen he badly slipped up with himself, though only two or three times, and he had not been totally sure of her age until later. Anyway, she was definitely very close to fifteen. Luckily, he had given her a dud name and, obviously, no address. This started at a charity disco where he regularly donated some bottles, and she threw herself at him. But they did, didn't they? This was the whole point. All that stuff about him looking like Charlton Heston on their home video, which was only three parts true.

'You've got to think these things right through, Winston. If we told Caring about that Citroën there's a good chance the job would be off. This is people getting very close to our tracks. You'd suddenly be a non-earner. Leopold's down there in Kew, looking to maintain the gravel quality on his drive, and waiting for a split from you, I take it.'

'Well, he got the place on the team for me.'

'Caring calls off and you go back empty. One thing that's fearsome is a disappointed bald midget.'

'That's two people already with skull deaths from this job, and we haven't even started.' He was talking straight ahead again.

'Two?'

'This boy you stood in for – Aston. Strange, really.'

'What's so strange?'

'Well, he gets his head smashed, so you come in. Then you smash someone else's head.'

Winston didn't say, You smash someone else's head, in case yours gets smashed, like Aston's, but that's how he was thinking. Ember turned on him and grunted: 'What happened to Aston wasn't about the job, haven't I told you that? Absolutely nothing. A sex vendetta. Police. Maybe you should see the woman. You'd

148

understand then how he could kill for her. Face, tits, hair, arse, naturally, but personality as well, a real way with her. These things add up to a lot of possessiveness and rage.'

'If you say. I'm believing everything you tell me from now on, Ralphy.'

'Look, make it Ralph, will you, or R.W. or Ember?'

At the club there was a car Ember did not recognise in the yard, an Escort, alongside Margaret's. It was too early for customers.

'See what I mean about coming to look for that bugger in the dock?' Winston said. He had tensed up.

Ember whispered: 'I'll drive out and we can ring and ask Maggie who's here.' He was afraid he would retch if they stayed.

He felt Winston glance at him. The sod was feeling on top again. 'No. I'll go in first. You wait.'

After a moment Ember forced himself to say: 'We'll both go. It's safer.'

'Wait. It's what I'm here for,' Winston replied. He sounded like a manager, back to work he understood. He left the Montego then and, on his way towards the rear door of the Monty, went close to the Escort and stared in. It could not be right to let him risk things alone like this, but Ember sat still. His legs and lungs were not feeling too good. In any case, as he had said himself, Winston was only doing his job.

After a few minutes, he came out and beckoned. Margaret and a man and woman Ember did not recognise were standing behind. He left the car, found he could stand all right and walked almost easily towards them, smiling right across the face to show that fear was the last thing Ralph Ember should ever be accused of.

'It's television, Ralph,' Margaret said.

'I'm Mike Yare-Gosse, and this is my research assistant, Avril.'

'About Ian Aston,' Margaret said. 'I've told Mr Yare-Gosse you probably wouldn't want to be involved, Ralph, but they insisted on waiting.'

'You identified the body, I think,' Yare-Gosse said. 'And he was a good member here. We're building a profile.'

'Well, a member.'

'We want to throw the case open to the public, you see,' Yare-Gosse went on. 'We have to show his life, the identification, the attack. As if we were doing a drama, but this is fact.'

149

'It's not something you could really be a part of, is it, Ralph?' Winston told him.

They were still talking in the yard. Keep it like this. Ember did not want to ask them back in to the club. That could be encouragement.

The girl, Avril, said: 'I've been doing some research on Ian's life, and it's obvious you were a real, trusted friend. That makes you such a valuable part of our project, Mr Ember. Unique. Possibly more important even than the parents. You were closer.'

'Not close at all. Not more than any number of members of the club.'

'Oh, come now. Called to identify the body?'

'That was just because they failed to locate the parents at once. It could have been anyone.'

'But the police did think of you, Mr Ember,' Avril said. 'They're selective about such things.'

'Well, I don't know why.'

Yare-Gosse said: 'I think I understand your reluctance, Mr Ember. You don't want to seem to be pushing yourself, looking for limelight in what is, obviously, a very tragic state of affairs. That's to your credit. And he used to meet Mrs Iles here? That could make things awkward for you with the cops? Licences and so on. I see that. Yet this programme could be a means of helping your friend, Ian, by bringing his killer or killers to justice.'

'Didn't he just say, not his friend?' Winston told them. 'Don't you ever listen?'

'Look, could we go back in and sit down in the club for a moment?' Avril asked. 'Easier to talk.'

'I have to square things up for lunchtime,' Ember replied.

'It won't take long,' Avril said. She had a very nice, respectful voice. 'But you are the horse's mouth, you know – what our trade calls a prime source. We regard you as crucial.' She turned and began to lead the way back into the club. Margaret followed her, then Yare-Gosse.

'Jesus,' Winston muttered to Ember. 'You've got to stop this.'

Ember shrugged. Great to see Winston down once again. It would be another of those situations beyond him. 'I can handle things,' Ember said. He liked that description, 'a prime source'. They would be rare. In a way, he supposed that really was what he was, a prime source.

They sat down near the bar and Maggie said she would make coffee. Avril remarked: 'Damn, you remind me of someone, Mr Ember, but I can't sort out who. A face I associate with the screen, too. You haven't done television work, have you? Or a brother? That ability to dominate a frame without trying, just by being there.'

'Afraid not.'

'I thought of Chuck Heston,' Yare-Gosse said. 'Immediately.'

'Of course,' Avril hooted. 'But younger, Mr Ember, naturally. El Cid himself. The profile, the noble shape of the head. I suppose you're always being told? It embarrasses you?'

'No, I've never heard that. Are you sure?'

'It's uncanny,' Avril said. 'You'd come over a treat even on all we can offer – the small screen.'

'Are we talking about actually going on television?' Ember said. 'I thought it was just information you wanted.'

'Information, yes, but also an appearance. My brief is to create what we describe as a narrative, as full a narrative as possible,' Yare-Gosse said. 'You're a central part of it, so, of course, we need you on screen.'

Margaret came in with the coffee and giggled. 'They want you to be on TV, Ralph? The kids will be thrilled out of their minds. But for heaven's sake get your hair cut.'

'Going on the box has got to be out,' Winston told them. 'Isn't it, Ralph?'

'I'm sorry, I'm not sure of your part in all this,' Yare-Gosse replied.

Winston did not answer. His voice might have gone for the moment. Ember said: 'Winston's a business associate. He helps me with a lot of major decisions.'

'Not on at all, Ralph, for the owner of a high-class club like the Monty with a reputation to get associated in the public eye with a murder and all that,' Winston muttered. 'It could do a lot of bad damage.'

'When you say business associate, what businesses other than the club are you into, Mr Ember?' Avril asked. She was about twenty-seven, not pretty, but lively and with happy eyes behind big-rimmed glasses. 'Would it have any bearing on what we're talking about – the life and death of Ian Aston?'

'Oh, scarcely, I think,' Ember replied, with a smile.

'None of this would take very long, Mr Ember,' Yare-Gosse said. 'We'd like to do a re-creation – that is, a visit to the morgue. So a sequence in the street, as if you were on your way there. Mute. And then an interview with our reporter, perhaps near where the body was found. The tip.'

'Make sure you do justice to the famous profile, Mike,' Avril pleaded with a laugh. 'No reason at all why an actuality programme shouldn't have a bit of glamour.'

'When's it going to be on?' Margaret asked. 'The kids will be bursting to tell them all at school. This would really be one up. You know how it is with girls. To us it's a dark, dark business, obviously, but all they'll be able to think about and talk about is daddy on telly.'

'Now, wait a minute,' Ember said, 'I haven't—'

'Goes out next week, Friday,' Avril told them. 'We can't keep it too long, because situations change. Someone might be arrested, in which case we'd be caught by *sub judice*. The studio stuff's live, of course, so we can take the calls and keep everything bang up to date.'

'Could we talk a minute, R.W.?' Winston said. He stood and walked out of the bar into the corridor.

'I don't know why he's so set against it, do you, Mr Ember? Ralph?' Yare-Gosse asked.

Ember found him quite decent for someone in this sort of work, sensible clothes with even a tie, and no arm twisting or loudness. 'Winston's always very cautious.' He leaned forward and spoke quietly to Yare-Gosse and the girl. 'Don't worry. I can manage him.'

Avril nodded and smiled, her eyes really alight behind the glasses. Glasses could suit some women as long as they had the legs and so on, he had always thought that. She said: 'I know you can, Ralph. I don't see it would hurt the Monty at all. You'll be a celebrity.'

He followed Winston out.

'I can't believe this, Ralphy. You're not really going to do it? Your fucking face everywhere. You're being sweetened. Charlton Heston, my arse.'

'Keep your voice down, right? And I told you about Ralphy.'

'Oh, security now, is it? Same time you're talking about poncing around in front of the network.'

'It's not broadcast until after the job. You don't think I haven't considered that? We're going to be masked up. No harm.'

'Anything go wrong down there and—'

'Something go wrong and we're in trouble anyway.' He did not want to think about it.

'Drawing a line from you to Aston, for Christ's sake, in front of millions.'

'The line's already there. That's why the police came to me for identification. Remember? You're not thinking straight again, Winston.' He kept it nice tempered, regardless.

'Caring will go mad. A tail in the dock, now this.'

'He doesn't know about the tail, and isn't going to, is he? Is he? The television he'll see the point of, because Caring *can* think right through, Winston. How do I explain it if I refuse? I stonewall and they'll start wondering and dig, dig, digging. This is a friend and member of the club. Wouldn't I want to do what I can to help catch whoever did him?'

'Except it might be Caring.'

'I wouldn't let him hear you say that if I was you. The way Caring will see this is, it could be a way of screwing that bugger Iles. Calls could come in that would nail him at last. All right, after the job we're not going to be bothered much about settling with Iles or any other cop, because we'll be rolling in it and fireproof. But, all the same. There's a lot of boys wanting Iles and maybe others hauled in and sent away. It's not just Aston. At least two more he owes for.'

Avril stuck her head into the corridor. 'All right, Ralph? Any points I can help with?'

'Piss off, will you,' Winston said.

'Up yours, Anorex. Any points I can help with, Ralph?' she repeated.

'I'll be there now.'

She went back to the bar.

'You can't wait to get yourself on that bloody box, can you?' Winston said.

The ugly sod was jealous. Why hadn't he seen it sooner? This bastard thought the girls would be so excited to hear their father was going on television they'd forget about him. He wanted that slimy moustache in lights. Back-seat Winston. No more looking after his toast and the rest of what this filthy molester had in mind. 'And keep away from Venetia and Fay, my little daughters, or I'll have your balls,' he said.

'What? What the fuck are you talking about now? Jesus, I hate working with people from out of town.'

Chapter 27

Standing with no clothes on before the bedroom Regency cheval mirror, Sarah Iles found there were moments when she was hardly conscious of the reflection of her body at all, only of the glass in its hinged mahogany frame: of the glass as glass, as lethal, glinting material, and the array of shapes it would break into if she shoved the thing over off its delicate feet. Wouldn't that be a monstrous thing to do to such a beautiful object? Yes, and the notion thrilled her. This mirror had come to Desmond as a gift from his parents' house. That was one of the differences between his parents and hers: hers bought them the horrible fruit bowl. Sarah had always loved the mirror's old elegance – the proportions, the warmth of the wood, the reeded, downswept legs. Vandalising the bloody thing now would be another way of fighting free from this house, these possessions, from her role, this marriage, that tribe, another club. So, in this sense it was not so far from the fruit bowl, after all. And, of course, they were both glass. There would be pieces even more knife-like than when she smashed the bowl, wouldn't there, pieces that came to a good point, and with long razor edges, tinged by age, maybe?

So how would you pick up one of those slabs of glass, to use it like a knife, without cutting your fingers to pieces? You wouldn't and you couldn't. Did it matter, some damage to the hand? There would be a lot of blood. But there would be a lot of blood, anyway. Sarah had put the baby on the big double bed while she dressed, and Fanny was gurgling away there cheerfully and pulling at a sheet in a charming, winning way, if you wanted to be charmed and won.

God, all that sad, self-humiliating whimsy Desmond had concocted about being sterile, to prove the child had to be Ian's and therefore worth cherishing by her. Yes, yes, QED. But what had made him think such tactics were needed? Oh, he was very clever, very police-clever: trained to see right through people and spot their weaknesses. Somehow, he knew she had come to resent the child and the sterility fiction was a police-clever way – such a stupid, police-clever way – of putting all that right. What must it have cost to label himself barren? Despair had taken Desmond over. Too bad, and too late: he was not the only one into despair.

She tried to escape her obsession with the glass and concentrate on her body. For a minute or two it did the trick. Desmond once said he and she were forever linked by a shared determination to make mirrors work overtime. Sarah thought she would flee the habit soon: the pregnancy could have done her worse damage, but things at flesh level were definitely not what they used to be. Skin was funny stuff, funny enough to make you weep. As an elastic wrap-around, it seemed second rate, liable suddenly to lose most of its sheen and come-on.

Several times she had heard Desmond groan before this glass, even watched him punch himself angrily in the gut. 'So what the hell happened to the beautiful people?' he howled once. What happened to one of them was he had his head ripped open on an illicit waste tip, by person or persons unknown, except to the person unknown, and to a lip-zipped police Force, and her.

She was conscious only of the glass again, the long stretch of it, and a few ugly grey-black spots where the silvering had decayed. As she posed in front of the mirror but failed to see herself, Sarah felt this was just as it should be. It was a household where she did not rate or properly exist, and did not want to, a household that belonged to Desmond and the baby. She belonged elsewhere, though where, now Ian was dead? Moving to the bed, she picked up Fanny and took her to the child's own room, adjoining theirs, and placed her in the cot. A crazy act of consideration: she feared the baby might be alarmed if the mirror did go over and the glass shattered. It was like suicides folding their clothes before walking into the sea. There was something else: once, only once, wasn't it, Ian had been with her in this matrimonial bed, and so it had become a happy place? Keep it like that.

Coming back into the main bedroom she approached the mirror with roundabout stealth, like a mugging target, then suddenly stuck one of her bare feet on one of its acanthus feet – Desmond's mother was always on about the acanthus feet – yes, fixed the foot to stop it skidding across the boards and gave the frame a violent, short push. The mirror toppled and fell with a bang, half on a rug, half on the boards. It bounced but the glass did not break.

Her first thought was, Thank God, thank God, a second chance. Get out of the house to normality as you did before. Find women on a bus. She had been saved again from something vile and incomprehensible. She loved the child, had longed for her to be born, and for most of the time took joyous pleasure in her company. So, where did they come from, these bursts of appalling, graphic intent? Was she off her head? She had gone lactation loony? Of course she had. It could happen to anyone and had happened to her. And why the hell shouldn't it, the stress here, the pain? Her identity was running away. She had read in the papers lately about an animal affliction called mad cow disease. She was a mad cow. Yes, mad cow, mad cow. What a mercy she had recognised she was sick and could identify and deal with these black spasms. Yes, yes, a true mercy.

Then she bent quickly, righted the cheval, got a really firm foothold on the acanthus fancy bits once more and this time, using all her will and misery, gave not just a dismal push but actually flung the thing down on the floor. 'Threw the fucking looking glass,' she muttered. With a marvellous, ringing clatter, the mirror burst apart and, even in the other room, Fanny began to yell.

Over a tiny area of her thigh, Sarah felt a sudden, intense pain, as if she had been scorched. The sensation subsided almost at once but did not go away and when she looked down she saw that a microscopically thin arrow of glass, about three inches long, had hit her and stuck there. It hung from her flesh like a banderilla in a bull, and carried a steady stream of blood, as if through a pipe, on to her foot and the floor. Leaning down, she grasped the sliver and tried to draw it out. At once she saw lines of blood start along her finger and thumb, though she felt no cut. As she tugged at the glass and watched her skin tent out, the burning pain increased to worse than before and she could not stop herself giving a brief, tortured shriek. God, she had closed the bedroom window, but there might be one open on the landing and the sounds would carry.

Eventually, she was able to tear the glass dart free and she dropped it to the floor, where it lay in the design of a rug like a misplaced streak of smudged red pattern. In the next room,

Fanny was now screaming in terror at the din and Sarah called out, 'It's all right, love. Mummy's coming,' and, as she said it, found herself looking about the room to spot what other kind of glass bits the mirror had produced. She stepped away from the blood around her feet, though her leg went on spurting, and dragged the dressing-table cloth clear to wipe her hands, scattering make-up across the floor. It would have been easier to take a bed sheet, but she still could not bear to stain a souvenir.

She turned and was walking back towards the wreck of the cheval and the scatter of pieces, the red, sopping cloth still in her hand, when she heard the sound of more glass breaking and then a woman urgently shouting her name, 'Mrs Iles! Mrs Iles! Please!' Next door, Fanny still bellowed.

Please what? It was not a voice Sarah recognised. She heard men's voices, too, and then there were hurrying footsteps on the stairs, several people, and a man said something, something that sounded like: 'Are you rolling?'

'Of course I'm rolling,' another man grunted.

The bedroom door was open and she stood near the bed, too shocked and confused to think of trying to get across to shut it. A woman she did not know suddenly appeared there: heavy-framed glasses, jeans, a long, thick white cardigan. Behind, were three men, one big and bald and wearing a silver and red anorak, with a movie camera up to his face, the lens pointing at Sarah. Alongside him, another man in the same style anorak carried a spotlight that glared into her face. For a crazy second the only thought Sarah had was, if she did not come out in mirrors would she come out on film? How much of her was left?

'Oh, God,' the woman said. *'Grand Guignol.* Where's the child? Please, Mrs Iles. Please.'

That word again.

The woman ran across the room right through the blood patch towards the far door, and the sound of Fanny yelling. The men with the camera and light followed her, crunching on glass. The third man, slight, small-featured, thirtyish, in a tweed jacket, remained near Sarah. He looked around and pulled her dressing-gown from a chair, then walked forward and helped her into it.

'She's all right, Mike,' the woman called from Fanny's room. 'Thank God, we're in time.'

'And what about you, Mrs Iles?' the man with Sarah said.

He had a small, childlike, worried voice, the one which had asked the question on the stairs. 'Will you sit down?'

The baby had stopped crying. Sarah turned and walked towards her room. The woman was bent over the cot, holding Fanny's hand and swinging it gently back and forth consolingly. The baby smiled. The cameraman was still filming.

The woman looked up at her: 'Is this unforgivable of us? Of course it is. But we were so afraid.'

'Afraid of what?' Sarah asked. She leaned against the door frame.

'We were in the road, hoping, frankly, to get some footage of you walking,' the woman said.

'Footage?' She looked down at her feet. 'Walking?'

'We heard the noise, even right down the drive – a crash and then the screaming.'

'I'm Mike Yare-Gosse,' the man in the jacket said. He was standing behind her. 'Midlands Television. We're doing a feature on Ian Aston's death. Perhaps you've heard. That's enough now, Chas,' he said, and the bald man stopped filming and lowered the camera.

'Afraid why? Of what?' Sarah asked.

'Oh, we thought an accident,' Yare-Gosse said. 'And I suppose that was right. You're cut and so on.'

'And you were worried about the baby?'

'About the baby, about the two of you,' the woman replied. 'Intruders, anything.'

'Intruders?'

She thought about that. 'We are, you mean? I am sorry.'

'And ran to the baby,' Sarah said. 'Why?'

'She's really fine,' the woman replied. 'I'm Avril Sampson, Mike's researcher.' She released Fanny's hand and stood up.

'I'm afraid we've broken a panel in your front door,' Yare-Gosse said. 'We couldn't wait.'

'Couldn't you?' Sarah replied.

'It was well meant, Mrs Iles,' Avril Sampson told her. 'We'll get it repaired, naturally.'

'I don't want you to worry about the film, Mrs Iles,' Yare-Gosse said.

'Worry? Why should I? I was only pussy naked and covered in blood.'

159

'None of it will be used, believe me,' Yare-Gosse said. 'Oh, unthinkable. I must say, you seem fine, except for the cuts and so on.'

'Of course. So why was he filming?'

The cameraman said: 'Only in case the baby—'

'It's a routine, Mrs Iles,' Yare-Gosse replied. 'For when we're going into a situation where we're not sure what we'll find. In case we miss something.'

'You expected to find the baby hurt? Why?'

'Believe me, we didn't know what we'd find. All we heard were the sounds of an accident and acute distress, Mrs Iles.' Yare-Gosse picked up the cheval mirror and set it straight. 'No serious harm. You'll get a new glass. Glorious acanthus feet. Regency?'

'Could we go somewhere and talk for a moment, Mrs Iles?' Avril asked. 'Are there bandages in the house? We should do something about your leg and hands. Perhaps I could make you some tea. You must be badly shocked. I'll carry my shoes so as not to spread blood.'

Yare-Gosse ran a hand lovingly over the cheval frame. 'Unfortunately, some of these beautiful old pieces can be very unstable.'

'But we do pull out of it,' Sarah replied. 'Go downstairs, I'll dress and join you in a while.'

'Shall I take the baby?' Avril asked.

'Leave her.'

'Yes, of course,' Yare-Gosse said, 'that's great.'

When they had gone, Sarah bandaged herself, put some clothes on and sat for a moment looking at the mess. How had she given these people house room? She hadn't. They had taken it, and could do what they wanted with her now. She was obligated. They had seen her helpless and off her head, had her in the can, whatever they said. When she went down they were all sitting in the lounge. Only the man who had carried the light stood up when she came in. Avril had made tea and handed her a mug. Sarah sat down opposite Yare-Gosse. What a sweet little character, like a boy in daddy's gear.

'The only purpose of our film is to help find whoever killed Ian Aston, Mrs Iles,' he said. 'We regard ourselves as very much an aid to the police.'

'How does hanging around my house fit in?'

'Mrs Iles, we have to give what we call in the trade a narrative.'

'Yes?'

'You're a vital part of that.'

'How? You mean as the Assistant Chief Constable's wife?'

Nobody answered for a moment and then Avril said: 'In a sense, yes.'

She saw Yare-Gosse sit up straighter and as leader take on the responsibility of saying the unspeakable. 'No, that doesn't fully describe your part, does it Mrs Iles? Look, we've spoken to all sorts of people. To Ian's father, for instance.'

'Obviously, we know a fair amount of background,' Avril said.

'Mr Aston, in fact, thought you might well be willing to help us,' Yare-Gosse explained. 'He believed you felt isolated.'

'So you lurk around, waiting to steal film of me in the street.'

'We didn't know whether you'd agree or not, Mrs Iles,' Yare-Gosse said.

'Take first, ask afterwards.'

'Like it or not, you are at the heart of the narrative, Mrs Iles.'

'Fuck the narrative,' she said, 'and fuck you.'

He lowered his miniature head and shrugged his miniature shoulders, maybe to show he sympathised with her rage. 'We hoped you might want to help clear up the mystery. Have, as it were, an interest in that.'

'You're going to link me with Ian Aston in your programme?'

'Mrs Iles, Sarah, we can't tell the story truthfully otherwise,' Avril said. She stood up and approached Sarah. Producing a handkerchief she held it to Sarah's mouth for her to moisten. 'There's blood on the side of your forehead. You must have touched it when doing your hair.' Sarah wet the handkerchief and Avril rubbed the spot. 'We gathered that perhaps you would be willing to speak – to say at least something. We gathered you might resent the way the investigation seems to have stalled. Again. There. That's fine, Sarah.' She went back to her chair.

'You gathered – gathered that I'd go on television and talk about – narrate – my private life, pillory my husband and his colleagues?'

'We thought you might long to see some progress.'

Yes, she longed to see some progress, but did not know what exactly progress might be. 'The police are doing all they can. They are led by one of the most gifted detectives in any Force.'

'Harpur?' Yare-Gosse said. 'We certainly hear some good of him. Probably more good than bad, which is the best one can say about most detectives. He looks big enough to take care of himself. But is he completely free to follow the lines of inquiry he wishes?'

'Why not?'

'Ah, but now you talk as an ACC's wife,' Yare-Gosse said.

'How else?'

'Mrs Iles, I say again, that's not the whole picture.'

No, they could say that – and say it again.

'Mrs Iles, Sarah – this is very, very delicate, don't think we fail to realise it,' Avril Sampson said, 'but we understand there is a possibility, a probability, that two previous unsolved local killings might be connected to the death of Aston.'

'Connected?'

Yare-Gosse said: 'Conceivably – I put it no stronger than that – conceivably the same killer. A similar sort of curtain drawn, a similar kind of convenient impasse, a similar sort of ineffectual supervision from the very top. Personally, I like Mark Lane very much, but one has to wonder how strong he is. New in the job.'

She stood, feeling rather shaky. 'I must see to the baby now. I think you should go. Please, don't wait outside. I shall be staying in. The Rougement Place neighbours are sensitive. Forget about the broken glass – the broken glass in the door. I don't want you or anyone connected with you back here.'

'Will you be all right? Are you sure?' Avril asked.

'You mean the baby?'

'Of course things will be all right,' Yare-Gosse said. 'Mrs Iles is fine.'

'But how will you explain to your husband – the mirror, the door?' Avril Sampson asked, her eyes full of phoney worry behind the goggles.

'I'm not at all a bad liar.'

Chapter 28

Just as they were getting into the car at the Monty, Winston said: 'Oh, by the way, Ralph, Caring and Harry, the new lad, are coming down to meet you afterwards.'

This was supposed to be as if he had only just thought of it, of course, so casual. Ember felt his knees and ankles almost go. There was the matter of the Citroën. 'What? Coming where?'

'Where we're going. They want to see you. It's urgent. Harry came up and tipped me the message.'

'What's wrong, Ralph?' Margaret asked.

'Why didn't you tell me before, Winston, you bastard? What's it about?'

'To see you.'

'Come on, Ralph. We'll be late.'

Ember drove and kept a real eye on the mirror this time. He tried to forget what Winston had said and move back to normal. 'Of course, you know what terrifies me most, don't you, and what I'm going to mention tonight?'

'What's that then, Ralph?' Winston asked.

'It's something I must fight for,' Ember replied.

'What's that then, Ralph?' Winston asked again from the rear seat of the Montego.

'Oh, Winst, this is one of his obsessions,' Margaret said. 'You won't get far, Ralph.'

'Latin,' Ember said.

The three of them were on their way to a parent–teacher association session at Ember's children's school. Caring and the new boy coming here? He began to shake a bit.

'They'll wait outside, in the yard somewhere,' Winston said.

'It's a school with a yard?'

The plan was Ember and Margaret would go into the meeting

itself, while Winston waited with the car. Christ, could anyone imagine this skinny, pony-tailed, rubber-banded, ginger freak in the actual, academic building with its statues of poets and that Copernicus, and among the other parents, maybe bumping into the headmistress, Mrs Cory? Fay and Venetia would never be able to show their faces again. Caring and Pete insisted that Winston had to be somewhere near at all times now, though. Well, in any case, was Ember going to leave Winston home alone with the two girls, the way they were about him? The bar staff could do the baby-sitting.

'Latin? That's a true anxiety?' Winston asked.

'Oh, yes. This is what is also referred to as the Classics, that realm,' Ember explained. He would show the sod he was not worried: discuss decent matters in a good voice. 'Schools all over are giving them up.' He still watched the mirror, and knew Winston was concentrating on the view out of the back window. There were no lights that stuck with them, though. He was sure of it. The solution to that problem with the Citroën had been risky, but it was turning out perfection, and stuff the fret.

'Ralph's concerned in case our daughters' school drops Latin from the curriculum.'

'That would be a major tragedy, a place of this calibre,' Ember said. 'Many girls go on to what's referred to as Oxbridge.'

'I'm quite a believer in education,' Winston replied. 'It can't do harm.'

Caring and the new one: it had to be about the Citroën. All right. The point was, try to corner someone like that Citroën driver and get him alive and conscious to a spot for questioning and there would have been fifty chances of complications – resistance, blood, yelling, reciprocal damage, witnesses. And then, after you've interviewed him, what do you do? Give him a splint or two and say, 'So kind. On your way now, and, pray, don't speak of this interlude'? He still had to be disposed of, and the vehicle. It was all so much defter, the way it happened. Make it quick, keep it simple, use the natural assets, such as gravity, a dock and dark water. That sounded obvious, but it took years to learn, and Winston had not reached there yet. Maybe not even Caring had. Ember would tell them.

'There's a question mark over Latin nationwide,' he grieved. 'I'm not one of those who've suddenly abandoned Mrs Thatcher on a couple of whims, but perhaps all this emphasis on the national balance sheet – bound to be deleterious for the Classics.'

The bank project was only three days off, and Ember did not really feel like turning up at the PTA at all. His nerves were pretty problematical, what with the job and the Citroën and now these television people sniffing around the death of Aston. Those sods had so much pull and were so bloody crafty you never knew what they might come up with. But Caring and Chitty had decided it was important for him to go to the school meeting, important to be seen keeping up all the normal commitments, as long as Winston stayed close to watch for trouble. In any case, Caring said he could not be more in favour of school functions for parents, not just because he hoped to jump the high-jump teacher at his kid's place, but as a way of showing you wanted your total money's worth and were on the ball. For a couple of seconds when they were talking about it, Ember had felt like telling him there was not going to be any trouble because the trouble was safe at the bottom of Young's. That would not have been clever at all, though, to put Caring in the picture, unless it had to be. Let sleeping vans lie. Now, Ember could smell the money that was coming, as long as there were no hitches, and he could also still smell the rough bother which had arrived for Aston because he slipped up somehow working for Caring, and which could get a replay.

'Kids don't want to bother with those old languages,' Margaret said. 'They can't see the point, nor their parents.'

'Because they think life's nothing but computers or being doctors or cleaning up on currency deals,' Ember explained. 'Which is all very well, but the Classics are about something deeper.'

He slowed down very suddenly, just to see if anything behind was caught off guard and came up close, but still nothing. Of course nothing. He had read that Citroën situation spot-on: this was a piddling little rival outfit, and if you knocked off one and got him water-logged the rest would receive the message and understand.

Ember said: 'All right, kids in the ordinary schools can do without Classics, maybe, because they're thinking about slob jobs such as in a factory or being a hairdresser, with no Latin dimension, but a school like this, private, with girls who will be in cocktail parties and so on when they grow up, they need to know all the great old tales. The Delphic Oracle. Somebody mention that in a lounge and a girl respond by looking like Miss Dumbo of 1997, or whatever, and what do people think? There's more to life than a lovely face or even pussy. As I say, it's all total crap, but calibre crap and with a ring to it.'

Sometimes, he thought he should have cleared the pockets of that lad in the Citroën. You had to leave a couple of windows a bit open or it would not sink quickly, and so there was always a danger that some stuff would float up. Is this what had happened? Probably there was a red patch on the surface for a while, though he had not been able to see it in the dark. That would have soon dispersed, though.

'Greats, they called the Classics at Oxbridge,' Ember remarked as they drew into the school grounds.

'That so?' Winston said.

Ember kept on. He would show how cool he could be, regardless. 'I'm glad you didn't make one of those stupid jokes, g-r-a-t-e-s, like fireplaces. No, this is G-r-e-a-t-s, because great subjects. Some of your really top people. It was known as reading Greats, not studying or learning, but reading – relaxed, absorbing a culture. People would say they were going up to their rooms to read some Greats with a glass of marsala wine. At the end of their university days, able to do all sorts. Harold Macmillan. Greats. Am I right?'

They left Winston in the back of the car. As Ember and Margaret walked towards the entrance, she said: 'My God, have you noticed our girls and him? It's a disgrace and dangerous. And he acts up to it.'

He could hardly take in what she was saying but muttered: 'I've spoken to Winston.'

'It's Venetia and Fay you should speak to.'

'Why don't you?'

'He's interested, anyone can see it, damn him. Smiling – no smirking, licking his lips, touching their arms.'

'You sound jealous of them,' he said. Suddenly all his nerves were being roasted. 'Yes. Christ. And since when, "Winst"?'

'Don't be idiotic.'

'You fancy some sleazy jerk like that? Interior décor? I know

the only interiors he wants to decorate. Jealous of your own kids
– a kid of eleven?'

'What the hell does he see in them? I mean, they're so
boring, Ralph. What can they talk about?'

'I can't believe this. What gets to you, his floor-brush moustache
or the knuckle scars where he's clobbered people?'

'Mr and Mrs Ember,' the headmistress declared, beaming. She
was at the door to greet parents. 'This is grand. Venetia and Fay
are doing so radiantly well. You must be very proud.'

Ten out of ten: Mrs Mavis Cory could remember both the
names and fit them to the right people. This was the private sector.
She really made a fuss. Ember knew what she was thinking as she
waved them towards the school's large, dignified old entrance hall:
put shit on a shelf and it thinks it's cake.

'Both so gifted in art,' the head went on. 'You'll see pictures
by them displayed in one of the corridors tonight – quite possibly
good enough to be on permanent show, indeed.'

'That's Ralph coming out in them.'

'You paint, Mr Ember?'

He forced recovery on himself again. 'I struggle.' Occasionally,
when he thought about the bank split, it was not just as instant
exit from the Monty, but he saw himself somewhere beautiful
and warm with his easel and perhaps a large soft hat, building
a portfolio. Bridges with a small river under he liked doing. He
needed the shady hat because he went deep dago in the sun and
hated not looking British. On these trips, he would be alone,
especially after that sickening give-away by Margaret just now.
Women: you never knew with them, even after all the trouble he
had taken, and never a leg-over with spare on Monty premises.
He would still act right, though, and make sure she and the girls
saw quite a whack of the cash.

You always met some right prick parents at these sessions,
people he would never mention the Monty to, nor Shield Terrace,
where it was. Any conversation, he said he was in catering and left
it at that. These others would be from Elms Enclave or the Loam
Estate, that sort of place: accountants, hi-tech factory owners,
dentists, all full of money noise. How many of them travelled
with their own bodyguard, though? They did not realise he was
like the Queen, and he had a quiet smile over all these bastards.
A pity he could not let Winston loose on a few of them.

Although his mind was nearly all somewhere else, he had his chance later to ask about Latin in a question-and-answer session in a room they called Big Moot, if you could believe it, and the head did say she took his point, which usually meant, Get knotted, mouse brain. 'No final decision on dropping Latin will be made before full consultation with all parties – parents, staff and governors,' she remarked, and that one usually meant she ran the place and would do what the fucking hell she liked. Ember was not satisfied, but he had done what he could. The future of the Classics in the world – could he be responsible for that unassisted?

When they came out, Winston was standing near the Montego looking edgy. 'There's some toilets, built over against the wall. Caring and Harry said Margaret to wait in the car, if she doesn't mind.'

'In girls' lavatories?' Ember said. He had read somewhere that the word 'toilets' couldn't be proler.

'There's not going to be many girl pupils about this time of night, Ralph.'

'Sit here alone in the dark?' Margaret said.

'It won't be long,' Winston replied. 'Caring promised.'

'Ralph, is this going to be all right? I mean, all right?' She could sound as if she really worried about him one minute, and yet was talking that panting way about Winston no time ago.

'Of course, love,' he said.

'Of course,' Winston told her. 'Caring – he avoids the phone and he doesn't want to come up the Monty just now for various reasons. This was a useful place, that's all.'

'I don't know,' Margaret said.

Ember disliked standing there talking to Winston, pinpointed in the headlights of the departing Volvos and Audis and BMWs. A Montego, plus Winston: together these did not spell the utmost status. They persuaded Margaret into the car and then Winston and he walked over to the lavatories. 'They leave these open? They're not vandalised?' Ember said.

'I think Harry did something with the door.'

'So what's it about, Winston?' If he refused to go what would happen? Was Winston supposed to bring him, bring him in any way necessary?

'Search me, Ralphy. I mean, Ralph.'

Ember stopped for a second. 'Listen, you haven't opened your mouth? About the dock?'

'Would I? Could I now? How?'

Three answers when one bugger would do. Ember grew more anxious. 'Just be bloody careful in here.'

'Caring seemed all right.'

'Nice. So, where's Pete Chitty?'

'Just Caring and Harry.'

That could mean any bloody thing. It could mean Pete lurking somewhere close for a special purpose, a quiet approach from behind when the discussions were proceeding in the lavs. Had Pete been the one who saw to Ian? These two, or three if Pete was around, they could have a K-frame each to assist at this meeting. Ember carried nothing, not even the wrench now. He had ditched that, in a different dock of course, though. And Winston? Would he have anything? Back in Kew all that while ago Leopold had said Winston usually went armed. But was that a help? Whose side was Winston on? He said he had not talked, but had he? Was this little get-together basically all his fault? Was he doing the shepherding now?

The doubts and fears piled up. At least they showed his brain was still working, despite the usual back and shoulders sweat and bad legs and the feeble voice. That was how panic generally hit him, though: he always saw all the dark possibilities with first-rate, foul clarity, but could not think what to do about them, except go over and over the list in his head in a different order.

A real calibre conference this, four men, and maybe five, in a girls' school lavatory at 10 o'clock at night, and one of the four or five Winston bloody Acre. You would not mistake it for OPEC. Just before they reached the cosy brick building Ember thought for a second of coming clean with Winston, telling him what he was scared of here, asking him if they could tackle it together, asking him, also, if he was tooled up. A silent scream for help. But what good was it coming clean with Winston if Winston was not going to come clean with him? The point about this playground and these lavatories were they were a jungle and he was on his own in it. First thing you had to learn in this sort of game was the difference between friends and enemies: there might not be one.

Ember's breathing could not have been worse, and his body heaved from hips to neck every time he tried to pull more air in. Even if he had had the Smith and Wesson with him he could never have hit anyone with it because his whole physique was moving about like a flag in a gale. How would that headmistress explain it to the kids, all the kids not just Fay and Venetia, if his body was found here in the innocent little lavs tomorrow morning wearing this grand, four-fifty quid suit brought specially to keep his end up at these school dos? Jesus, pleading for the life of the Classics one minute and dead alongside juvenile water closets the next, another Aston. He felt pretty certain that what this would be known as among some was irony.

Caring and Harry Lighterman were standing waiting at the far end of the lavatory, the six cubicles on their left, doors open. Ember glanced from the corner of his eye into each of them as he went towards the two men, but saw no sign of Chitty.

'As toilets go these are quality,' Caring remarked. 'No shortage of paper, and not that shiny, cheap stuff that skids. This school is in a very decent league, that's obvious, Ralphy.'

Harry Lighterman walked forward a couple of steps and put that dreamy-looking face close to Ember's. 'To me, Ralphy, you seem scared to death of something. What's the problem?' His voice seemed to cut through, saying all sorts without saying them.

'Scared?' Ember replied. 'Who? Me? Why?'

'I asked first,' Harry said.

'He's worried about the kids at school,' Winston told them. 'Latin.'

Caring Oliver said: 'Diabolical. I've felt the same sort of bother at school meetings. We suffer for our kids. This is parenthood. Ralph, I can't stop worrying about the Montego and this furtive walk-around in Pete's flat. Pete's great and careful and he tells me there was nothing to be found, no information. I don't know, though.'

'He wouldn't have germane stuff on show. Pete's a pro,' Ember replied. It was a thing people said – this one's a pro, this one's not a pro. It didn't really add up to much either way. It was just words. People could be a pro and still make big mistakes. Pilate was a pro.

'Still no sign of any trouble around you, yourself, Ralph?'

Harry asked. He went back and stood by Caring in the shadow of the end wall.

'Nothing,' Ember replied. He had just dug his grave a foot or two deeper if Winston had spilled or was going to.

Caring went into one of the cubicles and had a long, heavy piss. He did not flush it away, maybe thinking of the tank noise. It seemed all wrong, girls coming in here tomorrow fresh from studying verbs when he had done that. Afterwards Caring lowered the wooden seat and sat on it to talk, while they stood around the door. That seemed wrong, too, for him to be squatting there, even with all his clothes on. What it was, it lacked delicacy. This was another world.

'I'll tell you straight out, I'm scared we're going to get to this bank and find another outfit trying the same ploy,' Caring said. 'We've got planning and plenty of reconnaissance, but it's going to be nothing at all if we arrive there and the scene is already occupied by a strange crew. This is a farce, but this is a tragedy, also.'

'Caring wants you to get back down to Wales, Ralph, and check we're clear,' Harry explained in that way he had, straight out, no lead-up. 'You and Pete Chitty. He's outside in a car. This wouldn't be the Montego.'

'Go tonight,' Caring said. 'There's no time to mess about. Winston can stay with your family, in case of bother, and he'll go home now with Margaret. They'll all be looked after.'

Christ, he could say that again. 'I don't get it, Caring. What I mean, we didn't have contact with any crew down there, did we, Winston? We saw Denzil, full stop. I don't know any crew in that area or how to find them. Denzil's not germane to that.'

'Well, he could be, couldn't he?' Caring replied. 'Of course, you make really sharp objections based on a lifetime, as ever, Ralph, but this outfit are probably still buzzing around Denzil, looking for information. That's your way in. Pick up someone near his place, maybe. It's got to be tried. Anything else would be criminally slack.'

'Yes, criminally,' Harry muttered.

This was the thing with Caring, and it always had been. He worked on logic: not sense but logic. He got an idea and then he moved from it step by step, it did not matter if it was all wrong to start with, or if it was the wrong direction, he kept on going, bit by gradual bit, like a fly getting in worse on one of those sticky, hanging papers. You had to wonder in which special way Aston upset Caring's logic and had to be taken out. The thing about Caring was, he had so much method it could trap him. Take now: he was worried and the people he was worried about were in Wales. So, his mind said, send Ralph to Wales to find the people he was worried about because that was where the people were. Obviously. Send Ralph, although there was no real chance of getting to them, even if there had been time, and no real chance of finding out anything even if he did locate them. Jesus, these people called him Panicking Ralph on the quiet, but the way Caring went on was a kind of panic itself, a cool, thinking kind that might seem all right and sane if you said it quickly but was a total nothing when you really put the light on it and looked.

'I think we must take the chance they haven't got the date and time and won't be at the bank,' Ember said.

Caring sat back on the lavatory and smiled, leaning against the flush tank. In the poor light that worried face under the grey hair looked almost cheery for once. 'Ralph, you're old style, and I admire it, I do. In those days, you boys took the big risks, and more often than not they came off, just because of the bravery and boldness. Me, Harry, maybe Winston, too, we're brought up in a different way. It's the influence of technology, perhaps. I'm not convinced it's better than yours, Ralph, but that's how we are, and we can't change. There's something within which won't allow me to take chances – not until I've done everything to sort them out.'

'So get down there, will you, Ralph?' Harry said, still talking like a hammer on a nail. 'Give this twenty-four hours. Make it non-stop, intense work. If you can't come up with anything, that's it. Too bad. We've done what we could.'

'That's it, exactly,' Caring told him. 'I'm damn lucky to have someone I can feel full faith in, Ralph. Yes, back early the day after tomorrow, give a final briefing, especially to our latest arrival, Fritzy, and we're away. I'll feel a lot better about it if I know an expert's been down there and had a real poke about, Ralph.' He stood up, still smiling.

Christ, they were pathetic, this lot. Suddenly, Ember could not understand how he had ever been afraid of them. These moments when he could feel all-out confident in himself were

172

getting rarer as he grew older, but this was one. Yes, Caring had it right – these people were a new style, and it was a gutless, stop–start, old lady style. He felt bigger than all of them put together. They held meetings in kids' lavs and grew jittery over nothing. They did not have ideas, they twitched. They did not make decisions, they ran mad. They had to be taught a few things, and a school could be the best place. He wasn't going to rush to Wales overnight in search of bugger-all with the king of denim and he was certainly not going to leave his three females in charge of cock-happy Winston, a.k.a. Winst. That bastard was trying to look intelligent and concerned now, but he must think he had just won a ticket for an all-age, non-stop shagging weekend. Well, this would scare the bloody ginger out of his whiskers.

'Something happened that I wasn't going to mention,' Ember said. 'It didn't seem necessary. But if you're perturbed, Caring, it might be to the point. You see, I don't like mad chance-taking any more than you.'

Winston said: 'Ralph, are you—'

'Something happened? An event?' Caring asked.

What in God's name did that mean? If something happened, yes, an event. What else? Was Oliver saying he could not imagine Panicking Ralph Ember being capable of producing an event? So, let him listen. 'We had a tight situation,' Ember said. 'But it's settled. This will dispose of your worries – the only reason I'm bothering to talk about it.'

'We?' Harry asked.

'Winston and I.'

'Ralph takes over a bit, Caring,' Winston said. 'He's got background, that's what I was told, wasn't I? I have to accept he knows what he's up to.' He waved his hands about on every side, asking for understanding all round, the ponce, including from Ember. 'Ralph's great, a real plateful.' He smiled at Ember, but even in the dark it looked sick, and he smiled at Caring and Harry, but it was sicker.

'I'm trained to think of the job in view – the job, the job, the job, always the job,' Ember said.

'Well, yes,' Caring replied. He sat down again, on the side of the lavatory seat this time.

'Whatever has to be done for the safety of the job, do it, that's the thinking that's been made part of me. Over the years.'

173

'Thanks for the memoirs. So what the fuck happened, Ralph?' Harry asked.

'This was a fraught decision,' Winston said.

'Fraught? I wouldn't say that,' Ember remarked. 'Brisk, yes. The long and short is, the lad who went through Pete's place is out of the reckoning. My own feeling is he was their main man. There'll be no more intrusion – not Pete's place, or the Monty, or the bank.' He told them about the Citroën in the dock.

'We could have put you in the picture, obviously,' Winston said, 'but Ralph thought, don't upset you, Caring.'

'Poise, decisiveness, morale. These are what are needed,' Ember said, 'not just for this job, for all jobs. My object is to make sure they're not shaken, not in any way. There can be times when silence is the right policy, the only policy. I saw it like that.' His voice had come back and was great. It sounded like, Up you if you don't fancy it. This is Ralph Ember not some apprentice talking. 'But circumstances change. Caring, your worries now are a new element to be catered for.' He sent for a good, meaty, serene grin. 'So, there you go. No need for any trips to Wales, you see.'

Winston said: 'Caring, all this was pressure decisions, no time to consult.'

'Pressure decisions is what I was brought up on, luckily,' Ember remarked. 'As for Winston – well, he's got a way to go yet, but promising.'

Caring looked seizure material, all the good spirits gone, his face into top-to-bottom agony. Maybe it was *his* body the kids would come across tomorrow. He was very still, but groaned once.

Harry said: 'This wasn't seen? Nobody?'

'Would we be here?'

'How do you know, main man?'

'My feeling,' Ember said. It was the sort of good guess you made when you had experience This novice could not contradict. 'Yes, feeling. I don't claim he had a special sort of scalp.'

'Did you identify?' Harry asked. 'Papers?'

'Priorities,' Ember replied. 'That's what I had to keep in mind.'

'His papers with him in the dock?' Harry said. 'Christ.'

'If he carried papers. Do people like him do that?'

'Like what?' Harry asked.

'A main man.'

174

'But is he?'

'You fond of going round in circles, Harry?'

That kept this fly boy quiet for a while. Then he said: 'But, Ralph, I asked you just now, didn't I – any shadows reaching your way and you said—?'

'Yes, you did. You had a right to ask. But I didn't feel like telling you. You know the difference between asking and answers?'

Oliver had his hands over his face and said something.

'What was that, Caring?' Ember asked considerately, bending down to him, like a nurse over someone in difficulties on the pan.

'It's done?' Caring whispered.

'The van in the dock? Absolutely,' Ember replied.

Harry said: 'This is going to—'

'Thing of the past?' Caring said.

'Yes, exactly. The past,' Ember replied.

'If we can keep it like that,' Harry said.

Oliver looked up at Ember. 'Tell me, Ralph, is this how you'd have handled things in the old days, you and the others, the other big people?' He sounded weak, earnest, as if he really wanted the reply.

'Oh, yes,' Ember replied. 'No question.'

'And no come-back so far?' Caring asked.

'Not a thing, is there, Winston?' Ember replied.

'No sign, Caring.' Winston grinned. You could see he had suddenly come to see Caring would swallow it, might even like it. Now, Winston wanted it to look as if the dock solution was his idea as much as Ember's. Caring would know the opposite. That passenger, Winston, would never have had the balls.

'It could work, Harry,' Caring said quietly. 'We always thought it would be a small, nothing outfit. They wouldn't have staff to assign. It could be the main man. And some dud old Citroën. Doesn't it show they're paltry? Yes, I'm bloody certain it does.'

'Sure,' Winston declared. 'Paltry.'

This was it: Caring's old plod logic going again. He had to start from what there was, the van in the dock. It was done, it was past. It could not be changed. The news had rocked him, but his mind would make the best of it. He wanted to believe the

175

bank job could still go ahead, and he would think his way to that, regardless, step-by-steady-step.

'Exactly how I saw things at the time, Caring,' Ember said. 'But, obviously, it all had to be done a bit faster. Basically, wipe out the Citroën driver and it was wiping out the whole team.'

'That's the old training,' Caring replied. He stood up, half smiling, or at least a quarter.

'What I meant when I said it was a pressure decision, you see, Caring,' Winston told him.

Caring gazed at Ember. 'You may have done well here. All right, it might not be how I would have handled it, but that's only a question of taste.'

'Thanks, Caring,' Winston replied.

'The job, the job, the job,' Ember remarked.

'Can't fault it,' Caring said. 'Harry, go and tell Pete there won't be any Welsh trip. And say he'll get no more break-ins at the flat, either, thanks to Ralphy and the old tradition.' He smoothed down his suit, ready to leave, then turned and flushed the lavatory bowl. 'Hygiene's the least that children in a fine school like this can expect.'

Chapter 29

'Grand, Alec, Paul. Then when you've killed you drag him to here, Paul,' Yare-Gosse said, pointing at a spot near some assorted heaped refuse on the waste ground. 'I didn't want that in the rehearsals or his clothes will show dirt at the start of the piece. But we're ready to film now. So, the whole thing, right through, please. Paul, don't, well, kill yourself with the effort of dragging him. Make it slow. This is a heavily built corpse who'd take some shifting, and I want a decent duration, anyway, so we can put a few sentences of voice-over on it. The crude brutality must get across to viewers. You hold his feet to tug him, one up under each of your arms, and his head scraping along on the ground – sorry about that, Alec – hence the blood trail. We won't be looking close-up at your face, of course, but it would help if you could seem as defunct as you can make it, Alec, difficult, I know, for an actor so justly famed for animation. All right?'

Sarah was standing in the shadows under the footbridge, close enough to see and hear most of it, but out of the glare from the television lights: hoping not to be detected watching, hoping not to be detected weeping. She had come along on the quiet to look at her lover being murdered in a sketch. It was a dark, warm, almost pleasant night, with low-lying, thick cloud.

Laughing, the fair-haired man, Alec, got up from the ground, where he had lain after this final run-through of the killing, and brushed himself down. 'Next, King Lear,' he said.

He was not a bad likeness for Ian. Oh, Christ, he was a chillingly, unbearably, good likeness and she felt the tears rush down her face and fall from her chin, though she kept totally silent. Yare-Gosse knew how to cast. She should not have come. Hadn't these people done her enough damage already? No, she should not have come but knew there had never been the smallest doubt that she would, once she heard when they were doing the death.

It was an appalling sequence which she had deliberately visualised for herself a hundred times, and which had invaded her dreams twice. All the same, to watch it happen was agonising, even as a piece of drama, even shaped and improved and Yare-Gossed into a suitable episode for the network. She had the feel and odour and noise of this miserable place now, all of it extra to how she had pictured and dreamed things, and none of it fun. There was the bleak ground underfoot, the mud and grit and bits of broken bottle and half-buried bricks and stones. His body had lain in that stuff for hours and had been man-handled across it any-old-how before. Yare-Gosse and Alec and Paul would show her their version of that soon, if she liked to wait, and she did like – or found it impossible to leave. The smells here were of mud, of wet paper, and decaying, wet timber, of dumped chemicals and oil and paint, of urine-stained, sodden mattresses. And there were the sounds of trains and cars and the awful, rapid, scuttling foot-steps of Paul on the black soil as he ran from behind to make the attack. These were the foul exactitudes of the spot, additions to what she had been able to picture, bits of sickening fact, even though she was here for theatre. Des had a saying picked up from poetry somewhere, 'Human kind cannot bear very much reality.' She knew what it meant.

So, the actor, Alec, thought it was all rubbish, a nothing part, one he compared in joke to a star role: 'Next, King Lear.' She wanted to loathe him for his callousness and arrogance, for talking as if the life he played here added up only to a write-off. But, because of the way he looked, she could not loathe him – the hair and shoulders, his good, strong neck, even the boyish, snub profile, all matching Ian's – and the way he dressed. Of course, they had the clothes exactly right. That would be easy: brown bomber jacket, jeans, open-necked plaid shirt. Mr Casual. Mr Macho, but it had suited Ian. Anyway, he was not the kind to take advice from her on clothes. Yes, Mr Macho, up to a point.

She longed to step out from these shadows under the bridge and speak to Alec, not because it would be like speaking to Ian, but because it wouldn't. Anything to end the taunting resemblance. She could feel these conflicts in her response start to drive her off balance again, split her mind down the middle: the hatred for this posturing, twat actor, the love and yearning for the man he played; the wish to talk to him, but only so as to wipe him out.

As for Ian's walk, this undiscovered star could not manage it. He moved too briskly. She had scarcely ever seen Ian hurry. He ambled – the style of someone who took things as they came and rarely worried enough. Perhaps that was why he ended up dead on a tip. The actor went back to the entrance of the footbridge and prepared to emerge again, making for the public telephone.

Yare-Gosse called: 'Try and get a bit of edginess from the start, Alec. Chances are he knew he might be a target. This lad spent his life wondering who was behind him.'

No. Perhaps he should have. Once or twice she and Ian had discussed danger, but he had never seemed bothered. That was like him, and, in any case, he did not know Desmond and Desmond's range. Despite the shady work Ian handled, and the rough people he handled it for, there had been something almost innocent about him: she had loved that, and despaired of it. He was street-wise, but not about the classier streets. Ian expected an Assistant Chief Constable to behave like one. Did people with silver leaf on their cap go ape?

Yare-Gosse called: 'Ready when you are, Alec.'

In a moment, the actor came out again from the entrance to the footbridge and began his walk. He was still moving too quickly, though this time he glanced back a couple of times, as if afraid he was being followed. Just before he reached the booth, the other actor, Paul, emerged behind him from the bridge, running. He was slighter, darker, perhaps a little older, his face partly hidden by a scarf. He reminded her of nobody, and that would be how Yare-Gosse wanted it: his programme could not risk pointing a finger. Anyway, not even in her dreams had Sarah managed to identify the assailant. She was here to watch her lover murdered, yes, but here to watch her lover murdered by her husband? Nobody was saying.

Paul held something in his right hand, possibly a piece of masonry. Alec reached out for the door of the booth and looked around again, as if just hearing those light, hurrying footsteps. Seeing Paul, he threw up an arm, the way someone would to grapple with an attacker or to protect himself. But that did not work. Paul hurled himself forward, raised his hand and brought the object down three times. To Sarah at that distance and in the

179

half dark they looked like actual, heavy blows to the head and she almost cried out. In defence, Alec attempted two or three punches, but they were undirected and feeble. She thought Ian would have done better, though not enough better. Alec staggered momentarily before falling. For a couple of seconds he lay still on the filthy ground, then stirred and half struggled up. Paul leaned over him and struck down repeatedly towards the head, grunting with the effort. Weakly, Ian tried to squirm clear and to push the attacker off, but couldn't. Ian grew weaker still, finally sinking back and becoming motionless once more: she found she was thinking of him as Ian, not the actor, during these seconds and found, too, that she had turned away briefly at the end, gazing across the railway lines at the row of little houses, at anything, while he was hammered back to the ground.

When she looked again, Paul had taken hold of Alec's feet by the ankles and begun to drag him across the tip, face up, his arms stretched out helplessly behind. Paul must have thrown down the object he had been holding. The progress was as slow and laborious as Yare-Gosse had asked for, with Alec's head bumping over the littered surface. She thought of Western film episodes, when a character with one foot in a stirrup was dragged helplessly across the ground by a runaway horse. That had always looked desperately painful, but exciting to her, a piece of fiction in a far-off setting. This, now, was also a piece of fiction, with actors, lights, planned moves and mock blows, but she could not look at it like that. Instead, she saw Ian's body, still with some life in it then, being cruelly moved through the workaday rubbish and dumped out of sight from the road. Eventually, Paul dropped the feet, and crouched down again, as though to check the man on the floor was finished. Then he straightened and ran back towards the footbridge and out of sight. After a moment, the man on the ground moved yet again, painfully crawled a few yards, then collapsed.

'Cut,' Yare-Gosse shouted. 'Great. Almost right. Look, Alec, do you think you could bear to do it just once more? We'll have to try and clean you up. A couple of little points.'

Alec stood and was picking earth out of his hair. From where he had been standing, near a camera, Yare-Gosse began walking towards Alec in the middle of the patch of ground and no longer had to shout, so she caught only the beginning of what he said:

'The actual killing was a treat and the disposal but the anticipatory dread – that's where the "be sure your sins will find you out" bit is – and I'd like it even stronger if—'

Sarah forced her legs into movement. She must not watch it again, nor listen to that intelligent voice reduce life and death to meaningful telly shots. It was possible to slip out from under the bridge on the far side and perhaps get away unseen across another strip of waste ground and then into a block of small streets. She had parked her car out of sight in one of them and walked to the filming.

She reached the Panda and was just about to drive away when someone tapped the side window. Looking up she saw Colin Harpur. He went around the front of the car and she let him into the passenger seat. 'I enjoyed the show, didn't you?' she said. 'You were there? I didn't spot you.'

'I saw you. Did you have to come, Sarah?'

'I'm a Yare-Gosse groupy.' She looked back towards the footbridge. 'Is that how it happened? The savagery. The beating on the ground?' She began to cry again. 'Is it, Colin?'

'Nobody's sure. One doctor says one thing, another another.'

'Well, of course it was savage,' she said. 'Wet question. This is the death of a man. And towing him across the rubbish, like pulling a dead dog off the road. All the money would fall out of his trouser pockets. It'll make grand TV.'

'We can't stop them.'

She wiped her face with her palm.

'You've hurt your hand,' he said.

'Desmond told you about it, did he? The baby's all right. He's looking after her tonight. Listen Colin, if Ian was on his way to phone me when . . .' The weeping took control again for a moment. She grew angry with herself. 'This is soft. I'm making a meal of it. I was going to say I'm responsible for what happened – because of the bloody phone booth. As if I wasn't responsible in any—'

'Yes, it's soft. You're supplying answers where there are only questions.'

He was trying to be kind, but she turned on him, all the same: 'So why – why are there only questions?'

'How it is in my game. Until we get lucky.'

There was a weariness in the way he spoke which shocked her, weariness and distance. She glanced across at him, crouched and bent up absurdly in the little Italian car, and saw that he was staring ahead, his eyes blank, his mouth set hard. She realised suddenly how much she had been expecting and counting on his sympathy. She had been fishing for a magically concocted, tolerable version from him of what might have happened. God, pathetic: it was like a child seeking some soothing explanation from its parent for a terrifying experience, even while suspecting that the explanation would be lies. The memory of Harpur's support at the funeral was strong in her still, and she knew now that she had been hoping for it again. Yet he seemed switched off, almost as if he had forgotten she was there. Tonight, she did not rate with him and she felt as if she was stuck out on the edge of his consciousness, about to drop into nowhere. It seemed another symptom of that break-up of her selfhood, and fear hit her hard again, harder than ever.

'Colin,' she said, 'perhaps it's you who shouldn't have watched the filming.'

'I've always hated play-acting. Except panto. Things are bad enough in the world, without putting them under lights.'

She leaned across and put a hand on his, her left, unbandaged hand, which was nearer to him: she would not have wanted to seem to be angling for pity. In any case, Harpur suddenly appeared as much in need of comfort as herself. She liked that. He turned and gave her a grin, then bent his already bent head and kissed her on her forehead. She eased her face a few degrees squarer to him and his mouth moved down, as if it was only natural, and fixed on hers. Now she did use her bandaged hand, pushing her arm slowly around his neck and holding him to her.

'I watch you agonising over someone else,' he said glumly.

'And I'm married to someone else again, and had a previous affair with yet someone else, both chums of yours.'

'It's quite a situation.'

'Is it a situation?'

'I'd say so.'

'Thank God.' But she thought he seemed unsure, concerned. 'There was somebody else, yes? I mean, somebody else apart from Megan?'

'That had to end. It was destroying her family, driving her husband around the twist, almost homicidal.'

'I know the feeling.'

'We had to think of him – and the children. It hurt. It's over now.'

'I hope so.' To her, though, he still appeared troubled. 'Ah, you're worried about how Desmond's endorsement of the JFK three-way approach to sex might affect you?'

'You know about that?'

'But Kennedy didn't die of Aids, did he?'

'That's a point.'

Chapter 30

Ember and the others were in the car and on their way down to the money in Exeter when Caring said there had better be a few amendments in the way things would run. That was his word, amendments, one of his gentlemanly words. Well, it was hardly ever Caring's mode to shout or act wild, but Ember could see a lot of thought had gone on, some more of that distinguished Ollie logic. This was a 4.30 a.m. start and still as dark as fate because they needed to be at the bank manager's house nice and early.

Ember knew Caring was always like this, chewing away at the details of a plan right up to the last moment, trying to make it all-round perfection. The trouble was, he would be thinking of improvements so late that people did not know where the hell they were and you could get a really unfortunate situation. It was one of what were called paradoxes, where he wanted something better and best, but could turn the whole lot problematical by working too hard. On the seventh day God rested. Think, if he had kept fiddling about making a sea bigger there might have been no Isle of Wight. One thing Ember had learned from weathered people back in the old days was that you found yourself a good, simple way of handling your project, and then you stuck to it. But he did not say anything now. Sometimes it was easiest not to argue with Caring, as Aston might have found out. And, anyway, although Caring's ways might be upsetting, they worked. Take a look at his house and paddocks and his cars and his wife and his kids' school. In the back of the stolen Mazda with Winston Acre, Ember listened carefully, feeling sure somehow that any changes would be to do with him.

Caring was in the front passenger seat, with Peter Chitty driving. The other two boys, Harry Lighterman and the newest one, Fritzy Something, were staying down in Exeter already so as to pick up the switch cars and get them in place.

'This is the long and short of it: I'll want you to look after the bank manager's wife and children, Ralph,' Caring said.

'That could be a better idea, Oliver,' Chitty replied immediately. Pete usually did say things like this when Caring spoke. You would not meet a better echo than Pete. In the original plan Winston would stay at the house because if matters turned bad there might be some very forceful work needed with the family. Ember had been due to go as part of the actual bank team. Why else had he looked over the building on the visit with Chitty?

'That's more your sort of assignment, Ralph – the family,' Oliver went on.

'Anything you like, Caring,' Ember replied. He tried to make it sound as if the new duties were a sight tougher but he would somehow cope all the same. 'Ralph Ember will do it.' Remaining with the family had always seemed to him the cushiest job of the lot and he had felt gibbering envy of Winston for landing it.

'I need somebody top class there,' Caring said. 'Subtle.'

'Check,' Chitty added.

'Keep them happy, but secure,' Caring said.

'Count on me,' Ember replied.

Chitty said: 'If it came to the worst—'

'Count on me,' Ember told them.

'Which it won't,' Chitty said. 'The important thing is the manager must see that if he doesn't do the business for us his family gets—'

'He'll see it,' Ember replied, 'fear not.'

'Why it was going to be Winston,' Caring said. 'Winston's pretty, yet somehow people can also spot menace. Combination's a great pull to the birds, yes, Winston? But Ralph's just as credible, and more. Ralph's got the weight. There's a history of rough triumphs in those eyes of Ralph.'

'They've seen some victories, Caring,' Ember replied.

'We take the manager down to the bank before any staff arrive,' Caring said. 'We ring you from his private office and you get one of the family – mummy or a kid, it doesn't matter – to tell him to make sure he goes through with it. Probably better a kid. There's a whole life in front of a kid, all being well – confirmation, careers and so on. Obviously, it will be your job to make sure whoever it is says the right thing, something desperate, not brave or encouraging.'

'Defiance? None of that, don't worry, Caring,' Ember replied.

'We keep the line open and brief you as things proceed, Ralphy. The staff turn up. We get them to act reasonably. We wait for the time-locks on the strong room to spring at nine twenty-five a.m. and then all that's needed is for the manager to open the combination locks as well. Any failure by him, we'll need sounds over the phone of genuine carnage from his house, Ralph. That could be crucial pressure. Real hostage distress, you understand? We won't want to hang about. There'll be customers after nine-thirty.'

'As I say, rely on me,' Ember replied.

'One thing you don't have to worry about is Ralph going soft,' Winston said.

Caring nodded: 'The Citroën. Yes.'

'Not just that,' Winston replied. 'I can't explain. Living up there, at the Monty, I've really come to know Ralph.'

Chitty laughed: 'Oh, I see, he's been blind-eyeing while you helped yourself to family pussy, and now he's your great mate, yes, Winst? *Quim pro quo*, like?'

'It's immaterial,' Caring muttered. 'As long as everyone knows his own commitments. You hold them till nine forty-five, Ralph. Now, that's important. Right up until nine forty-five, don't go early. You tell them, no alarm for another hour after you've left or the manager suffers. But the wife probably won't believe that, and she'll be right. We're not taking him from the bank. He'd be a lumber. By nine forty-five there's going to be a general shout anyway – customers will see to that. Smash the phone. Not just disconnect. It could be a plug-in thing and all she does is put it back in the socket. Turn left out of the house and there's a car for you, a grey Granada, around the corner twenty yards up the road on the left. Keys in it. Then right, right again, pick up the signs to Tiverton and make for the next switch point as before, the lay-by. We'll have a look at it now, on the way down. A blue Rover and a brown Audi, I hear from the boys. The Rover's yours. Keys for it in the Granada. Then home. Share-out in the car park of the Pier pub, out on the foreshore at ten in the night. It's big and remote. And it will be nice and dark by then.'

Chitty said: 'Don't forget to take your mask off when you leave the house. It's a respectable area.'

'All sounds good. Straightforward,' Ember replied. He tried to sort out what they were really saying. One of the basics in business was, Read between the lines. Caring must have finally decided it was too big a risk to have him in the bank. Maybe Chitty had been on at Ollie. Pete was an assistant, but he saw plenty and said his piece. They would be thinking, Panicking Ralph – a crack-up that could fuck everything. The thing was, they would probably regard that business with the Citroën as a panic, not something that had to be done. They might be scared he would go unpredictable again down at the bank. Caring kept on going through this spiel about the past and victories and he must believe some of it, or Ember would not be here now. Under it all, though, Oliver had that word – that bloody cruel word, Panicking – he had that for ever in his head's filing system, and that was the germane one. Well, when it came down to it, thank God. There was going to be big stress down there, waiting for the time-locks, taking care of the staff and customers as they arrived, working on the manager, carting the cash. Plus, possible trouble from this other outfit. There had to be easier ways of earning a split. Let Winston handle it. Winston could be jumpy, too, but he'd be all right in that sort of situation, no time to think and the chance of violence. Caring had seen this at last. Yes, thank God.

Terrorising a couple of kids and a woman – that should be a push-over. All psychological. There wouldn't be any need to get butcherous, surely, whatever Caring said. That manager would show wisdom. They were picked for being good at sums, not for valour. Valour? What would he get out of that? Anyway, at that end, Winston would be available now to loosen him up. Three hundred grand for a bit of baby-sitting and socialising was fair money.

Just south of Tiverton, they drove into the lay-by and stopped. It was a good spot, probably part of a previous, replaced road, and shielded from the new one by trees. The Rover and Audi were there, looking very capable, and pointed towards escape. The others jumped out for a pee. That would be nerves as much as anything. Ember badly wanted one himself, but stayed in the car: if you'd been top bracket in the old days you were not going to take aggro from your bladder now. Caring always seemed cool and logical but he pissed a lot, and you had to do what you could to get one up on these people. All right, Caring and Pete had him marked down as Panicking, only fit for a part of the job that could be handled by somebody's aunty, but at least he did not need a wet every ten minutes through fright. They would see him waiting for them untroubled in the back of the car and know that Ralph W. Ember was a very different quality from Ian Aston. Not somebody to take liberties with.

They drove into the bank manager's street at just after 7 o'clock, which was about right. Ember did not feel too shaky. That was the thing about his collapses, they could never be forecast – they zoomed out of nowhere. It was light now. Chitty took them past the house slowly. There seemed to be nobody up yet, so they would wait. 'Your Granada, Ralph,' Caring said, as they passed the end of the side road. 'Harry and Fritzy have done it right. Of course.'

Chitty turned and parked at a good distance and on the opposite side of the street. They watched from there. Caring said: 'In case of total disaster—'

'Which is impossible,' Chitty remarked.

'Nobody who is taken gives the police even one name, not one,' Caring went on. 'This isn't a regular team. There's Pete and me, yes, but the rest are from everywhere. The police can't just look at one of us and then trace a gang. So, silence.'

'Who talks to police?' Ember replied.

'It's been known. Deals,' Caring said.

'But, anyway, none of that's going to happen,' Chitty declared.

'This it?' Winston asked. Curtains upstairs were drawn back.

Chitty drove slowly down the street and stopped near the drive. They left the car and walked swiftly towards the front door. Ember's legs felt really great, like someone else's, someone aiming for the Distinguished Service Order by advancing against fearful odds. As soon as they were in the drive all but Chitty balaclava-ed up. He went ahead, knocked the door and turned his back while he waited. The other three stayed out of sight. Ember heard the front door open and, as they all moved, saw Chitty pull on his balaclava before turning. A fair-haired boy of about seven in heavy rimmed glasses and green, spaceman pyjamas stood holding the door and they rushed past him. He was going to yell, but Winston grabbed him, his hand over the boy's face and mouth. Caring shut the front door behind them. Then he, Chitty and Ember raced up the stairs, all with K-frames on show. Winston came behind, carrying the boy, still gagging him with his hand.

From one of the bedrooms, a woman called something, maybe asking who had been at the door, and Caring and Chitty moved at once towards the sound. They pushed open a door and Ember heard half a scream and then Caring said: 'Close the curtains again, please, and come away from the window. Then both of you sit on the bed.' There was a delay and then a bit of a thump before Caring said in a hurt voice: 'I told you, pull the cunting curtains, didn't I?' Winston pushed past Ember to show them the boy and make the point there had better be no trouble. The kid's glasses were still there, but slanted on his face, not over his eyes and only fixed to one ear. That sort of language in front of a kid, it was untoward. It was a surprise coming from Caring.

Opposite Ember another door opened suddenly and a girl of four or five in a lilac track suit looked out. When she saw Ember in the mask and with the pistol, she began to close the door again, but he stepped quickly across the landing and held it open with his free hand. 'Don't be afraid,' he said. 'It's only a mask. And this is a toy gun. It's like a game.' He knew he was good on baby talk.

'Which game?'

'Some fun.'

'No, it isn't. Why are you in my house?'

'We've come to see your daddy.'

'Others?'

'Yes, in mummy and daddy's bedroom.'

'Who asked you in?'

'Your brother. Now I want you to come downstairs with me.'

'No.' She tried to shut the door again.

'Everyone's going downstairs. It's part of the game.'

'That's a real pistol, stupid.'

Winston backed out on to the landing from the other room, still carrying the boy. He had taken his hand away from the child's mouth now to let him breathe and Ember saw the terror in his face. It was bad, but could not be helped. After Winston came the mother and father, both dressed. The father had a cut on the side of his cheek and the start of a prize black eye. The woman kept a hand on the boy's arm, comforting him. She was murmuring: 'We must do what they say, Robert. Don't make a

189

noise, dear.' There was the sound of a telephone receiver being smashed and then Caring and Chitty came from the room behind the others.

The girl ran past Ember to her parents. 'Mummy, who are they? Why are they in our house? Is daddy hurt?'

'Hold your mummy's hand and we'll all go downstairs,' Caring told her. 'We won't be staying long.'

'He said a toy gun, mummy.'

'Just hold your mother's hand and go downstairs,' Chitty told her.

The father held out his hand and the girl took it.

'Daddy's girl,' Caring said. 'That's all right.'

Winston went down the stairs with the boy, then Caring followed, descending backwards, with the pistol pointed up towards the rest of the family. Chitty followed. Ember found the lavatory and emptied his bladder. His pride at the delay held him together. This was maturity and composure. This was know-how.

They went into the lounge, at the front of the house, where the curtains were still closed from the night before. 'Good,' Caring said. 'Now, everybody sit down.' A telephone stood on a small table and he went over and picked up the receiver to check it was all right. 'Good, again.'

Shock seemed to catch up on Robert, the young boy, and he began to cry against his mother's shoulder and to rub at his mouth where Winston's hand had been, as if trying to wipe off a taint. Ember could understand that. She was no looker, with legs like a Jap wrestler's. You would think a bank manager could afford to move up a class or two.

Caring spoke to the manager. 'Here's how it runs, then, Mr Kale. You and I and one of my friends will go in your car, you driving, down to the bank. One of my other friends will come behind in our Mazda. And one of my other friends, this one, here, will stay with mummy and the children. He's a good one, a decent one – has his own idolised children, same as self – and it takes a lot to make him unpleasant, but he certainly can get unpleasant, especially if things start going wrong. I want to stress that. A pro. Well, that isn't going to be the case here, I know. Look, I'm sorry if this sounds like Humphrey Bogart a bit, but it's hard to fight free from those films we've all seen. So, we'll go into the bank and immediately get in touch with my friend here, by telephone. Then, in due course, you'll open up the vault and when we've done what we have to we'll disappear, and you'll come with us, Mr Kale. My friend will disappear from your house at the same time, and once we've put you down, Mr Kale, the whole matter will be over. There's a good chance you won't have to talk to your house on the phone at all. You can come home and catch up on breakfast in peace. Well, up to you, entirely. I don't know how anything could be simpler, do you?'

The manager was young for that sort of job, Ember thought, not much more than thirty-five. Like the wife, he was fat, though, with thick, red cheeks, and his breathing sounded pretty poor, maybe because of the stress and damage. He had one of those faces you could remember from kids at your school, really porky and ripe, and useless at everything except playing with himself and knowing about apostrophes. There would not be any more trouble from him. The woman had stayed pretty calm, her eyes on the children most of the time, though occasionally she stared at Ember and the others, as if trying to picture how they looked behind the masks and remember their build. She would be listening to their accents, too, he reckoned. Well, a good mixture. She was small and heavy lipped, with rimless glasses. Ember would have bet she was clever. Fat ones were often cleverer than the others because of their chemistry. This had been proved. He thought of her giving evidence somewhere, and making a bloody good job of it, if they could see her ugly little face over the edge of the box. He felt himself start to get out of control. Why was he the one who had to stay with this sharp little round bitch – so she could do a real study of him and fix him in her head? Perhaps he should never have agreed to that television show, after all. He was on his own here, and no sight of the takings until tonight at the Pier. Chancy? Unduly.

'So smarten yourself up, Mr Kale, would you?' Chitty said. 'Give that spot where you had a fall a bit of a wipe with a handkerchief? Your sort of job, you don't want to look like a Saturday night affray, do you?'

Kale rubbed the blood off.

'Myself, I love this house,' Chitty went on. 'It's got a happy feel to it, a family feel, and that's not as easy to achieve as people might think. I don't mind a bit of untidiness and dirt, as long as the spirit's right. Do you know what I mean, Mrs K?' It was not a bad room – red striped wallpaper, like a middling hotel hoping for the historical touch, and furniture that would do in the vestibule.

'We can make a move,' Caring said. 'The next sequence is not too easy. One of my friends and I will be in the back of your car, Mr Kale, but down low, because we'll still have the balaclavas on, and you can't drive out from your property with people like that on view. You go as usual to the bank yard and park near the door and you let us all in. From then on it's simple enough. One of my other friends will follow us in the Mazda, but a good way back, because he won't have his balaclava on, obviously, and we don't want you doing a memory job in the mirror.'

Caring and Pete Chitty prepared to go out with Kale between them. Winston would get behind. All of them had put their K-frames away.

'Tell him to do what we say, Mrs Kale,' Chitty told her.

'Yes, tell your husband,' Ember said. He cracked his voice like a whip. These people – the Kales, Ollie, the kids – all of them, had to believe in him.

This fat little cow stared up at Ember from her chair and then looked across at the other fat little sod, her hub. 'Do what you think's right, Tim,' she said. It was cool, no trouble with the words. It was a code? Who knew, they might have discussed many times what to do if this situation ever came, and they had a drill. Jesus, she might bring problems later.

Chitty said: 'Yes, he will do what he thinks right. He wants to come back and find this place like when he leaves it, filthy but home, and everyone in it in fair shape.'

Kale turned to Ember: 'They're not part of this, my family.'

'That's the point, isn't it? They don't have to be,' Ember replied. 'Don't make them part of it.' Again he got some roughness into his voice, not blood-bath but very hard. Sometimes he wished he looked less like Charlton Heston: people thought that underneath it all he must be big-hearted and stuffed with integrity. But, Christ, he had a mask on.

At just before 8 o'clock, the four left. They would meet Harry Lighterman and Fritzy in another car near the centre. It was spot-on for time-tabling. They wanted to get to the bank before anyone else arrived and also keep the waiting down to the minimum. There would be an all-night security man to deal with but that should be easy because they would be going in with a key through the manager's usual door and only a little earlier than he normally arrived. The guard would not be rushing for any alarm button until it was too late. They should be in and on the phone to Ember at about 8.40. Caring's research said nobody called at the house in the mornings, no milkman or newspaper boy or friends of the children on their way to school. It all looked great, so far.

'Well, you kids will have a morning off from classes today,' he said.

'I'm only in nursery,' the girl replied.

'From nursery, then.'

'I don't go on Tuesdays or Wednesdays.'

'Robert needs some clothes,' Mrs Kale said. 'It's cold. He's got to go to his bedroom.' She said it as if this was obvious and there would be no argument. The boy stood up in his green pyjamas.

'Stay there.' Ember went into the hall, leaving the door open, so he could still watch them, and took a coat from the stand there. He brought it back and handed it to the boy.

'Silly, that's mummy's coat,' the girl said.

'Not to worry.'

'He can't wear a lady's coat.'

'It's not for long. Part of the game.'

'What game?' the girl asked.

'Dressing up. Put it on, Robert,' Ember said. 'You can wrap it around twice.'

The woman twitched, but said nothing. The boy put the coat on a chair and went and sat close to his mother again. Ember still had the K-frame in his hand, but slipped it into his pocket now. This was a woman and children, for God's sake. He sat down near the door. The three of them stared at him, the kids because they probably did not know where else to look, the woman putting it all into the little fat memory and trying to make him feel bad. He was having a bit of a sweat around the face and neck, but reckoned that could be only the balaclava, not fright. At least this bitch could not see it.

'You have children?' the woman asked. The voice said she could not believe he led an ordinary life somewhere. Did she think he spent all his time with a mask on, waving a pistol in people's lounges, scaring kids?

'That was just something my friend said,' Ember told her. 'Bull.'

'You haven't got children?'

'No, nothing like that.'

'How do you know about games, then?' the girl asked.

'Well, I can remember. When I was a boy myself. *The Bells of St Clement's.*'

'Hasn't he got children, either?' Mrs Kale said.

'Who?'

'Your friend, as you call him. The one in charge.'

'Who said he's in charge?'

'The one who hit Tim.'

'Hit daddy?' the girl said.

'You saw, darling.'

'Hit? On his face? I thought he only fell.'

'He's all right,' Ember told her.

'Why did your friend hit him?' the girl said. 'You said a game.'

'Has he got children?' the woman asked.

'No.'

'I suppose you'd lie,' she said.

'You don't need to know about us. An hour, we're gone for ever. You ought to forget everything. Understand? There's no medals in it. This conversation – to get at my accent?' Ember replied.

The woman shrugged. 'We've got a wait, haven't we? What else do we do but talk?'

He could see how the manager might have come to end up with her. He had not married her, she had married him. She took charge, that gritty brain, those tough, dark eyes.

The boy sat up straight suddenly, then stood. 'Where are you going?' Ember said. 'Sit still.' Suddenly, he was almost shouting. Robert picked up the coat and put it on. It swallowed him and reached the floor. He looked like a *TV Times* picture about poor children in Victorian days. The girl laughed and then Robert himself began to giggle. He took a few poncy steps in front of his mother, swinging an arm and trying to walk like a woman, in this no-style, beige, tweed coat. Ember laughed, too. 'Brilliant, Robert,' he said. The girl went to a heap of toys in the corner and pulled out an imitation air-hostess hat with Trans-Universe printed on it. She fitted it on the boy's head. 'Smashing,' Ember said. The boy sat down with his mother again.

'I think after all you have got children,' she said.

'No. Perhaps one day.'

'When you've got a stack of money?' she asked.

'Maybe.'

'You're taking the bank's money, are you?' the boy said. 'Dad's helping you take the bank's money?'

'It's not his fault,' Ember replied. 'You shouldn't think he's bad.'

'Because he's scared what could happen to us?' the boy said.

'What could happen to us?' the girl asked. 'That gun's not a toy, is it? That was telling lies and silly to say this was a game, if you are hitting my dad.'

'But if he says, no he won't help?' the boy said. 'If you're a manager, you've got to look after the bank's money. That's why he's a manager.'

'He would usually, I know,' Ember replied. 'But today, he hasn't got a chance.'

'I can tell you've got children,' the woman said. 'The way you listen, and give an answer. You're in tune.'

He liked that, and for a second was going to tell her he had two daughters and always tried to see their point of view, even about something grubby like Winston. Then he realised this smarty was leading him on, building a nice little dossier. If she had been taller and had better eyes she could have joined the police: the legs were right. Anyway, six or seven more minutes and they should be on the phone. 'We can watch television,' he said, and went to switch it on. It was news about boat people in Hong Kong. He felt sorry for them. When you saw something like that, the lesson was, you made sure you always had the money to buy yourself out of a hellish situation. This was a long way away, yes, and different conditions, but you could find yourself and your family in a spot wherever you lived, and money would almost always put things right. Look at the vessels they had to use, look at the immigration waiting for a sweetener. Cash could have done the whole magic.

The woman, looking at the screen, said: 'They're a plague.'

'Skinny,' the girl added.

'All they get is rice,' the boy told her.

'They want a home,' Ember said.

'They want, they want,' the woman muttered.

The phone rang. He pushed a settee against the door before he answered it.

'Where were you, Ralphy?' Pete Chitty said. 'I thought they'd overwhelmed you.'

'How goes?'

'Great. More or less great. He's going to be nice, aren't you, Timmy? What's the chatter?'

'Telly.'

'Keep the K-frame in front of them, Ralphy. Keep them low. Be mean.'

'What else?'

'Any difficulties, Ralph, and I'd say make the little girl the star. There's something special between her and daddy. That happens, doesn't it? Doesn't it, Timmy?'

Ember looked at the girl, who was crouched forward in front of the television, studying the Governor of Hong Kong and his worries which he could ditch any time and come home, her knuckles pressed against her mouth. Mrs Kale saw him watching, and her face tightened and twitched again.

'You've won them over?' Chitty asked.

'Something like that,' Ember replied.

'You sound all right. Dominating. Me, I'm up for a time, then fraying. I don't go for it. I mean, where's these other fuckers?'

'Which?'

'You know which. The competition.'

'We're in the clear,' Ember said. Jesus, what the hell was Chitty doing, pumping his sudden anguish down the line? There was no point. Ember had enough at this end already. This phone was for communications, not therapy.

Chitty moaned: 'Oh, we drove in here, to the yard, and all the others joined us – all as planned, fine.'

'That's it then. No fret.'

'Is it? I see cars parked around, men in some. Look, are these people waiting for us to do the business and then take it all? The funny outfit – Wales? Hi-jack?'

'Wales is nothing.' This was what you could get with people with no real form to them like Chitty in his youth clothes. They could be all right right up to the moment, really hard and all mouth, and then when they got into the immediate environment here come the shakes and the imaginings, worse than any of Ember's panics. This boy was sitting in a banker's seat in a grand office where good, honest, commercial deals with a lot of noughts to them were put together and it all knocked him sick, because he had no real background. He wanted to be home with his art prints and rainbow furniture, and even when he was there he could go uncoordinated and hurl footwear. It was what was called their psyche. You never knew what sort of people you were getting in with when you started work of this sort. They'd split open with no reason, like fruit left too long. 'Of course there's cars parked. It's a city. Men in them? They're getting their gear together, the briefcase and *Financial Times* before going in for another day. Who's listening?'

'Only Kale. The others are taking another look around.'

'Don't let them hear you talking like that. It could throw people, make it all shaky.'

'You're scared you're going to be stuck up there for nothing? Might be.'

'No. It's clockwork.' Ember could see the woman and the boy gazing at him, the woman still so sure of her bloody self. You'd think they did a hostage turn every couple of weeks. Those short fat ones had confidence, it was well known, because they were all tight up together in a package, no weak bits straggling on the edges.

Ember heard another voice. Caring came on the line: 'It's shaping, but I think it would be an idea if one of them had a word now with Mr Kale. There's no trouble, but just to make sure there won't be any. That seems logical to me. There's a word for it. Pre-emptive?'

'If it's running well maybe it would be better, —'

'No,' Caring yelled. That was rare, for him to crack.

'What?' Ember asked.

'I thought you were going to use my name.'

'Never.' Christ, yes, he had almost said it. 'One of the first things I ever learned, no names.'

'All right.'

'No, but I say this, if it's going fine, why should—?'

'Get one of the kids.' Ember heard him turn his head away from the receiver. 'Mr Kale, come and have a little talk, before the crisis moment. A breath of home.'

Ember put the receiver down on the table and said: 'Your husband wants to talk.'

'I don't think so,' the woman replied. It was very quiet, like saying no thanks to a cup of tea, brick-wall quiet.

Ember stood up and turned to speak directly to the little girl. God, why didn't he know her name? 'Come and tell daddy you're missing him and want to see him home soon.'

'I think I do,' the girl replied, after a think about this. 'But I want you to go away first.'

'Yes, I'm going very soon.'

'You'll leave her alone,' the woman said. 'I won't have you touch her or go near her.' She looked about the room, as if searching for a weapon.

Ember picked up the receiver: 'Are you there, Mr Kale? I'm bringing your daughter.'

'Let me speak to my wife. I want to know everything's all right.' You could tell he had porky lips. He sounded bad, too much spit greasing his words, words sliding into one another, swallowing one another like scum down a sink. Ember felt better again. All this pressurising might be unnecessary.

'Yes, everything's all right, Mr Kale. I'm going to fetch your daughter.' He put the receiver down again.

In a rush, the boy stood and placed himself in front of his mother and sister, walking like a man this time, this lad in an air-hostess hat and the dull, comical coat hanging off his shoulders and dragging the ground, his eyes terrified behind the glasses. He did not speak. Perhaps he could not speak. Standing and pushing himself into that spot might have taken everything he had.

Could you hit a kid of seven in women's gear? You had to admire him. 'Robert, out of the way, love,' Ember said. To his horror he found himself reaching into his pocket for the pistol. 'Move. Time's very short. I've got a job to do here.' Where in God's name was that rough-edge snarl gone?

The woman stood up, too, now. She grabbed at one of those all-joints table lamps, pulled it from the socket, trailing wire. Ferociously, she swung the lamp at him, out of reach. 'I'll yell,' she said. 'The kids will yell. There'll be people in the road now.'

He wanted to shout at this dumpy cow about the Citroën, so she'd know what she was playing about with. Ever seen a blood patch on black dock water, Mrs K? He felt his back and shoulders moistening up and knew that in a couple of moments he might not be able to move because of nerves, so he reached out and gripped the lapel of the woman's coat on the boy and shoved him hard to the side, out of the way. Robert fell against the side of one of the easy chairs. It was like a little, pissed old woman in a party hat tumbling from a bus. He stayed there.

Ember turned to face the woman as she hit him for the first time with the lamp. It caught his arm. He still had a hand in his pocket on the gun, and maybe she thought she could disable him in time. Now, she started to yell and scream, no words, just an angry, non-stop din, the rotten little face rottener. Then the boy began to howl, too. The bulb in the lamp flew out and exploded like a firework when it hit the floor. Next time she hit him, it was lower down, and she was either going for his balls or his hand in the gun pocket. It did no damage, only gave a bit of pain in the hip. He pulled his hand out, but no gun, and as she lifted the lamp once more, fixed on her wrist and held her helpless. She tried to butt him then, but was too short. Where the hell had this manager found her?

'Shut up,' he said. 'Just shut up.' All at once it was too much.

But she let go louder. The little girl suddenly ran around whimpering behind Ember, trying to get out of the room, but when she came to the settee across the door she turned back to the telephone table and picked up the receiver.

'Daddy,' she screamed into it, 'daddy, please, daddy, come home.'

The din, this room – they put him off. They had spent money on the furniture and the curtains and wallpaper, but not enough money. There was no theme, no taste. When Kale was promoted they probably went down to some big store and splashed about a bit with the credit cards, listening to all the sales talk, and ending up with a van load of high grade rubbish. Ember felt soiled at having to scare kids and a woman in such a tatty place. He said to Mrs Kale: 'Keep quiet. You needn't. I'm going. I'm sick of this. I can't do it.'

'Of course you can't,' Mrs Kale said.

'I'm getting out. I've got daughters of my own, for God's sake.'

The woman said: 'Anyone could tell. Go, then.' But she was not going to believe him, just like that. She started to yell again, and so did the boy.

He bent her hand back and made her drop the lamp, then threw it over into a far corner of the room where it crashed against a radiator. On the television now a woman started doing physical jerks, thumping about on the floor. The little girl was crying into the telephone, only getting out an occasional word: 'Please. Daddy. Help us.'

Ember was into more or less total, recognisable panic all right, but a morsel of his brain still functioned. If he did it right, he could get out of here now and still be entitled to collect. Who was going to know when he left? He wanted safety and escape from this furniture. He wanted peace and the money – not especially the money, but all the same the money. He had been a boat person too long.

Every way, it was important to put this phone out before he took off in the Granada. He needed maximum time to get clear, and he did not want Caring and the others able to check whether he was still in position. Dragging the screaming woman over to the little table, he took the receiver from the child without trouble. The porky voice was gabbling away at the other end, shouting so loudly he could hear the words even while the child still had hold of the instrument.

'Gloria, darling, get the man, get the man to the telephone,' her father called. He could be weeping. 'I heard a shot. Tell the man I'll do anything, anything.'

Ember put the receiver to his ear. Kale was still talking. 'He needn't hurt anyone any more. What's the banging on the floor, all the noise, Gloria?'

Alongside Ember, the woman continued to scream. Then Caring came on the phone. 'Great,' he said. 'Can you hear?' He shouted. 'That screaming. What the hell are you doing to them? Didn't I say you were perfect for that end? Enough now. It's as planned here. Someone said an explosion. You've been firing, for Christ's sake? We don't want deaths, do you hear? No deaths, not kid deaths. Twenty more minutes, then go. No need for any more of that. Now, please. Ease up, right?'

'Twenty minutes enough? You sure?'

'Jesus, you're enjoying it? We're going to open up the vault now.'

Immediately, Ember cracked the receiver against the wall, pulled the settee clear of the door and ran from the house to

200

the Granada, tugging the balaclava off as he went. Once outside the town, he turned off the main road and detoured in country lanes. For a time he stopped on a stretch of high ground and tried to admire the view, although his heart was banging away and his eyes felt steamed over. He knew he must not rush: he had to arrive at that car-switch lay-by after the others had come and gone in the Audi. Then they would know he had done things right at the house and remained there up to the last.

He gave it half an hour before rejoining the main road. When he arrived, the Mazda was in the lay-by and the Audi had gone. Great. Yes, they would realise they were dealing with a hard case, if they still had any doubts before. He left the Granada and began the long drive back in the Rover. The boys, Harry and Fritzy, had made sure it was full of juice. They were very useful people. The whole team were class. Ember began to feel relaxed again, proud to have been part of the raid, even from a distance. That had been an important job. Obviously, leaving early had hurt nobody, nobody in the house, and nobody in the raid.

He was within fifty miles of home when the News on the car radio reported a disastrous attempt to rob a bank in Exeter that morning. Three men had been killed and one was in custody. At this stage, it was not clear whether all or any of the three were robbers or police or bank staff. No names had been released. However, it was known that some of the robbers had escaped with a large amount of money, perhaps more than a million.

Ember's eyes seemed to flood once more and his neck grew rigid, so that he could hardly turn his head. He would have liked to pull off the motorway again for a while and try to recover some calm. He forced himself to keep going, though. You could not be less conspicuous than doing seventy in the middle lane.

Chapter 31

When he reached home, Ember saw at once that Margaret had heard the news, too, a face like women at a pit disaster. Although he had not told her the job was today or where, she could work out what a 4.30 a.m. start meant.

'Thank God,' she said, when he walked in. He had left the Rover in a multi-storey and come the rest of the way by bus. 'Ralph, who's gone?'

She wanted to ask him about Winston, that was obvious – had Acre been one of the three stretched out under a blanket in the street or the bank? – but she knew she couldn't, not just like that, not at the start, anyway. Putting her arms around him, she squeezed his shoulder and his arm in a sort of joke, checking he was undamaged, as if he was the one she worried about. He said: 'All I know is what's on the News.'

'What went wrong?'

'I've got to get out of these clothes.' In the bedroom he changed his suit, shirt, tie, shoes and socks. Then he took them all out to the yard incinerator and started a fire with petrol. He burned everything, plus the balaclava. The K-frame he had dropped in a brown stream while spending time with the rural view above Exeter. Margaret had the 4 o'clock News on the radio when he returned, but there was no more detail, except they were now saying the haul might reach a million and a half. Not long afterwards, the girls came in.

'Where's Winst?' Venetia asked.

'His name's Winston,' Fay said.

'Where is he, dad?'

'He's gone.'

'Gone?' Venetia asked.

Ember was aware of Margaret staring at him, trying to read

whether the word meant something extra. And who amongst this lot cared about Ralph W. Ember? 'So what's the latest about the Latin?' he replied.

'Search me,' Venetia said.

'What's that supposed to mean?' Ember said. 'Is that the way they teach you to talk there, slang from a Ronald Reagan film?'

'What's all the filthy smoke in the yard?' Venetia replied. 'Horrible smell.'

'Gone where, dad?' Fay asked. 'Mum, where's Winston?' She wanted to treat what Ember said as a leg-pull, but there was also a trace of anxiety in her voice.

'Is your headmistress keeping Latin or not?' Ember asked.

'She's keeping it so far,' Venetia replied. 'Worse luck.'

'I don't trust her,' Ember said. 'She's got soft option written all over her.'

They were talking in the Monty bar and now all went up to the flat. Ember walked to the lounge window and looked out along Shield Terrace. Venetia came and stood by him, watching, too. 'When's he coming back? Where's he gone?'

'Who?'

'Daddy! Winst, of course.'

'He's not coming back.'

Fay was fiddling with the television controls, looking for her tea-time programme. 'Daddy, don't be silly.'

'He's not.'

Venetia turned from the window. 'Mummy, he is, isn't he?'

'I don't know. No, I don't know at all.' She sounded worse than either of the girls.

You could almost see it as comic, couldn't you? Well, why didn't he laugh? Here he was, crippled by worries – about the police, about the share, about quitting Kale's house too early, about any settling up for that – and all he could hear was every female in this place gasping for that long, ginger jerk, who might be dead by now. With any luck he would be. Those bloody great stringy legs and the horse tail moustache: he had to be a juicy target.

Abruptly, Fay stood up in front of the television set, ignoring the programme. Her face had gone white. It had hit her that Ember might mean what he said. She ran from the lounge and he heard her make for the spare room where Acre had slept. Had been supposed to sleep. In a moment, there came a great wail of distress.

Venetia went to join her and Ember heard them sobbing together. They did not come back to the lounge.

'They'll get themselves thrown out of that school, if they talk about some offal like Winston Acre there,' he said. 'He could be all over the papers.'

'Three dead, one taken,' she replied. 'I mean, how many of you were there altogether.'

'Six.'

'My God. Three dead out of . . . If . . .'

'But there might have been another crew, or police or bank people.'

'You sound as if you weren't even with them, Ralph.'

'I was with them. I had the intellectual end – the family.'

'Yes?'

'We've got to be open in an hour,' he said. 'That's important.'

'Of course.' She was sitting in front of the children's programme on the television, the sound off, and not seeing it. Wherever he was today, television added a flavour. 'Couldn't you ring Caring? Or Pete Chitty?'

He was still at the window. 'You know what Caring's like about the telephone, and especially now. I've got to go very, very carefully. Think of Aston, will you?'

'Aston? Why? You haven't done anything that—'

'Done, not done, it doesn't matter. Jesus, Maggie, there's going to be blame flying all ways. This was a catastrophe. People will be vindictive. They won't stop to think.'

'Yes, but—'

'I lie low.'

'Just see if he answers. Ring off when he picks the phone up, if you like.'

She wanted to find what the odds were, as simple as that. If Caring replied it showed he was not dead, so there would be one more chance that Winston might be. And if Chitty also answered, two more chances. Her face looked agonised. It occurred to him that she might ring them herself. Of course, they were both unlisted but he had their numbers in his little book and, walking to the desk, picked it up and put it in his pocket. She watched him. Good. Bloody good. Let her see he had her faithless game worked

204

out. Christ, though, when he had come through this there would be a few matters to put right between her and him. She could not mess him about. Did she realise that if things turned out well, he would still be alive and free and very seriously rich? A million and a half around, according to the News. It was still possible that nobody would ever know he left the Kales' too early. It was still possible the police would not trace the raiders or him. It was still possible Caring or Pete was all right, or both, and that they had the cash, not the other team. It was still possible the profits would be at the Pier car park tonight for dividing, and there might be more each now. With luck, Ralph W. Ember could be a very desirable commodity before too long. Didn't she see all this?

Of course, Winston Acre might be alive and free and seriously rich, too. But did she really believe a wild London youngster like that might look back in her direction, the daft, middle-aged housewife? Winston would want to be enjoying himself at Kew and so on once more, into the great life he had there, among the antique shops and bistros and décor. And didn't it matter to Margaret that Venetia and maybe even Fay—? He could not formulate that thought in his head. Chitty had formulated it in his sweet way and nearly driven Ember nuts. But did all that mean nothing to Margaret? He had always treated her too well, this was more than half the trouble. All the trouble.

'I'll go for the share tonight,' he said. 'You'll need to look after the club for a while.' They would have his slice among them if he failed to show up. Also, if he did not go it would be like admitting he had fallen to pieces at the house. There might be only one or two there, and they could cut it right down the middle between them, and one of them could be Winston. Could he let that happen? For a start, the clothes and shoes he had burned were worth a couple of hundred, and this was the second pair of shoes to go that way. All this, small scale matters: but the principle counted.

'Are you sure, Ralph?' She made it sound as if he was brave and even crazy to go for the share-out.

'It's a place with a lot of good cover – a big car park near the foreshore. I can look around first, see what's what. The least thing problematical and I'll stay out of sight.'

'It's a million and a half, isn't it?'

The point about Margaret was she could think very clearly about two things at once.

Venetia came back into the lounge, her eyes bleary from crying. 'Didn't he say anything – goodbye?'

'Winston's in this strange job, love,' Ember said. 'He never knows when he's going to be called suddenly.'

'But he could still have said goodbye – even a note.'

'Oh, he did,' Ember replied.

'A letter or something?' she asked, really brightening.

'No, but he asked me to explain to you and Fay and to say cheers.'

'Only cheers? Like with a drink? Did he say me first or Fay? Now, think, daddy. Who first?'

'And he said to ask you – he was really concerned about this – he said to ask you not to speak to anyone about him living here. Not to anyone, whatever happens.'

'Whatever happens? What sort of job?' Venetia said.

'Something important for the State, I think.'

'With an elastic band on his hair?'

'Where's Fay?'

'In her room doing a big weepy and moaning that her life is over, the silly little smell.'

'That's enough,' Margaret said.

'Well, he might come back,' Venetia replied.

'I've no information to this effect,' Ember said.

Chapter 32

Driving his Montego, Ember entered the car park of the Pier public house at about 9.30, half an hour early. A scattering of vehicles stood in the big, shadowy space, none he recognised, and none occupied, as far as he could tell in the dark. He put on wellington boots, left the car at once and climbed the earth sea-wall to the foreshore. If he kept low on the other side he could watch vehicles arrive without being spotted himself. Wellington boots always made him feel pretty good and strong: they were what labourers wore, and like the boots of cavalry soldiers in the old days – people who were used to getting on with things, doing the job, no fussing. He enjoyed the stiff, strong way they made you walk, like someone who meant to get there sooner or later.

The sea was coming in and he could hear it behind him, slowly creeping forward over the long mud flats, not crashing breakers – again, getting there eventually, though. It might not be pretty here, even in daylight, but it was Nature, and all sorts of valued birds thought a hell of a lot of that mud. An occasional flurry of rain rushed in from the sea and rattled against the brightly lit windows of the Pier. He did not mind the rain and cloud: the darker the better. He wished he had kept the K-frame, though, ditched when he had been so fearful. He could have done with it now, when he was fearful again, though interested for the moment in a bit more than being only safe. He had the whiff of big money, just like old times, and that always got to his psyche. God knew how many years it was since he had used a pistol. All the same, he reckoned he still could, if he had to. And just to have a gun and show it could have been a help, anyway. Here, now, he might need every bit of help available. The Pier's car park had all the handy cover he described to Margaret, which meant others could use it, too. Anybody looking for him would see the Montego and know he must be around. Why he had brought it: he was here to make contact and collect and freight the gains home. The car was also a give-away, though.

Radio News had come up during the evening with the names of two men killed at the bank. One was Timothy Drake Kale, the manager. The second – described as a raider – Ember had never heard of, presumably from the other team. So, that lot had got there, despite everything. God, what a shambles, two outfits, one job. It almost grieved him to hear about Kale. Perhaps he had shown some valour eventually, after all, and paid for it. He thought of the little girl, screaming at her father down the telephone to come home and save them, though there had been no real need: they had never been in any danger. That wife would take over all right, run the house, bring up the kids, until she terrorised someone else into marrying her. In the papers, Kale would probably be described as a high-flier, even if he did not have the lips for it. Bank people and that kind often became high-fliers once they were dead. The killing of a manager meant the police would be very tough and very tireless. Ember wished now he had decided to keep his watch from among the trees at the other side of the Pier. The sea-wall was so open and an obvious place to choose. Too late to change now, though. It would be crazy to cross the car park.

At around 10 o'clock a string of vehicles began to arrive, full of late drinkers for the pub. Their headlights swept the sea-wall as they approached and he had to keep very low. Was it hopeless to be here at all? Would anyone show after so much carnage this morning? The ones who had made it away were probably still running, and maybe laughing if they had the cash. He would give it until 11 and then possibly try what Margaret suggested, a call to Caring or Chitty, no talk, just a check. And if one of them answered? He wasn't sure what he would do then. A visit? The thought made the sweat start, even here in the rain and wind from the sea.

It was just before 10.20 when what looked like Caring's silver Daimler drove into the car park and did a little tour until its lights picked up the Montego. The Daimler pulled in alongside it. Ember stayed where he was and watched. The driver seemed to be alone in the car, though support could easily lie flat waiting in the back. The driver switched off his lights, climbed out and went and stared into the Montego. Then, he stood near the Daimler and looked urgently about. As far as Ember could tell from that distance, he was not talking to anyone keeping down in the Daimler. It looked like Caring, that long grey hair nicely back over his ears.

Ember went lower down the sea-wall and walked swiftly along the foreshore to a spot which he judged would bring him out just above the Daimler. Very cautiously he climbed up. When he could look again, Caring was in the car and had switched on his lights. A moment later, the engine started. He was leaving. Ember, panicking, but panicking about his share, not his skin this time, quickly took the few extra steps to the top of the sea-wall, waving both his hands and yelling: 'Wait, I'm here,' He thought how bright he was not to call Caring's name, even in this sort of stress. He had learned. But people going into the Pier turned at the noise and stared as he ran down the slope of the sea-wall. He had not really handled things too well. Would he be memorable?

Caring saw him, thank God, thank God, and switched off the engine and his lights, then pushed open the passenger door. 'Ralphy. Nobody else? Seen any signs at all?'

'Nothing.'

'Why the fuck were you up there? Boots? There's no time to fool about. But you're all right?'

'What about the others?' Ember asked. 'Is it OK, the boots in the Daimler? It will brush out.'

'Harry Lighterman's fine. He's got his lot and gone. It seemed best. Yours? On the back seat, Ralphy. Take it. I'm pissing off fast. A long way.'

Ember turned and picked up a parcel done in red gift wrapping, with smart yellow string and a bow. There were three others the same on the seat. 'You've taken a lot of trouble, Caring.'

'Patsy, my wife. She's keen on appearances. Look, it's down, Ralphy, less than we'd hoped. A balls-up. Well, you heard, I expect. We had to settle for what we could. There's a hundred and twenty grand there for you. You earned it.'

Ember hugged it to himself. 'I never really expected you to come.'

'I said I would, didn't I?'

It was the great old system and order that Caring believed in. What you said you would do you did unless you were dead.

'Pete Chitty? Winston? The new boy, Fritzy?' Ember asked.

'Christ knows. I thought they'd be here. Hoped. We got

209

separated. It was chaos, Ralphy. You did fine where you were, as expected, but at our end, just chaos. Well, we couldn't hang about.'

Ember realised suddenly that Caring feared he himself had let the operation down, left too soon, abandoned people. Ember understood. Such a gorgeous treat to see someone else suffer for that. Even in the dark you could tell Caring's worried face was super-worried tonight and twisted with guilt.

'Ralph, it became impossible. Another couple of minutes, we'd all have been taken.'

'I know you did all you could, Caring. I'm not blaming you. Not a damn bit, believe me.'

'Thanks, Ralphy. It means a lot – a voice from a veteran. Harry and I, we had the luck, that's how it looks. And he's bloody good with the K-frame.'

How to check the fucking truth about the size of the haul? 'They said a million and a half, Caring.'

'That's media. If it had gone right, maybe. Believe me, though, Ralphy.'

Ember looked back at the other parcels.

'I don't know, Ralph. Will they ever be able to use it now, you mean? Somebody they've got inside, at least one.'

'Maybe you hold some of it, me the rest, in case they turn up.'

Caring looked back at the parcels. 'Three.'

'Shall I take another two?'

That might level it up: no knowing what he and Lighterman had for themselves, the sods. Ember felt strong enough to push Caring tonight. It was part that Caring looked so low, part the wellies. 'If you're going to disappear, I mean, Ollie. I'll be still at the Monty, anybody want to call for his share. Sort of banker.'

Caring started the engine. 'It could make sense.'

Ember leaned over and took two more of the parcels.

'I'm getting out of the country,' Caring said. 'Patsy's staying, at least a while. There's the daughter in school, and we can't pull her out of there overnight. It's not that sort of place.'

'Did you ever get your leg over that teacher? The one who liked *Hard Day On the Planet*?'

'What?'

'Fan of Loudon Wainwright the Third, wasn't she?'

'If Pete Chitty is – What I mean, if they get an identification of Pete Chitty they'll make the connection and come looking for me. Or whoever's inside – if he talks. Patsy will say I'm out of the country on business. Right, too.'

'Talk? That won't happen, Caring,' Ember said. 'Our sort of people don't. Good people. It's been a privilege.' He pushed again. 'Tell me, now it's all over, who did Aston? What was it about? I mean, was it Iles or did Aston fall down on—?'.

'And it's been a privilege to work with you, too, Ralph. A nice reminder of better, established standards.'

'Pete's got to be all right. He wouldn't get hit or caught. Too sharp.'

'Of course. But just in case.' He switched on his lights. 'Why the hell they call you Panicking I'll never know, Ralphy. You're like a rock. You can get your girls into the Cheltenham place, too, now. They've got real Latin there.'

'You'll be all right, Caring. Keep the driving moderate. Don't do anything untoward that would attract attention.'

'Fair enough. I know that money's going to be all right with you, Ralph. For the boys.'

Ember opened the door. The Daimler started to reverse before he was properly out. 'And don't persecute yourself – your conscience. You did all you could, Caring,' he called, slamming the door. Fucking gutless wonder. You gave them to the firing squad. Ember could see what had happened: the Caring logic turned into fright and break-down. The logic told him he was in trouble and could not wait for the rest, so he ran.

When the Daimler had gone, he put the parcels into the boot of the Montego, locked it and thought for a minute of walking over to the Pier for an armagnac to bring back some stability. Would a dump like that have armagnac? Then he found his legs were not too good after the excitement, and it was at least twenty yards. The boots felt heavy. He could change into his shoes again, or drive nearer the pub. But, in any case, it was probably stupid to hang about here. The others might still turn up, looking for their slice, including that shag, Winston.

211

Chapter 33

Next morning, Ember was sitting in the bar of the Monty wearing his dressing-gown and feeling more or less jubilant, when those two police vandals arrived, Harpur and the ACC, Iles. Ember and many club customers always said it was a living mystery that people like this pair had been given high rank in a police force, especially such a totally malfeasant lout as Desmond Iles. Ember and his wife often took their breakfast coffee in the bar after the children had gone to school, and today he had forced himself to stick to normal ways. Nothing fresh about the raid had come up on television or radio News.

The Monty bar was more comfortable than the kitchen, and Ember liked the sense of space, and the handsomeness of the panelling that dated from the club's former status as a business-men's select meeting place. Empty of members, the Monty still had a lot of style, and he found starting the day here could often be a big help.

A piece of mail had angered him this morning. That was all right: he needed something to take his mind away from its real worries. 'Through the post,' he shouted. 'Through the bloody post. How do you like that, Margaret? She's afraid to tell me face to face and couldn't even send the letter home with one of the girls. This is arm's-length. "Keep your distance, Mr Ralph W. Ember, pray. Here's my decision, like it or lump it." Second-class stamp.'

His wife said: 'There are more important things to talk about. Latin! We thought it would go this way, Ralph.'

'More important things? Perhaps. It's just that I hate – hate cowardice. That's what it is, Margaret, nothing less.' He began to read the letter, giving a loud, sickly imitation of the educated voice of the girls' headmistress, so that the words echoed around the Monty and Margaret had to smile. *Dear Mr Ember, I know*

that you and Mrs Ember are very concerned about the question of
the continued teaching of Latin here. I am writing to give what I
hope you will regard as some very good news in this regard.

'The two-timing bitch.'

From next term I intend to introduce a stimulating new course
entitled Classical Studies for girls throughout the school. This will
involve a thorough grounding in all aspects of classical culture
– history, literature and, yes, even some of the quite complex
philosophy of those times! Girls leaving the school will, in fact,
know as much about the way of life in the classical period as they
do about any other area of history, such as Victorian times or King
Alfred!

I do hope this will strike you as an acceptable compromise.
Of course, it is a matter of the greatest regret to me that owing to
staffing problems we cannot continue to teach one of the classical
languages, and I know you will share my feelings.

'Slimy sow.'

But, in opting to deal with the classical period in English only,
I am, I fear, only following a trend general to many of our schools
and, yes, even to many universities. Perhaps in the future I may be
able to restore the teaching of Latin to the timetable, though I realise
this is no great consolation to you, since Venetia and Fay may by
then have progressed from the school. For the immediate present,
though, I'm afraid Latin teaching will cease at the end of the term.
Please do try to think well of my admittedly imperfect solution to
the difficulty.

'Well, yes, it's a sop, but she's doing her best,' Margaret said.

'Electra, Minerva, the Cyclops, done in English? It's not the
same, can't be. Are you telling me that school where Caring's
kid goes—'

'He's leaving her there, regardless? After all you've told me?'

'Are you trying to convince me a really calibre school like that
would even consider doing the Cyclops in English? Yes, yes, the
yarns are total, fart-arseing rubbish, but it has to be Latin rubbish,
that's the whole point. How can you have some one-eyed giant in
English? It's untoward. I tell you, Maggie, I'm seriously thinking
of pulling Venetia and Fay out of that place now and—'

There was a banging at the door and someone called, 'Ralph,
are you in there? Open up, sweetie.'

'Iles?' Margaret said.

Ember drew the dressing-gown around himself more closely, like a woman afraid of showing too much.

'So someone's talked, promises or not,' Margaret whispered.

'I don't know, do I?' he said.

Margaret went to open the door.

'Here's a picture of leisure then,' Iles said, coming in. Harpur followed. 'Are you the lucky ones? Colin and I have been going to and fro about our business, which is the business of the Queen, all night. Haven't I seen that fucking eventide home garment before, Ralph? It's not you, lad. Get something in keeping, something princely. You're looking bad – worse than Colin and I after trekking the motorway. Rough news in the post? Only runner-up in the Nobel Peace Prize thing again?'

'Just our routine call, Ralph,' Harpur said. 'Licensing formalities. Fire doors, membership book – the usual.'

'And we'd like you to come on a little outing with us,' Iles said. 'In a moment.' He stepped across to Ember, took the letter from him and read it quickly. 'Oh, no wonder you're distressed. Ralphy, we're as on a darkling plain where ignorant armies clash by night. Isn't it too bad, though: you do what you can to be a bastion, Ralph, and then this?' Iles threw the letter on to the table in disgust. 'Mrs Ember, you've got a cultural gem here. Why don't you just take the girls out of that school, Ralphy? Find somewhere of real quality for them?'

'Well, there's no other private day school around,' Ember replied.

'Boarding?' Iles said.

'That costs,' Ember said.

'Yes, but kids' education: can one stint? The Monty not doing too well?'

'I suppose you're right, Mr Iles. We might have to think about sacrifice.'

'It's in your nature, Ralphy,' Iles told him. 'You're famed for it.' The ACC sat down opposite. 'Yes, as Colin says, in one way our routine visit. Always a treat, Ralph, Mrs Ember.'

'What little outing?' Margaret asked.

Ember studied both police faces, trying to spot the theme. What all-night business? He could never tell what Iles was thinking. His features showed very little, except contempt, and it was like sitting in front of a death mask. Harpur looked friendly enough, but

214

Harpur always did. You could not trust that, either. Ember gripped the edge of the table to stop himself visibly trembling. 'Margaret will get you a drink, gentlemen?' He could not have managed it himself. Iles asked for what he always called his 'customary old tart's choice', port and lemon, and Harpur had gin and cider mixed. He was studying the membership book.

'Some names of distinction emblazoned here, Ralph,' he said.

Margaret had stayed standing at the bar. 'So why have you come?' She had begun shrieking a bit. 'Why?'

Margaret could be like that now and then, not able to keep things temperate and subtle. In some ways she reminded Ember of Mrs Kale – full of fight, even if fighting could not be of any use. Of course, she would think these two knew something additional from Exeter and were sitting on it, something about darling Winston. He said: 'Mr Iles and Mr Harpur come up here regularly, love, to cast an eye. As they said. You know that.'

'And to see if we can lend support with the Save Latin Campaign,' Iles added. 'What's happening to the Classics in this country is an offence, nothing less. *Crimine ab uno disce omnes*, I suppose you'd say, Ralphy.'

'Here's poor old Pete Chitty's name in the membership list,' Harpur remarked.

'Ah,' Iles said sadly.

'Chitty?' Ember asked.

'For Pete Chitty and those marvellous bits of denim I always had a very soft spot,' Iles said.

'What about him?' Margaret asked. She tried to keep her voice sane, though without making much of a job of it. Of course, she wanted to hear he was dead. That would make the three. Wasn't it wholesome?

'What outing you ask,' Iles said. 'Oh, Young's Dock. We want Ralphy to come over there with us. Shortly.'

'What? Why the dock?' Margaret asked.

'Why?' Ember said. He could barely get the sound out.

'Will you go to the funeral, Ralphy?' Iles asked.

'What funeral?' Ember said.

'I know you think of club members as being like your own family,' Iles went on.

'Peter Chitty?' Margaret said. She looked as if she might start giggling with relief. 'But what's happened? Please.'

'That's what I meant about working all night,' Iles replied. 'Chitty caught it in that bank thing down in Exeter. You saw the TV? We were called down there last night. Not police shots that did him, I might say. A gang battle over a special money load. Three .38 bullets in his chest. He died on a verge. Blood over the grass. I always think it looks worse, like an animal.'

'Oh, God,' Ember whispered, 'it's good of you to come and tell us.'

'Elementary courtesy, Ralphy,' Iles said. 'We understand club feeling, you know. Don't people sometimes say police are like a club at the top? They don't always mean it well, I'm afraid.'

'This is so tragic,' Margaret remarked.

Ember worked at his voice and commented: 'But, from what I've seen on the News and read in the papers, he could be said to have had it coming. It sounds harsh, yes, but I can't think otherwise. He seemed a nice enough person, yet to get mixed up in such things. Guns. Asking for it. How could he be part of that? How?'

'Exactly,' Iles replied. 'Will you go to the funeral, Ralph?' he asked again.

Ember said: 'I'll take an armagnac, if I may, Margaret.' Sometimes it could do the trick. 'Funeral? Chitty? No, indeed. A parade of villains behind a villain.' He wished now he had been in the flat when they called. He felt trapped, sitting with his legs under one of the club tables and with Iles so relaxed and near, right opposite, in a custom-made navy pinstripe suit that must have cost at least five or six hundred and was definitely not run up by Len Large the tailor in Corporation Street. To Ember, the size of the room seemed of no relief any more. He was pinned in a corner of it. Margaret gave him a hefty brandy and Iles pushed his glass forward for another port and lemon.

'Flowers from the Monty then?' Iles asked. 'One of those wreaths in the shape of the book of *Revelation*, and with a text in primroses? "He that killeth with the sword must be killed with the sword." Myself, I adore gangland funerals. The mourners! Faces that seem naked without bars to look between.'

'This club will not be associated with it in any way, even though he was a member, and an acceptable one, as far as any of us could tell,' Ember said. 'I have to think of the reputation of the Monty.'

216

'We really can't be responsible for how members behave away from the club,' Margaret said.

'There's a lot of money missing,' Harpur remarked.

'I heard that,' Ember said. 'More than a million it said on the radio.'

'A lot more,' Harpur replied.

That Caring shit.

'Quite a few people still loose,' Harpur said. 'I expect you can guess where we're looking, Ralph, if Chitty was involved.'

'Caring Oliver?'

'Well, I didn't say it,' Harpur replied. 'The name didn't come from me.'

'Another member, yes, Ralphy?' Iles said. 'You'll have to tighten up the entrance procedures, you know. Sometimes it sounds as if you wouldn't blackball Charlie Manson from this place.'

'People come with first-class recommendations, Mr Iles – from vicars, business folk, professors, that sort of calibre. The club tries to be discriminating.'

'Why Young's Dock?' Margaret asked.

'We talked to somebody in Exeter,' Harpur replied. 'You might have heard they've got one man inside. He wanted to fix a deal with us. They often do, before the charges. He asked particularly to talk to us. And it was about Young's Dock.'

'Not another member, I hope?' Margaret asked.

Ember saw she wanted to know if it was Winston. Jesus, of course it was bloody Winston, and he had told the lot.

Iles said: 'Let's make a move then, shall we, Ralph? I have to pack for a conference.'

'How's your wife and the baby, Mr Iles?' Margaret said, as the three men left.

'Brilliant,' Iles replied. 'Considerate of you to ask.' In the car on the way to the dock he said: 'The lad they picked up is called Winston Acre, a Londoner. Obviously, you've never heard of him, Ralph.'

When he dressed, Ember had put on a thick thermal vest to soak up the sweat, because he knew things would be bad. It was a gamble: he might sweat from the heat as well now. If they were on their way to Young's Dock it meant Winston had opened his mouth about the Citroën, didn't it? So, how was he supposed to play this? His mind hardly functioned. He could not think. Instinct said always act ignorant. You could not hurt yourself ignorant.

'Winston? Black?' he asked.

'Ginger. Tall,' Harpur said. 'We didn't swallow it all at first, but the divers have been down and it's right.'

'We're always pulling vehicles and rogues out of Young's you know, Ralphy,' Iles said. 'It's a collecting point.' The ACC drove the Orion. Ember sat in the back with Harpur.

'We don't know how far the connection with our patch goes, you see, Ralph,' Harpur told him.

'You've spoken to Caring Oliver?'

'To his wife. He's abroad on business,' Harpur said. 'Wouldn't he be, though?'

'Excess baggage problem, I should think, with that amount of loot,' Iles commented.

'It's a real stack,' Ember said.

'Confirmed by the bank today as £1.8 million,' Harpur replied. 'And, of course, people shot or caught, and one or two we think who took off scared with nothing, so very big helpings for the people left.'

'I see that,' Ember remarked.

'As to local connections, the wife of the manager says she thinks the masked lad they had looking after them in the house had an accent from these parts,' Harpur went on. 'That's about all she can tell us, though. Except he said he had daughters, apparently. And he really lit up with stress.'

'Yes?' Ember said. 'Would a pro advertise his family circumstances?'

'Quite,' Iles replied.

'Misinformation,' Ember said. 'It's in the news these days.'

'I'll buy that,' Iles said. 'Good Lord, it could describe you, otherwise, couldn't it, Ralphy, except for the stuff about going to pieces under stress?'

They drove on to the dock. The Citroën van, filthy with mud, stood on the side near a mobile crane. Ember felt nausea close around him like a noose. The heavy vest hung soaking against his chest and shoulders. He thought the time might have arrived to start telling them what they already knew but what they wanted to hear from him. It was why they had

218

arranged this visit. It might make things easier for him in the long run.

Iles stopped the car and turned. 'We pulled what was left of a general duties villain from Wales out of this vehicle, Ralph. The Citroën windows were part open, so comprehensive fish damage to the corpse. But it was still possible to see he had died from blows to the skull.'

Oh, Christ, those sweet, thick parcels in the loft at the Monty with the jolly paper still on them, though the yellow string and bows gone now, to enable counting.

Iles said: 'Our friend, Winston, tells us Pete Chitty did the job on Citroën man.'

Ember stayed silent, could not speak.

'Winston says Chitty told him how it happened, the whole sequence. Winston was living at his flat before the job, apparently.'

'Yes?' Ember replied.

'That's what Winston says,' Harpur told him. 'Of course, it's one of the oldest tricks in the game: someone in Winston Acre's situation gives the police information that can hurt nobody, in the hope of softer treatment. If you can stick a crime on a lad who's dead, great, lies or not. What worse can happen to him? We're forever running into posthumous confessions via friends. Had it very lately, and it worked.'

'You don't believe this what's his name, Winston?' Ember said.

'Colin's telling you it's a well-known ploy by people looking at a long sentence. He's not saying we don't believe him.' Ember saw it was another of those times when you listened to what was said but had to hear something extra.

Harpur added: 'I went through Chitty's flat not long ago. No sign of anyone else living there. He would have lodged elsewhere and is covering for his host. It's probably shit about Winston being close to Pete at all. But you won't talk about my little expedition, Ralph. Not an official visit.'

'Yes, Winston might be shielding someone and still trying to get what he can out of a deal. You know how it goes, Ralphy,' Iles said. 'Only fools and vicars believe there's no loyalty among thieves. It's as good and strong as police loyalty, often better. Think what happened to Stalker. Sometimes the cop club's a treacherous place.'

A police recovery truck drove past them and in a little while men started to winch the Citroën up on to it. As they were finishing an estate car and an Escort arrived at speed and a gang of television people climbed out. They persuaded the men with the truck to let the car roll back on to the dock side and filmed it there.

'This will really kill the kind of malevolent, slanderous programme they wanted to do,' Iles said happily. 'The whole thing is resolved now. You see, Ralphy, I'm inclined to take this boy Winston's story as true, despite everything, including Harpur's bilious quibbles.'

'Yes?' Ember remarked. 'Well, if this Winston's got all the details.'

'Exactly,' Iles replied. Then he asked quietly: 'Do those injuries remind you of someone else's at all, Ralph?'

And suddenly, Ember realised why he might have been brought here today and given a message without being given a message. But he said: 'Remind me? How do you mean? Someone else's injuries? Can't help you. I'm a dumbo.'

'Skull damage? Identical. Another of your unfortunate club members. Clubbed.'

'Oh, you mean Ian Aston?'

The television people had noticed Iles in the car and a woman approached.

'They'll want you to pose by the Citroën, sir,' Harpur said. 'Vindicated.'

Iles started the Orion and drew away, waving nicely to her as they went.

220

Chapter 34

They were in bed, lying side by side on their backs, listening to a couple of the Monty's late-stay members trying to get their car started in the yard. A minute ago, Ember had entwined his fingers in Margaret's but without any response. He freed his hand now. They had talked it all through, or almost all.

'Winston will go down for ever, even though he's done some singing,' he told her. 'Armed robbery, probably murder. Plus the way he looks.'

'Caring deserted him?'

'How it looks. And he's a good lad basically. Well, he covered for me, didn't he – though I realise that could have been because of you. Or because of one of the girls. Or both the girls.'

'Don't say that, Ralph. Don't.'

'Which? About you or the girls? Anyway, it's more likely he did it because that's the way good lads like Winston operate. It's the code.'

She turned away, perhaps crying. 'And the police believe him?'

'The police want to believe him. It deals with Iles's problem, doesn't it? If they can show Pete Chitty killed the man in the dock they can say he did Aston as well. Dead to rights. Same injuries.'

'They took you down there to—'

'To let me know they knew what was what.'

'So what is what?'

'Oh, that they suspected Winston wasn't close to Chitty – didn't stay with him and never heard any confession from him about the man in the Citroën. And to tell me they thought I was in the manager's house.'

'And—'

'And they won't be doing anything about it because it's more

221

convenient as things are. Chitty wiped out is a gift all round. So everybody keeps quiet. I'll visit Winston, eventually. Take him gifts. He deserves that, at least.'

'So will I.'

'Why not? A moustache comb.'

She was quiet for a time. Then she muttered: 'You say there's one of them still on the loose, looking for his cash?'

'Fritzy? As far as I know. If he comes here we tell him Caring and Harry Lighterman have it. Which is true, the sods, and more. Likewise should a little bald guy named Leopold turn up claiming Winston's share. Anyway, I'll be out of this place soon. Give it six months or a year, so nobody's going to ask how I can suddenly afford it. Come if you like. Or move nearer to Long Lartin jail for your visiting. I'll set you up there.'

'Ralph, the Winston thing, it was only—'

'And I'm going to shift the girls from that dump of a school.'

In the yard, the sick car eventually coughed and coughed again then somehow managed to keep going. Doors slammed and it moved away wheezing towards the street. There was something degrading about having members with a vehicle like that. The police were right: he ought to be more fussy.

The Cheltenham place would do all right for Venetia and Fay, and there would be no money problems. Boarding could be convenient now. And, the thing was, Caring could not show himself down there, or anywhere else in Britain, for a century or two. Almost certainly it would be worth taking a look at the teacher he had been lining up. Screwing his bird might take away some of the bad taste about the split, and Ember would not seriously object to doing it to the music of Loudon Wainwright the Third.

Chapter 35

They were in bed, lying on their backs. Sarah said: 'Where are you supposed to be?'

'Keeping the streets safe, as ever,' Harpur replied.

'What about you? Do you feel safe?'

'Fairly. A rugby referees' conference in Scarborough, isn't it?'

'Two nights.'

'I did check he'd arrived.'

She put her hand in his. 'It's not just that you like the risk, is it, Col? I mean, if Desmond . . .'

'I don't think he killed Aston.'

'No? Why don't you?'

'I don't. He wouldn't. It was a private matter.'

'So?'

'The ACC sees himself as a public servant.'

'Who, then?'

'It might even be Chitty. Some of that lot. Probably.'

'But you can't be sure of the truth?'

'As your husband says, only juries know the truth. And television, of course. It's going to say Chitty in Yare-Gosse's rearranged programme. And Mike Yare-Gosse isn't one to have the wool pulled over his eyes, now is he?'

'No? And the other two they say Desmond did?'

He turned to face her: 'That could be different. Those two had to be seen off. The courts had failed us, as the courts often do. Possibly he did help out there, a public duty. Only possibly. Look, Sarah, the country's sweeter without that pair.'

'My God. But, my God, you're police, aren't you? Well, aren't you? Law, aren't you? Anyway, I didn't really mean that – when I said safe.'

'I know. Hygiene. How many people am I making love to,

223

and does the line stretch to every high-risk centre in the world?'

'Something like that.'

'It felt like only one. But the right one.'

She released her fingers and moved them gently across his chest. 'I'd heard you were shot in a vital area during that Preston ambush. I noticed no ill-effects.'

'Kind.'

The baby began to cry softly in the other room. 'I'll go to her in a minute.'

'Well, say in a few minutes.'

'Yes, that will do.'